D1458419

NO PLACE FOR A LADY

NO PLACE FOR A LADY

Western Stories by Women Writers

edited by

VICKI PIEKARSKI

Sagebrush
Large Print Westerns

First published in the United States by Five Star Westerns

First published in Great Britain by ISIS Publishing Ltd

Published in Large Print 2004 by ISIS Publishing Ltd,
7 Centremead, Osney Mead, Oxford OX2 0ES,
United Kingdom
by arrangement with
Golden West Literary Agency

British Library Cataloguing in Publication Data
No place for a lady : Western stories by
women writers. – Large print ed. –
(Sagebrush western series)
    1. American fiction – Women authors
    2. Western stories – Women authors
    3. Large type books
    I. Piekarski, Vicki
    813' .0874089287 [FS]

ISBN 0–7531–7114–7 (hb)

Printed and bound by Antony Rowe, Chippenham

For Colette
Friend and a woman tough enough
to have made it on the frontier

Contents

Foreword ix

The Woman at Eighteen-Mile by Mary Austin 1

Shootin'-up Sheriff by Cherry Wilson 13

The Drought by Dorothy Scarborough 53

Wilderness Road by Janice Holt Giles 78

Brother Shotgun by Jeanne Williams 103

The Widow's Stallion by Phyllis de la Garza 124

Callie by Cynthia Haseloff 150

Sidesaddle by Rita Cleary 170

The Indian Witch by Marcia Muller 185

Saddle Pals by Patti Hudson 199

For Two Dollars by Jane Candia Coleman 208

Thursdays at Snuff's by Gretel Ehrlich 227

Contents

Foreword

Western American fiction in its traditional form — the heroic adventure story — is generally perceived to be a genre written by men, for men, about men. Notwithstanding this male-centered focus, a surprising number of women in the 20th century were able to carve out for themselves rather successful careers writing Western stories. In most cases their accomplishments have gone unrecognized. They have been overlooked by literary historians, scholars, and students of Western fiction. Their contributions are not represented in anthologies of Western stories, and with the passage of time their lives and stories have become all but lost to literary history. Part of the reason, surely, that much of the Western fiction written by women has been overlooked is due to where the stories originally appeared.

In the first half of the 20th century the primary market for Western fiction by women, or by men, was the magazine market, especially pulp magazines. Printed weekly or monthly on cheap pulpwood paper, pulp magazines had an almost insatiable need for stories with which to fill double-columned pages that displayed little advertising. Pulp magazines provided a format through which writers could practice and perfect their craft. Conrad Richter, who wrote briefly for the pulps, credited this experience with teaching him how to plot out a story. For the author who could produce quickly and steadily, the reward, regardless of gender was a regular income. Additional income, prior to the advent of paperback reprints in the1940s, could be generated through hardcover book sales, both first editions and reprint rights. For some women the only available book market for their longer fiction was among British publishers, and many women never published at all outside the magazine market. Yet even publication in book form did not guarantee women writers a place in literary history as it often did their male counterparts.

Another factor that has contributed to the obscurity of female writers of Western fiction was that their identities were often concealed through sexually ambiguous pseudonyms, most commonly the use of initials. The problem associated with this practice is illustrated by what happened to Jeanne Williams when she began writing novels for young boys. Her editors had convinced her that boys did not read books written by women so she used the byline J. R. Williams on her first three young adult books. When the first of these novels, TAME THE WILD STALLION, won the Cokesbury Book Award in 1957 from the Texas Institute of Letters as the best juvenile of the year, Williams did not learn of the award until two weeks after the presentation ceremony because the organization could not locate any male author named J. R. Williams. Whether this practice was begun by editors to fool a reading audience they believed to be composed largely of misogynistic males or by female authors themselves to garner an unbiased reading from an editor and thus gain entry into a male-dominated field may never be known. Jeanne Williams has told me that she cannot remember how it came about, when she was writing for the pulps, that a sexually ambiguous byline was often attached to her stories. Nonetheless, the fact remains that even as late as the 1980s almost any woman attempting to publish a traditional Western story automatically affixed a sexually blurred identity to her work. There are a few exceptions: one was Dorothy M. Johnson who established a loyal following for her stories through their publication in *Collier's* and *The Saturday Evening Post* prior to their appearance in book collections. Yet, clearly, for the majority of women writers what had begun as a perceived necessity became a restrictive tradition. Only recently has there been some sign of abatement in this practice.

Who were the principal women who wrote adventure stories of the West in the 20th century and what are their contributions? Any survey must begin with B. M. Bower, who was one of the first women to write traditional ranch romances. A contemporary of Owen Wister, she pioneered the romantic cowboy story in her own inimitable and unsophisticated style, de-emphasizing violence and gun play — at least until late in her career. She stressed a sense of light-hearted, frequently slapstick humor, as well as a sense of family often focused exclusively on groups of male characters. It was the success of her interlinked Flying U stories —

originally appearing in pulp magazines and eventually in hardcover books as fifteen novels and short story collections featuring Chip Bennett and/or members of the Happy Family — that, along with the longevity of her forty-year career, secured a place for her in the literary history of the Western story. Indeed, Bower seems to be the token female Western writer favored by scholars, although the entire scope of her work — some seventy novels and hundreds of short stories — has yet to receive the kind of thorough critical assessment it warrants.

Emerging on the scene ten years after Bower began writing, Honoré Willsie Morrow attempted in seven novels to expand Western storylines to encompass feminist ideas as well as political and social issues. Over the years her work has generated a modicum of critical attention, although much of it has been directed at her historical novels set outside the American West or at her biographical novels, particularly the fictional trilogy about Abraham Lincoln known collectively as THE GREAT CAPTAIN (1930). Morrow was born in Ottumwa, Iowa in 1880. Although in her adulthood she visited the West and wrote about the West, she remained an Easterner, closely tied to her New England roots, a circumstance unusual among women Western writers. She was published in many of the slick women's magazines of her day, contributing non-fiction and fictional pieces, only some with Western themes.

Morrow's first novel, THE HEART OF THE DESERT (1913), ran to six printings and is certainly of literary interest because the white heroine ends up happily married to a full-blooded Indian. The narrative concludes with the couple kissing and literally riding off into "the desert sunset". Assuredly a literary event since a similar miscegenation theme in THE VANISHING AMERICAN by Zane Grey, serialized eleven years later in *Ladies Home Journal*, was deemed so potentially shocking for readers that the author was forced to have Nophaie, a Navajo, die before he and the white heroine could marry. Even fifty years after Morrow's novel it was still considered taboo for an interracial marriage to be shown ending happily — in Jane Barry's A TIME IN THE SUN (1962) the heroine's Apache husband dies. Morrow's subsequent Western novels deserve attention, but for other reasons: their concern with women's issues and political and social themes as in EXILE OF THE LARIAT (1932). That Morrow could write such unconventional Western stories and have them published was most likely due to the fact that Frederick A. Stokes was her publisher, a company well known for its controversial list of titles.

Compared to Bower or Morrow, Cherry Wilson is virtually unknown today. Yet in her twenty-year career she produced over 200 short stories and short novels, numerous serials, and five hardcover books, and six motion pictures were based on her fiction. Readers of *Western Story Magazine*, the highest paying of the Street & Smith publications where Wilson was a regular contributor, praised her stories in letters to the editors and ranked them next to those of Max Brand. Wilson moved from Pennsylvania with her parents to the Pacific Northwest when she was sixteen. She gained some experience writing for newspapers as she and her husband led a nomadic life. When Bob Wilson fell ill in 1924, the couple stopped traveling, took up a homestead, and to earn money Wilson decided to write Western fiction. Acceptance of her first story by *Western Story Magazine* began what would prove a long-standing professional relationship with Street & Smith magazine editors.

If thematically Wilson's fiction is similar to B. M. Bower's, stylistically her stories are less episodic and, with growing experience, exhibit a greater maturity of sensibility. Her early work, especially, parallels Bower rather closely in that she developed a series of interconnected tales about the cowhands of the Triangle Z Ranch. There is also a similar emphasis on male bonding and comedic scenes — "All-in" tells how the cowpunchers acquire instruments to form the Triangle Z all-brass band, and "Triangle Z's All-Brass Serenade" has the band serenading a Spanish *señorita* with an imperfect rendition of "Old Black Joe"! She also varied the series by borrowing an idea from Peter B. Kyne's THE THREE GODFATHERS (1913), making her cowpunchers co-operative caretakers of an orphan in seven of the stories, beginning with "Hushaby's Partner" (1926). Perhaps the most unusual and interesting of the Triangle Z stories is "Shootin'-up Sheriff" (1929), contained in this collection, in which a town is taken over by women. Again like Bower, Wilson stressed human relationships and humor in preference to gun play and action. In fact, some of her best work can be found in those stories where the focus is on relationships between children and adults, as in her novel, STORMY (1929), and short stories like "Ghost Town Trail" (1930) — a fascinating tale with an eerie setting and a storyline filled with mystery — and "The Swing Man's Trail" (1930) in which a boy doggedly pursues a herd of rustled cattle that has swept up his family's only cow. In the late 1930s she appears to have been plagued by health problems, and it was probably this that brought her career to an end early in the following decade.

The dust jacket of the first edition of THE OUTCAST OF THE LAZY S, published in 1933, stated: "Eli Colter needs no introduction. His stories of the Northwest have been widely read." The author was actually Eliza Colter who had been competing successfully with male writers in the pulp magazine market since the early 1920s and would write her last stories when in her sixties. Colter's Western stories have little in common with the more ambient world found in Bower or even Wilson. They are gritty, tough, violent, and episodes often become littered with bodies. When film director Howard Hawks said of Leigh Brackett that "she wrote like a man," he meant it as a compliment. The same could be said of Colter. There is virtually nothing about her fiction that would indicate the writer was a wife and mother.

Born in 1890 in Portland, Oregon, Colter was afflicted for a time by blindness when in her early teens. This experience taught her to "drill out" her own education, and that's what she continued to do throughout her life. She lived briefly in the States of

Washington, Georgia, Louisiana, and California. She played piano accompaniment to motion pictures while learning how to write. Although her first story was published in 1918 under a *nom de plume*, she felt her career as a professional really began in 1922 when she sold her first story to *Black Mask*. Colter wrote more than 300 stories and serials, mostly Western fiction. She appeared regularly in thirty-seven different magazines, including slick publications like *Liberty*, and her stories were often showcased on the covers of Fiction House's *Lariat Story Magazine*. She published seven hardcover Western novels. Colter was particularly adept at crafting complex plots out of the traditional Western storylines of her day — range wars as in "The Ghost of Skull Pass" (1938), cattlemen versus homesteaders as in "Mustang Marshal" (1944), and switched identities as in "The Rattlesnake Kid" (1949). No matter what the plot, she somehow always managed to include the unexpected. It might be a mystery element as in "Treasure Trail" (1937) or a shocking scene like the calculated poisoning of the sheriff's wife in "Canyon Rattlers" (1939). That Colter actually showed female characters being killed by the villains — in "Canyon Rattlers" and again in OUTCAST OF THE LAZY S (1933) where a woman is shot in cold blood — was decidedly unusual and outside the accepted conventions of Western stories written by chivalrous male authors of the times. Her villains represent the embodiment of evil — quite possibly a reaction to the constant rash of stories about redeemed outlaws. That Colter had a loyal readership is illustrated by the fact that in pulp magazines where almost no author could have more than one story in a single issue under one byline Colter's byline was often carried on two stories.

Chloe Kathleen Shaw, who wrote most of the time as C. K. Shaw, shares much in common with Colter though her active career in pulp magazines spanned only two decades. Shaw, like Colter, wrote "like a man," and her stories appeared in many of the best-paying pulp markets, *Dime Western, Western Story Magazine, Lariat Story Magazine,* and *Star Western.* More times than not a C. K. Shaw story would be headlined on the front cover. Although she did write stories in which women do figure prominently for romance Western pulps like *Rangeland Love Stories* under the byline Kathleen Shaw, in the majority of her Western stories the woman's point of view is notably absent and often there are no female characters whatsoever. She seemed naturally drawn to characters living on the fringes of the law and frequently her stories are about outlaws. While Shaw shared to an extent Colter's inclination toward pursuit stories — searching for a lost father or for a lost son — as well as stories about good and bad brothers, physical violence is less prevalent in her fiction than in Colter's.

Shaw was born to a long line of ranchers on a homestead in the Cherokee Strip and grew up in eastern Oregon where, she once observed, the "mail arrived according to the conditions of the road, likewise our doctor and our law." If Colter was a master of the well-made plot, Shaw's forte was her ability to create interesting casts of characters through whom and between whom she was able to develop a suspenseful and unpredictable interplay. Especially good examples of her character-driven fiction include "After Ten Years" (1927), "Gunhand's Rep" (1939), and "Three Way Double-Cross" (1942). She was a highly polished and talented writer who, like Colter, throughout her career probably fooled the majority of her readers as to her gender.

Some women became involved in writing Western stories because their husbands successfully wrote them. After her marriage to Fred Glidden who wrote as Luke Short, Florence Elder was urged by her husband to try her hand. She began writing stories under the byline Vic Elder. How much real help her husband was remains a mystery. She once related how, when she was stalled at a crucial point in a story, she asked Fred what she should do. His laconic reply was: "Put in a little action. That's what I do." Action stories, however, were not what Elder was writing. "The Chute to Love", her first published story, was sold in 1935 to *Rangeland Romances* for $50. She continued to write stories for the Western romance magazines for about seven years, until the birth of her third child in 1943. "The Wild One" (1936), while uncharacteristic, remains one of her best stories. In it the hero tries to capture a wild stallion to prove himself to the heroine when, in a surprising reversal, he falls in love with a half-Navajo woman who teaches him the importance of letting the stallion remain free.

Elsa Barker, married to Western poet and short story writer S. Omar Barker, had a much longer career than

Elder. She published over 200 Western stories in the magazine market under her married name, seven Western novels published only in England under the byline E. M. Barker — RIDER ON THE RAMHORN (1956) and COWBOYS CAN'T QUIT (1957) are two good examples and both were serialized in *Ranch Romances* — and had a Dell comic book based on one of her novels. Born in 1906 in Sibley, Illinois, she grew up in New Mexico. In addition to her own writing, she typed all of her husband's manuscripts — approximately 1,500 stories, 1,000 poems, and at least 1,000 fictional pieces. Many of Elsa's stories rely on the conventional plot elements of the ranch romance. There is some impediment to love — usually the failure of one of the lovers to recognize their love for the other — that results in a series of misunderstandings and complications. Her story "Grammar Glamour" (1939) is a fine example of this type of plot and appeared in one of her primary markets, *Ranch Romances*. It can be said that she was at her best when writing about women and what they know. As Bower before her, Barker would have her females perform a logical, but unpredictable, action for a woman in a difficult situation. In "Kitchen Courage" (1940) the heroine curtails the advances of the villain through the use of her oven — she turns up the heat so that the jam jars inside eventually explode, burning and cutting the villain who is seated nearby. This scene brings to mind Bower's novel, TROUBLE RIDES THE WIND (1935), that has the heroine shove a potato in the villain's mouth to stop his torrent of swearing.

By the 1950s the pulps were being replaced by the more compact original paperbacks. *Ranch Romances*, which survived until 1971, changed its editorial format sufficiently to offer one of the few remaining markets for fledgling Western writers, men and women alike. Authors like T. V. Olsen, Elmer Kelton, and Jeanne Williams were among the last of a new generation of Western writers still able to learn their craft in the short story magazine market. Whatever their seeming limitations, the pulps permitted writers greater artistic latitude than did the slicks with their more rigid editorial policies dictated by advertisers. Jeanne Williams could write a conventional story like "Spanish Dagger" (1955) and have it published in *Ranch Romances* as well as an offbeat story like "Brother Shotgun" (1957). The latter, which appears here, is one of her best short stories and one of her personal favorites. Williams met with far more resistance to her experimentalism once she began trying to publish books. While the direction her Western fiction ultimately took was the historical novel rather than the traditional Western story, her first novel, RIVER GUNS, is definitely a traditional Western, originally serialized in *Ranch Romances* in 1957 and published in book form in England in 1963.

Since the 1960s a number of women have entered the arena of the traditional Western story having published first-time hardcover and paperback fiction that was commercially successful in a genre that had been groping for new directions for some time. The critic for *The New York Times Book Review* stated in his review of DAY OF THE HUNTER (1960) that "sometimes a talent gallops out of the brush with a story so natural, so compelling in ramifications and handling, as to confound both the pundits and the veteran practitioners. DAY OF THE HUNTER by A. Ahlswede is such a performance." The initial "A" was for Ann, born in 1928 in Pasadena, California. Her experimentation with the basic structure of the traditional Western resulted in three highly regarded Western novels produced in the same number of years. Subsequent printings of DAY OF THE HUNTER carried her full name, as did HUNTING WOLF (1960) and THE SAVAGE LAND (1962). This last still stands as a classic story of greed that successfully challenged the basic structure and tenets of the traditional Western novel while aspiring to an elevated plateau of literary accomplishment.

Lee Hoffman, a writer whose name was sufficiently ambiguous without use of an initial or two, won the Spur Award from the Western Writers of America for THE VALDEZ HORSES (1967), a poignant story about a Mexican horse breeder and a colt named Banner. Hoffman was born in 1932 in Chicago, Illinois, and began writing stories, many of them Westerns, as a hobby while in the sixth grade. "When I run up against that 'How can you, a mere woman, write Westerns?' attitude," Hoffman once commented, "I mention that in my youth I owned a number of horses, did some trail riding in Colorado and Wyoming, and once worked as a shill to a horse trader in Kansas. I don't go into details about the trail riding being connected with a stay at a dude ranch, or the job with the horse trader only lasting a couple of weeks. He got arrested." Although she first wrote original science fiction paperbacks, Don Wolheim at Ace encouraged her to try a Western story. The result was GUNFIGHT AT LARAMIE (1966), the first of seventeen Western novels, including several comic Westerns like WILEY'S MOVE (1973). In these books Hoffman demonstrated just how adept she was at reworking the elements of a traditional story, particularly by showing her male characters to have frailties.

In much the same fashion Michigan-born P. A. Bechko produced seven Westerns in the 1970s and two in the 1990s. Her first novel, NIGHT OF THE FLAMING GUNS (1974), was marketed by an agent who was surprised to find out she was not a man. With BLOWN TO HELL (1976) Bechko, like Hoffman, ventured into the terrain of the comic Western. Similarly like Hoffman, Bechko proved able to compete successfully in the marketplace and to inject a comic element sorely needed during the 1970s when porno Westerns were at the zenith of their popularity among New York publishers.

L. J. Washburn was born in Lake Worth, Texas, in 1957. Livia became interested in Western films in her teens when, due to poor health, she was confined indoors and watched a lot of television. It was meeting her future husband, James M. Reasoner, which eventually steered her in the direction of writing her own Western stories. Before turning to Westerns exclusively, she experimented with blending her two favorite genres — detective and Western fiction — creating a series detective who works in the West. She followed this series with five traditional Western novels, beginning with EPITAPH (1988), which exhibited her ability to create offbeat characters and situations.

In the early 1980s, Cynthia Haseloff wrote five traditional Western novels under the pseudonym C. H. Haseloff, most of which placed a heroine at the center of the story. In the 1990s, after a ten-year period of silence, Haseloff returned to writing, this time using her actual name. Born in Vernon, Texas, the history and legends of the West were part of Haseloff's upbringing in Arkansas where her family settled shortly after she was born. She wrote her first novel, RIDE SOUTH! (1980), with her mother's encouragement. This unique story is concerned with a woman, a mother, searching for her twin daughters who have been taken captive by Indians. Haseloff proved in this book, as well as in others — MARAUDER (1982), DEAD WOMAN'S TRAIL (1984), THE CHAINS OF SARAI STONE (1995), and SATANTA'S WOMAN (1998) — that female characters can attain heroic and nearly mythological proportions within the framework of a traditional Western story. Her talent, like that of Dorothy M. Johnson, whose works she copied out in longhand when teaching herself how to write, rests in her ability to tell a story with an economy of words and perhaps, more importantly, with an overwhelming sense of humanity, as well as in the seemingly effortless way she uses language.

The women writers surveyed here, as well as others, often have had an uphill struggle to practice their art.

Despite the lack of encouragement or support from the publishing establishment, the critics, and, over the long term, the literary historians, mostly they persisted and often they prevailed. And, despite the odds working against them, they have made lasting contributions to the traditional Western, contributions that warrant recognition.

It has been eighteen years since I put together my first anthology of Western stories by women, WESTWARD THE WOMEN (1984). Since that time I have discovered new voices — some buried among the musty old pages of pulp magazines and others in books, both old and new, some not yet published. I wanted to share these discoveries.

The twelve stories I have chosen for this volume represent ninety-one years of women writing about the West. Their settings stretch from the Kentucky frontier to those in Oregon and the Southwest, from the 1770s to contemporary times. Their topics range from good times to bad times, happy times to sad times, from pulling up stakes to setting down roots. These are stories of men and women — seekers and finders — who made their way to the West and made their way in the West. Each story displays a unique artistry that stems from the heart of these writers in their abiding connection to the landscape, the people, and the history of the American West.

Vicki Piekarski
Portland, Oregon

The Woman at Eighteen-Mile

MARY AUSTIN

In the closing paragraph to her third-person autobiography, EARTH HORIZON (1932), Mary Austin wrote: "It is not that we work upon the Cosmos, but it works in us." The desert, "the land of little rain," as she called it, worked in Austin, shaped her life, shaped her thinking, shaped her art. "The Woman at Eighteen-Mile" is a story within a story in which the female narrator is in search of the "biggest story of the desert ever written". It first appeared in *Harper's Weekly* (25/9/09) and was collected in LOST BORDERS that same year, one of four Austin story collections.

❦

I had long wished to write a story of Death Valley that should be its final word. It was to be so chosen from the limited sort of incidents that could occur there, so charged with the still ferocity of its moods, that I should at length be quit of its obsession, free to

1

concern myself about other affairs. And from the moment of hearing of the finding of Lang's body at Dead Man's Spring I knew I had struck upon the trail of that story.

It was a teamster who told it, stopping over the night at McGee's, a big slow man, face and features all of a bluntness as if he had been dropped before the clay was set. He had a big blunt voice through which his words rolled, dulled along the edges. The same accident that had flattened the outlines of his nose and chin must have happened to his mind, for he was never able to deliver more than the middle of an idea, without any definiteness as to where it began or ended and what it stood next to. He called the dead man Long, and failed to remember who was supposed to have killed him and what about.

We had fallen a-talking 'round the fire of Convict Lake, and the teamster had handed up the incident of Dead Man's Spring as the only thing in his experience that matched with the rooted horror of its name. He had been of the party that recovered the body, and what had stayed with him was the sheer torment of the journey across Death Valley, the aching heat, the steady, sickening glare, the uncertainty as to whether there was a body in the obliterated grave, whether it was Lang's body, and whether they would be able to prove it; and then the exhuming of the dead, like the one real incident in a fever dream. He was very sure of the body, done up in an Indian blanket, striped red and black, with a rope around it like a handle, convenient for carrying. But he had forgotten what set the incident in motion or what became of Lang after that, if it really were Lang in the blanket.

Then I heard of the story again between Red Rock and Coyote Holes, about moon-set, when the stage labored up the long gorge, waking to hear the voices of the passengers run on steadily with the girding of the sand and the rattle of harness chains, run on and break and eddy around Dead Man's Spring, and back up the turgid pools of comment and speculation, falling in shallows of miner's talk, lost at last in a waste of ledges and contracts and forgotten strikes. Waking and falling asleep again, the story shaped itself of the largeness of the night; and then the two men got down at Coyote Holes an hour before the dawn, and I knew no more of them, neither face nor name. But what I had heard of the story confirmed it exactly, the story I had so long sought.

Those who have not lived in a mining country cannot understand how it is possible for whole communities to be so disrupted by the failure of a lode or a fall in the price of silver, that I could live seven years within a day's journey of Dead Man's Spring and not come upon anybody who could give me the whole of that story. I went about asking for it and got sticks and straws. There was a man who had kept bar in Tío Juan at the time, and had been the first to notice Whitmark's dealing with the Shoshone who was supposed to have stolen the body after it was dug up. There was a Mexican who had been the last to see Lang alive and might have told somewhat, but death got him before I did. Once, at a great dinner in San

3

Francisco, a large positive man with a square forehead and a face below it that somehow implied he had shaped it so butting his way through life, across the table two places down, caught at some word of mine, leaning forward above the bank of carnations that divided the cloth.

"Queer thing happened up in that country to a friend of mine, Whitmark . . ." But the toastmaster cut *him* off. All this time the story glimmered like a summer island in a mist, through every man's talk about it, grew and allured, caressing the soul. It had warmth and amplitude like a thing palpable to be stroked. There was a mine in it, a murder and a mystery, great sacrifice, Shoshones, dark and incredibly discreet, and the magnetic will of a man making manifest through all these; there were lonely water holes, deserted camps where coyotes hunted in the streets, fatigues and dreams and voices of the night. And at the last it appeared there was a woman in it.

Curiously, long before I learned of her connection with the story, I had known and liked her for a certain effect she had of being warmed and nourished from within. There was about her a spark, a nuance that men mistook — never more than once, as the stage driver told me confidently — a vitality that had nothing, absolutely nothing but the blank occasionless life of the desert to sustain it. She was one of the very few people I had known able to keep a soul alive and glowing in the wilderness, and I was to find out that she kept it so against the heart of my story. Mine! I called it so by that time, but hers was the right, though she had no

4

more pertinence to the plot than most women have to desert affairs.

She was the Woman of the Eighteen-Mile House. She had the desert mark upon her — lean figure, wasted bosom, the sharp upright furrow between the eyes, the burned tawny skin, with the pallid streak of the dropped eyelids, and, of course, I suppose, she knew her husband from among the lean, sidling, vacuous-looking Borderers; but I couldn't have identified him, so like he was to the other feckless men whom the desert sucks dry and keeps dangling like gourds on a string. Twenty-five years they had drifted from up Bodie way, around Panamint, toward Mojave, worse housed and fed than they might have been in the plowed lands, and without having hit upon the fortune which is primarily the object of every desert adventure. And when people have been as long as that in the Lost Borders there is not the slightest possibility of their coming to anything else. And still the Woman's soul was palpitant and enkindled. At the last, Mayer — that was the husband's name — had settled at the Eighteen-Mile House to care for the stage relays, and I had met the Woman, halting there with the stage, or camping nights on some slower passage.

At the time I learned of her connection with the Whitmark affair, the story still wanted some items of motive and understanding, a knowledge of the man himself, some account of his three months' *pasear* into the hills beyond Mesquite, which certainly had to do with the affair of the mine, but of which he would never be persuaded to speak. And I made perfectly sure of getting the rest of it from the Woman at the Eighteen-Mile.

It was full nine o'clock before the Woman's household was all settled and she had come out upon the stoop of the Eighteen-Mile House to talk, the moon coming up out of Shoshone land, all the hollow of the desert falling away before us, filled with the glitter of that surpassing wonder, the moon-mirage. Never mind what went before to draw her to the point of talking; it could have come about as simply as my saying: "I mean to print this story as I find it," and she would have had to talk to save it. Consider how still it was. Off to the right the figures of my men under their blankets stretched along the ground. Not a leaf to rustle, not a bough to creak. No grass to whisper in the wind, only stiff, scant shrubs and the sandy hills like shoals at the bottom of a lake of light. I could see the Woman's profile, thin and fine against the moon, and when she put up her hand to drag down the thick careless coil of her hair, I guessed we were close upon the heart of the story. And for her the heart of the story was the man, Whitmark.

She had been, at the time he came into the country seventeen years before, that which the world knows so little what to do with that it mostly throws away a good woman with great power and possibilities of passion. Whitmark stood for the best she had known; I should have said, from all I learned, just a clean-minded, acute, tolerably cultivated American business man with an obsession for accomplishing results.

6

He had been sent out to look after a mine to which the title was not clear and there were counter machinations to take it away from him. This much may be told without breach, for, as it turned out, I was not to write that story, after all, at least not in the lifetime of the Woman at the Eighteen-Mile. And the crux of the story to her was one little, so little, moment that, owing to Whitmark's having been taken with pneumonia within a week afterward was rendered fixed beyond change or tarnish of time.

When all this was going forward the Mayers kept a miners' boarding house at Tío Juan, where Whitmark was in and out, and the Woman, who from the first had been attracted by the certain stamp of competency and power, began to help him with warnings, intimations of character and local prejudice, afterward with information which got him the reputation of almost supernatural penetration.

There were reasons why, during his darkest time, Whitmark could find nobody but the Indians and the Woman to trust. Well, he had been wise enough to trust her, and it was plain to see from her account of it that this was the one occasion in life when her soul had stretched itself, observed, judged, wrought, and felt to the full of its power.

She loved him, yes, perhaps — I do not know — if you call love that soul service of a good woman to a man she may not touch. Whitmark had children back East and a wife whom he had married for all the traditions of niceness and denial and abnegation which men demand of the women they expect to marry, and find savorless so often when they are married to it. He had never known what it meant to have a woman concerned in his work, running neck and neck with it, divining his need, supplementing it not with the merely feminine trick of making him more complacent with himself, but with vital remedies and aids. And once he had struck the note of the West, he kindled to the event and enlarged his spirit. The two must have had great moments at the heart of that tremendous coil of circumstance. All this the Woman conveyed to me by the simplest telling of the story as it happened: "I said . . . and he did . . . the Indian went . . ."

I sat within the shallow shadow of the eaves experiencing the full-throated satisfaction of old prospectors over the feel of pay dirt, rubbing it between the thumb and palm, swearing over it softly below the breath. It was as good as that. And I was now to have it! For one thing the Woman made plain to me in the telling was the guilt of Whitmark. Though there was no evidence by which the court could hold him, though she did not believe it, though the fullness of her conviction intrigued me into believing that it did not matter so much what he was — the only way to write that story successfully was to fix forever against Whitmark's name its damning circumstance. The affair had been a good deal noised about at the time and, through whatever illusion of altered name and detail, was bound to be recognized and made much of in the newspapers. The Woman of the Eighteen-Mile saw that. Suddenly she broke off the telling to show me her poor heart, shriveling as I knew hearts to warp and shrink in the aching wilderness, this one occasion rendering it serviceable like a hearth-fire in an empty room.

"It was a night like this he went away," said the Woman, stirring to point to the solemn moonlight poured over all the world.

That was after twenty-two months of struggle had left Whitmark in possession of the property. He was on his way then to visit his family, whom he had seen but once in that time, and was to come again to put in operation the mine he had so hardly won. It was, it should have been, an hour ripe with satisfaction.

"He was to take the stage which passed through Bitter Wells at ten that night," said she, "and I rode out with him . . . he had asked me . . . from Tío Juan to bring back the horses. We started at sunset and reached the Wells a quarter of an hour before the time.

"The moon was half high when the sun went down and I was very happy because it had all come out so well, and he was to come again in two months. We talked as we rode. I told you he was a cheerful man. All the time when it looked as if he might be tried for his life, the worse it looked the more his spirits rose. He would have laughed if he had heard he was to be hung. But that night there was a trouble upon him. It grew as we rode. His face drew, his breath came sighing. He seemed always on the point of speaking and did not. It was as if he had something to say that must be said and at the moment of opening his lips it escaped him. In the moonlight I saw his mouth working and nothing came from it. If I spoke, the trouble went out of his face and when I left off it came again, puzzled wonder and pain.

9

"I know now," said the Woman, shaking forward her thick hair, "that it was a warning, a presentiment. I have heard such things, and it seems as if I should have felt it, too, hovering in the air like that. But I was glad because it had all come out so well and I had had a hand in it. Besides it was not for me." She turned toward me then for the first time, her hair falling forward to encompass all her face but the eyes, wistful with the desire to have me understand how fine this man was in every worldly point, how far above her, and how honored she was to have been the witness of the intimation of his destiny. I said quickly the thing that was expected of me, which was not the thing I thought, and gave her courage for going on.

"Yet," she said, "I was not entirely out of it, because . . . because the thing he said at the last, when he said it, did not seem the least strange to me, though afterward, of course, when I thought of it, it was the strangest good bye I had ever heard.

"We had got down and stood between the horses, and the stage was coming in. We heard the sand fret under it and the moonlight was a cold weight laid upon the world. He took my hand and held it against his breast so . . . and said . . . oh, I am perfectly sure of the words . . . he said . . . 'I have missed you so.' Just that, not good bye, and not *shall* miss you, but, 'I *have* missed you so.'

"Like that," she said, her hands still clasped above her wasted bosom, the quick spirit glowing through it like wine in a turgid glass — "like that," she said. But no; whatever the phrase implied of the failure of the

10

utterly safe and respectable life to satisfy the inmost hunger of the man, it could never have had in it the pain of her impassioned, lonely years. If it had been the one essential word the desert strives to say, it would have been pronounced like that.

"And it was not until the next day," she went on, "it occurred to me that was a strange thing to say to a woman he had seen two or three times a week for nearly two years. But somehow it seemed to me clearer when I heard a week later that he was dead. He had taken cold on the way home, and died after three days. His wife wrote me . . . it was a very nice letter . . . she said he told her I had been kind to him. Kind!" She broke off, and far out under the moon rose the thin howl of coyotes running together in the pack. "And that," said the Woman, "is why I made you promise at the beginning that, if I told you all I knew about Whitmark and Lang, you would not use it."

I jumped. She had done that, and I had promised light-heartedly. People nearly always exact that sort of an assurance in the beginning of confidences; like a woman wanting to be told she is of nobler courage at the moment of committing an indiscretion, a concession to the sacredness of personal experience which always seems so much less once it is delivered, they can be persuaded to forego the promise of inviolateness. I always promise and afterward persuade. But not the Woman of the Eighteen-Mile. If Whitmark had lived, he would have come back and proved his worth, cleared himself by his life and works. As it stood, by the facts against him he was most utterly given over

11

to ill repute. The singularity of the incident, the impossibility of its occurring in any place but Death Valley, conspired to fix the ineffaceable stain upon his wife and his children, for, by the story as I should write it, he ought to have been hung. No use to say modestly that the scratchings of my pen would never reach them. If it were not the biggest story of the desert ever written, I had no wish to write it. And there was the Woman. The story was all she had, absolutely all of heart-stretching, of enlargement and sustenance. What she thought about it was that that last elusive moment, when she touched the forecast shadow of his destiny, was to bind her to save his credit for his children's sake. One must needs be faithful to one's experiences when there are so few of them.

She said something like that, gathering up her hair in both hands, standing before me in the wan revealing light. The mark of the desert was on her. Heart of desolation! But I knew what pinchings of the spirit went to make that mark!

"It was a promise," she said.

"It is a promise."

But I caught myself in the reservation that it should not mean beyond the term of her life.

Shootin'-up Sheriff

CHERRY WILSON

For nearly a decade Cherry Wilson turned out tales about the cowpunchers of the Triangle Z Ranch, all of which appeared in Street & Smith's *Western Story Magazine*. At least thirteen of these light-hearted, humorous stories were published. While "Shootin'-up Sheriff", which appeared in *Western Story Magazine* in the June 15, 1929 issue, pokes fun at women in positions of power and the temperance movement, it is important to remember when and for whom these stories were primarily written. Humor in Wilson's stories was often generated by rôle reversals. This is clearly demonstrated in many of the Triangle Z stories that feature the co-operative efforts of the ranch hands in the raising of Pard, the orphaned baby.

∽⊘ℭ∾

Frequently, and with eloquence, Jerry Paxton informed the cowboys of Triangle Z Ranch that he was not a social arbiter, Solomon, or father confessor. He was a sheriff, the sheriff of Pima County, Arizona, to be exact. He was not possessed, by virtue of his office, or any divine attributes, nor required by it to judge horse races, baby shows, patch up squabbles, or relay proposals of marriage. But Triangle Z could not seem to savvy that! And they were eternally inventing a new game, in which he, Jerry Paxton, was "it," forever getting him into one jackpot after another — each worse than the last.

Hence, the mere sight of the Triangle Z brand on the bay horse outside the window of his office at Gunsight filled Jerry with instant and justifiable apprehension. He had no way of knowing what they wanted today, but he knew it was sure to mean trouble of an extremely painful and personal nature; and apprehensively listening to the scuffle of boots on the step, he grimly vowed to himself that whatever they wanted this time, they would not get it!

As a precautionary measure, before facing the door, he pulled his good-humored old face into an inhuman scowl — only to have it spread out in a grin that went twice around and lapped over in his relieved recognition of the pair coming in. Here were two members of Triangle Z who had always respected the dignity of his office — Hushaby and little Pard, the two-year-old orphan he had fathered from infancy.

Hushaby, a big, homely, sad-eyed buckaroo in a red shirt, green bandanna, and Mexican sombrero, carried the little, black-eyed buckaroo — for if Pard was not a buckaroo, his little pink rompers notwithstanding, nobody was. He had been raised in a bunkhouse, cradled in a packsaddle, and had cut his teeth on a six-gun — as Triangle Z would tell a man. Get the boys started, and they would rave about Pard till the cows came home. And Jerry's interest in the pair was scarcely less than Triangle Z's. It always renewed the old sheriff's faith in his fellowman to see the big, still buckaroo's worship for the baby who had no claim on him.

But the sheriff had hardly more than set out a chair, before he felt a twinge of his first alarm. The very way Hushaby sagged into it told him something was wrong, something mighty serious, to judge by his aspect. Even little Pard knew. For, sitting there on Hushaby's knee, his big, solemn black eyes devouring Jerry, he was far more serious than a baby should be.

"Great hop toad!" The sheriff surveyed the woebegone pair in amazement. "What's the calamity? You look like you ain't got a friend on earth."

He was startled by the haggard and heartbroken countenance Hushaby raised. "I . . . I wouldn't have, Jerry," miserably faltered the big buckaroo, "if them I got knowed what I am."

"Rats!" snorted Jerry inelegantly. "We know what you are . . . a square-shooter. They don't make 'em better. We know what you been, too, if that's what's worryin' you . . . Derringer Reese, a regular smoke-'em-up till you fell heir to Pard here, an' come to Triangle Z, where the boys heard you singin' them hushaby songs to him, an' pinned a new label on you. What are you that your friends don't know?"

"A thief," groaned Hushaby, clutching the baby, "the orneriest kind of a thief. The sort o' two-legged varmint which robs pore leetle orphans."

"You're loco." Jerry lapsed back in his chair. "Loco with the heat."

Wearily Hushaby shook his head. "That's what the boys think out to the ranch . . . but they don't know. Jist the same, Jerry, I will be if this keeps on. It's gittin' so I ain't accountable for my acts. Every day it gits worse. Fer every day I'm a-stealin' over thirty cents from this here leetle man."

Jerry tugged his weeping-willow mustache in sober thought. The Triangle boys had the right hunch. Pard had nothing to steal. And if he had, it couldn't be safer in a bank than with Hushaby. Didn't he spend every cent of his wages on that baby's upkeep? He never even went on an occasional spree, but worked like a dog all day punching cows for Triangle Z, and was up half the night looking after the baby. That was it! All work and no play had given him a hallucination. Jerry was sick with pity.

"Thirty cents a day," confessed the 'puncher, so drearily that little Pard's face puckered in sympathy, "is what I'm a-stealin' from him. I been at it most two years now . . . seven hundred an' two days, by the calendar on the bunkhouse wall . . . which makes two hundred an' thirty-four bucks which I've stole to date. An' tomorrow will tack thirty cents onto that, an' the nex' day . . ."

"Hold on, Hushaby!" Jerry lifted a hand restrainingly, and added, in a tone meant to be soothing to a man laboring under an awful delusion: "We've had a long, hot spell. Can't recall a longer hot spell before. Hitch your chair around to the winder, Hushaby . . . there's a

16

breeze comin' in. An' when you're all cool an' calm, suppose you tell me where Pard got all this money which you allege yourself to have stole from him."

But Hushaby protested pathetically: "I ain't batty! He got it from his pappy. You know how his pappy, Tim Casey, was pals with me when I was Derringer Reese, and how Tim married a *señorita* down in Chihuahua who died when Pard come? An' how a guerrilla bullet got Tim in less'n a week? An' you know how Tim give me his baby when he was dyin', and said . . . 'Take him back to God's country, Derringer, an' bring him up to be a regular *hombre*'? But that," said Hushaby sadly, as Jerry signified his familiarity with this much of the story, "is just half of the trust Tim put in me.

"Tim told me," continued Hushaby mournfully, as the sheriff leaned forward, intent to hear more of little Pard's history, "as how he had two thousand bucks in the bank at Bear Paw, New Mexico. He writ me a order on it, an' give me the key. 'Yank that money outta cold storage . . . ' was his dyin' words, Jerry . . . 'an' put it on interest at six percent, so the baby'll have a start when he gits of age.' But I couldn't do that an' keep Pard. So I let it stay, when it shoulda been makin' thirty cents a day. An' every day it ain't, I'm the same as stealin' that much from him."

Jerry saw the point in a hazy way. But he was far from convinced of Hushaby's sanity.

"If you got a order an' key," he demanded logically, "why, in the name of jurisprudence, don't you go and git the money? Bear Paw's just over the state line . . . a four-day ride from here."

"But I can't go there!" cried Hushaby. And his blank hopelessness drew a whimper from the worried baby. "I dassent show my face in Bear Paw, Jerry. Oncet . . . when I was Derringer Reese . . . I stampeded that place. They got charges enough ag'in' me there to send me up for the rest of my life. They'd take Pard away from me!" His head dropped despairingly.

Pard reached up, got the green bandanna in his dimpled fists, and, elevating himself, faced Jerry, his little feet planted uncertainly on Hushaby's knee, his little arms about Hushaby's neck, his hot little cheek pressed to Hushaby's. It was a picture of innocent love and trust that touched the old sheriff's heart. And, being touched, Jerry characteristically waxed sarcastic.

"So you got the habit!" he accused Hushaby. "You're as bad as the rest of Triangle Z. You want I should go git that money. Think it's right in my line of duty to traipse to a town two hundred miles off for a *hombre* what's raised such a ruction in it that he dassent go back there hisself."

"No-o," said the 'puncher, after considering it gloomily. "That wouldn't work, Jerry. But I'm mighty obliged to you just the same. You see, Rimrock . . . he's the banker . . . wouldn't give it to you. He'd honor a order straight from Tim to me, but not if it come through a third party."

"Waal," inquired Jerry suspiciously, "where do I come in?"

"Why," pleaded Hushaby, and little Pard's eyes seemed to implore Jerry, too, "I figgered as how if you'd go with me an' sorta pave the way . . . tell 'em I was

18

plumb reformed, an' sorry fer what I done . . . they'd mebbe let me git Pard's money an' go free. You see, they'd believe you, Jerry."

There it was again — that blind and sublime faith in his ability to perform any old miracle they wanted performed!

"By the way an' incidentally" — Jerry was satirical again — "what did you do that Bear Paw got it in fer you?"

Hushaby's dark face was stained with a blush of honest shame. "Aplenty!" he moaned. "You see, I'd been with a trail herd all summer, an' jist got paid off when I rode into Bear Paw. You know how it is, Jerry, when a *hombre* ain't been in a town or human comp'ny fer months?"

Having been a range man for more years than he had been a sheriff, Jerry knew.

"An' cravin' a leetle innocent pastime, I . . . I shot all the winders out of the Montezuma Hotel."

"Waal," decided the sheriff judicially, "that ain't no penitentiary offense."

"Then I . . . I seen a barrel a-settin' in front of the Mesquitery, an' I shot a hole in it, an', bein' thirsty, I drunk a lot, an' it . . . it was cider, Jerry . . . an' hard. So I don't recollect plain what-all I done. I just mind bangin' away at the street lamps, an' sloshin' around in the dark, with some yahoo yellin' as how I'd opened the fire plugs an' flooded the town, an' . . ."

"You'd best end your recollections there," Jerry struck in, "an' pray Bear Paw's done the same. However, you don't need to see anybody but this man

19

Rimrock. Slip in town, go to the bank, git Pard's money, an' sky-hoot back to Triangle Z."

But this simple procedure was out of the question, because, as Hushaby owned, more despondently: "I done more to Rimrock than I done to Bear Paw."

There was a long, solemn pause. "All right," prompted the sheriff, prepared for the worst, "what did you do to Rimrock?"

"I . . . I made a monkey outta him!" Hushaby's face flamed again. "I didn't know who he was, when I rode my hoss into the Montezuma, bustin' into a room where him an' a lot more long-faced *hombres* was convened . . . a directors' meetin', I heered later. An' it give me the willies, Jerry, to see 'em convenin' so solemncholy. So I made Rimrock . . . him bein' the longest-faced one in the lot . . . do a fandango to cheer 'em up. When that didn't faze 'em, I made him speak a piece . . . 'Mary Had a Leetle Lamb,' it was. An' seein' that didn't jolly 'em none, I . . . I made him sing that song . . . you know, Jerry . . . 'I'm wild and woolly an' fulla fleas, an' hard to curry below the . . .' "

"I know." Jerry was all but inaudible with horror, merely to hear of such liberties having been taken with the sacred person of a banker. "An' then?"

"Why, then . . . I run outta ammunition."

"Thanks fer small favors!" cried Jerry fervently, trying vainly to associate the perpetrator of this outrage with the mild, gentle, and pitifully penitent 'puncher before him. "Still," he predicted, as Hushaby's face dropped a couple more notches, "a lot of water's run under the bridge since then. Mebbe Rimrock's left Bear

20

Paw. He might even be dead. One never can tell what's happened."

But the big 'puncher knew better. "He'll be there," he moaned, "an' he'll be hostile. I heered he was advocatin' to hang me, if caught, a long time after. But if you'll tell him, Jerry, how I'm repentin' of it, ask his pardon fer me, an' explain about me an' my baby, he might let bygones be bygones an' give me Pard's money."

The cat was entirely out of the bag at last. In the sight of Sheriff Jerry Paxton, it was a mighty black cat. Instinct warned him to harden his heart and treat it rough. But it was as unthinkable to him as to Hushaby that a helpless orphan be cheated out of his thirty cents a day. And he was influenced by the courage Hushaby had shown in coming to him. Hushaby could have kept quiet about that money. Instead, he had owned up like a man, was willing to risk arrest and imprisonment rather than let the loss go on. He deserved any help the law could give him.

"Reckon a deputy could handle the business here," he gave in — and Hushaby grinned through the rift of hope in his gloom while little Pard was as happy as a baby could be to see him normal again.

But by way of apology for what he considered his weakness in being led into this worst of all jackpots that Triangle Z was ever to get him into, this trouble of such a painfully personal nature that he was never to think of it, even years later, without a shudder, Jerry remarked sententiously: "I don't wish it said that a orphan asked Jerry Paxton for bread an' he gave him a stone."

★   ★   ★

Old Xipe, god of the ancient Aztecs, had rolled midway down the western heavens to shoot his golden arrows, when, four days later, a little cavalcade halted on the summit of Lost Burro Range. It consisted of a hard-bitten old frontier sheriff on a bald-faced roan, a rangy bay, bearing a moody 'puncher and a darling youngster, and a pinto pack horse. Below them, a couple of miles or so, but deceptively near in the thin, clear air, sprawled the town of Bear Paw. Beside them was a white road sign, boldly lettered:

ARIZONA-NEW MEXICO

This was the state line. Once Sheriff Jerry Paxton stepped over it, he left behind all his vested authority, and became merely a citizen of the common or garden variety. And for Hushaby it was the dead line. Here, he was a respected member of society, there, a deep-dyed desperado, a fugitive, wanted on numerous, serious charges, subject to arrest and conviction that might shut him from the sight of men, orphaning Pard all over again. And conscience forced him to cross that line.

"But not today," vetoed Jerry firmly. "It's three o'clock now. The bank's closed. An' we ain't runnin' no more risk than we got to. I'll go down in the mornin'. But you stay right here in ol' Arizony, till I see how the land lays."

So they made camp on the home side of the line, under the roadside piñons. Hushaby's face was gray with strain as he thought of the morning. Not that he had lost faith in Jerry's ability to placate Rimrock; but there was a chance that he might not — and a chance of losing Pard was enough to break Hushaby.

Morosely he stripped the packsaddle from the extra horse, and, hanging it upside down between two piñons, gently laid little Pard — drowsy from the long ride and July heat — in it to sleep; noting, for the first time, how his little feet hung over the edge, and thinking of the many, many times he had bedded Pard down in it like this, when he did fit in, with plenty of room to stretch and squirm. He was proud Pard had grown. But there was a pain in his heart — as on that day Pard had taken his first, wobbly step — a pang that only a mother could understand.

And Jerry, relaxed under the trees, watching this tableau, wished that Rimrock could see it, too. He wished that the whole town of Bear Paw could have taken this four-day trip — seen that pair as he had seen them. For nobody could see Hushaby with the baby and believe there was a bit of meanness left in him. Not that he fussed over Pard much. It was just the way he looked at him — with his homely face shining plumb beautiful, like a lamp had been lighted within him.

Jerry had conceived a high respect for the man Bear Paw knew as Derringer Reese. He still kicked about coming, but that was merely on principle. He would go a lot farther for Hushaby, and do a lot more than just relay his apology to a hostile banker. He did not share Hushaby's fear as to the outcome. No man could be hard on a reformed outlaw with a baby on his hands, and a sheriff to vouch for him.

23

So his sleep was as untroubled that night as was Pard's, nestled under the blanket on Hushaby's arm. But the ex-outlaw saw the big yellow stars blossom and fade on night's black field. Thoughts kept him awake. Terrible thoughts of what he'd done before he got Pard — could it have been he? Happy thoughts of his blameless life since at Triangle Z. Dread thoughts of what the morrow might bring. Hushaby was tempted to slide out in the night with Pard. But, no — that wouldn't help things. No matter where he went, that thirty cents a day . . . He could not steal another penny from his baby!

Jerry saw the marks of this vigil in his face next morning, pityingly noted how he pushed back his flapjacks and bacon, left his coffee untasted. And he said, to cheer him: "Buck up, Hushaby. Nothin's so bad but it could be worse."

And when Hushaby couldn't buck up, Jerry decided to go into town. It was early, but he said kindly: "I'll scout around till the bank opens an' git a line on how things stack up. Then I'll know better how to tackle Rimrock. But whatever I do, be sure I'll have your best interests at heart."

He shook hands with Hushaby, chucked Pard under the chin, and hit the downgrade for Bear Paw. Once he looked back. The big fellow and the little fellow, who was not knee-high to him, were standing side by side under the piñons, wistfully watching. And, anxious to relieve their suspense, Jerry spurred to a gallop that brought him to town on the double-quick.

Years ago, duty had brought him to Bear Paw. It was a wild, wide-open border settlement then, dirty and odoriferous to a degree that still clung to his memory. But, traversing the long street of sun-blistered and warped, false-fronted shacks, Jerry was not thinking of Bear Paw as he had first seen it, but as it must have looked to Hushaby that night when he rode into it with money in his pockets and trail fever in his blood.

He saw, on his left, the Mesquitery, where hard cider had lit the spark that blew Hushaby up. It was not in operation now, for the door was padlocked. And there was the Montezuma Hotel, where Hushaby had ridden his horse into a meeting of bank directors, making a monkey out of the president, and necessitating this round-about way of withdrawing Pard's money from his bank. There were the fire hydrants he had opened, the street lamps he had smashed — everything.

Yet Jerry could not believe that this had all happened here. Not because of Hushaby's changed personality — but Bear Paw did not look as though anything exciting had ever happened to it. The town was so quiet he could have heard the very clocks tick. The streets were so clean that a right finicky man could have "et off them." The windows were so brightly gleaming that he could see three of him — his real self and, on either side, a reflection of it. And there was not an odor about Bear Paw he could catch — unless it was the odor of sanctity. For, though this was Saturday — when ranchers and 'punchers should be in town, doing their trading or making whoopee — it had all the earmarks of Sunday. There was but a man or two to a block. And

25

they weren't bunched together in social fashion, but moping along alone, stepping as if on eggs, and talking to themselves plumb pious.

His mystification growing by leaps and bounds, Jerry saw a cowboy he knew come out of a store with a glass of jam — one Profanity Jones, a former Lazy K waddy, whom he'd run out of Gunsight. As Jerry watched, Profanity hooked his spur in a bag of beans, and fell flat, smashing the jam jar to smithereens. His face was villainous as he picked himself out of the mess. And Jerry, edging his horse over, sure that Profanity would live up to his name and downright eager to hear it — thus already did Bear Paw affect him — was dumbfounded to hear the cowboy murmur — "By sassafras" — and look around like a scared rabbit.

All this was getting on Jerry's nerves, when he saw the jail ahead, and forgot Bear Paw in the birth of a brilliant idea. He would go there, make himself known, and sound out the sheriff as to the sentiment here against Derringer Reese. If he could win the officer over to Hushaby's cause, he might take him along when he apologized to Rimrock.

So, tying his horse outside, Jerry strode into the office. After the glaring sun, the gloom in here blinded him. But he readily made out the glitter of a sheriff's star on the figure behind the desk, and bore down on it, with hand outstretched, and the hearty, fraternal greeting: "Git up, ol' hoss, an' meet Jerry Paxton . . . your brother in the law."

He all but dropped dead the next instant, for the star was pinned to the blue-serge breast of a woman! An

26

ample woman! A veritable Amazon, with a cold, blue, inquiring eye, and a this-rock-shall-fly-from-its-firm-base-as-soon-as-I chin expression.

"I am the sheriff," she said, with polite frigidity, rising. "Did you wish to see me?"

Making a superhuman effort, Jerry blurted: "Heck, no!" Then, realizing how ungallant that sounded: "I . . . I mean I wasn't prepared for your bein' a lady. I'm the sheriff of Pima County, Arizona, an' I wished to see the local sheriff about a man . . ."

"You won't find him here," she said coldly. "We don't harbor suspicious characters in Bear Paw, and men with criminal records give us a wide berth. You can take my word for it that your man isn't here."

None knew that better than Jerry. His man was safe in old Arizona. He thanked his stars for it, the while he debated how to tell her about Hushaby. Sparring for time and poise, he did what he always did in moments of stress — began to work on a cigarette. But he fumbled the job when he saw her lips go thin, and her index finger stiffen toward a placard tacked over her desk.

No Smoking! it said.

"A vile habit!" Scathingly she denounced him and it. "One we've about stamped out here."

Jerry, cravenly pocketing the makings, was unaware that he was already muttering to himself, quite like the other men of Bear Paw.

"In fact," said the awful female with much satisfaction, "you will find this town exemplary in every respect. The law is enforced. My program is one of crime prevention, as well as detection and apprehension. Smoking is frowned on. Swearing a punishable offense. Gambling, rigidly banned. No form of nightlife tolerated. And Bear Paw has a clean bill of health . . . thanks to a man."

"A man?" Shocked unbelief quivered Jerry's mustache.

"Strange as it may seem, and is," was the reluctant admission, "a man is responsible for Bear Paw's present condition."

Feeling it a public duty to run him down and massacre him, Jerry gasped: "Who . . . for Pete's sake?"

Bear Paw's sheriff was too intent on her answer to notice his expression.

"Derringer Reese," she told him. "The outlaw . . . Reese," she went on, heedless that paralysis had affected her visitor, "proved the last straw. A little over two years ago, he invaded this town . . . shot it up, as the phrase goes. His felonious action aroused the women into becoming politically active. We organized. And, at the next election, we ousted the men, electing a straight women's ticket . . . sheriff, marshal, mayor . . . a woman to every office in city and county. We've not been in power two years yet, but we've accomplished a lot. No one who saw Bear Paw before can fail to perceive the effects."

Timidly but feelingly, Jerry affirmed: "I ain't no exception."

She thawed a bit to him. "Instead of having the town full of rowdies once a week, corrupting the morals of the young, with speak-easies flourishing, and poker

28

dens, we have a clean little city. For recreation, there is the church . . . also the movie . . . films, of course, selected by a special committee. Usually we have an educational film. Last week Bear Paw was privileged to see *The Life of the Boll Weevil*. And this week the picture is to be, *Salmon, The King of the Fish, from Ocean to Table*."

Jerry's pity for Bear Paw was only exceeded by his concern for Hushaby.

"Look over the town," the sheriff invited, with the zeal of a born reformer. "You may pick up some ideas for the moral improvement of your own county."

Jerry's eyes flared. His county! Where a man could swear at his own risk, smoke when, where, and what he liked, and prowl of nights! Where a man could be a man! Pattern his county after this — this white sepulcher! The mere thought gave him spunk enough to bring up the subject heavy on his heart.

"About this here Derringer Reese, the man who made you what you are today . . ." — he approached it delicately, guiltily, as her cold eyes fixed like searchlights on him. "What would you do if he came back?"

"What would I do?" She jerked up eagerly. "Put him in that good, strong cell back there. Why, we built this jail in that happy anticipation."

"But if he'd reformed?" faltered old Jerry, trembling in his cowboy boots, losing hope of evoking her sympathy. "If he was plumb sorry for what he'd done? If he had a ba . . ."

29

"I wish he would come back!" Her desirous gaze went right through him. "To arrest that perfectly terrible Derringer Reese . . . just the feather my cap needs."

Shocked by her revengeful disposition, in terror lest she read his mind in another minute, Jerry beat a quick retreat. He meandered aimlessly upstreet, debating what next. They sure had it in for Derringer Reese in this women's town. Ladies ruled the Bear Paw roost, and the female of the species — Hushaby better turn tail for Triangle Z. But Pard's money . . . ?

Seeing the bank ahead, Jerry started that way, determined to throw Hushaby on Rimrock's mercy. He was a man; he might understand, might let Hushaby sneak in after dark, and get Pard's money. But, almost there, Jerry remembered that Hushaby was responsible for the present condition of the town — which would make him plumb poison to a Bear Paw man. And his nerve, badly shaken by his interview with the sheriff, seemed to have utterly failed him.

He had no proof that Derringer Reese had reformed. Just his word. At home it was as good as a bond, but he was far from home. What Jerry needed was direct evidence to show Rimrock — proof that Hushaby would not make a monkey out of a banker again. Moping upstreet, morbid as any Bear Paw male, he turned his brain wrong-side out, suddenly seizing on another bright thought. He had it. Pard! That baby was living testimony to the change in Hushaby. All Pard was, he owed to him, and he was so cute he'd melt any heart. Jerry turned back for his roan. He'd hotfoot it to camp, and fetch Pard to convince Rimrock. Yeah, the baby would help them out of this difficulty.

He betrayed so much optimism when he galloped into camp that Hushaby sprang forward, crying eagerly: "You fixed it, Jerry? Rimrock's goin' to give me Pard's money?"

"Don't bust a latigo." Jerry hadn't the heart to tell the worried buckaroo the direful results of his old rampage in Bear Paw. "Rome, you know, wasn't built in a day. I come back fer Pard. I need him for evidence."

Fear shot through Hushaby. "You can't take him, Jerry!" he cried fiercely. "Not without me! Not to a place where I can't go. No, Jerry, I can't trust him to nobody . . ."

"Good grief!" exploded the sheriff, with some justification. "The people of Pima County trust me to handle their bandits, maniacs, an' even murderers! Reckon I can look after a two-year-old fer an hour or two. Ain't I traipsed two hundred miles to help you?"

But Hushaby had caught that slip. Jerry had had a run-in with somebody. He couldn't risk Pard where there was trouble. "I'd trust my life with you, Jerry," he said piteously, "but not this baby."

"If you don't," returned Jerry bluntly, "you may lose him for considerable more than a hour or two."

Hushaby's shoulders sagged in mute resignation. Wordlessly he picked up the canteen, wet a corner of his bandanna, and with it tenderly washed Pard's little round face. He slicked his black hair back with a rough, damp palm. Then, pulling his dress off over his head, he

31

put his pink rompers on, and delivered him over to Jerry.

"You'll bring him back?"

The old sheriff's eyes smarted at the agony that looked out of Hushaby's. "As sure as there's a heaven," he vowed. How mockingly that vow, in all its solemnity, was to return to Jerry.

"Good bye, Pard," choked Hushaby, blindly waving as the roan moved off.

Pard strained back, bewildered and hurt. Every day Hushaby left him at the bunkhouse and rode off to work. But he had never left Hushaby. His world was turning topsy-turvy, but he played the game as he had been taught.

"'Bye!" he said, waving his little fist back. "'Bye! 'Bye!"

And the big fellow called, as he covered his eyes, "Take him quick, Jerry!"

Manfully little Pard swallowed his sobs, downing so many of them that Jerry felt the little form quiver and shake in his arms. It worried him. Bad for a baby to hold in that way — might bust something!

"Thar, thar, Pard!" He fibbed to comfort him. "Hushaby won't be far. Betcha he's in Bear Paw afore we are. Ol' Jerry'll find him."

Then the strangely assorted pair rode into the town where a man couldn't draw a long breath without committing a crime, pulling up this time before the bank.

It was a one-room, one-horse affair, and dead as a doornail. When Jerry entered with Pard, there was not a

32

soul in it except the long-faced individual behind the wicket, whom he knew from description and instinct could only be Rimrock. Appreciating for the first time what a daredevil Hushaby must have been to make game of this iceberg of a man, the old sheriff shifted Pard more conspicuously to his breast, and introduced himself.

"Rimrock" — Jerry's self-assurance oozed fast, once he was embarked on his apology for Hushaby — "I come to talk to you, man to man. We're both old enough to know how even the best of us makes mistakes . . . lapse from grace and . . . Rimrock," he repeated, wholly disconcerted by the banker's unbending reserve, "I've come in behalf of a *hombre* what's got business with your bank but can't tend to it fer hisself, because . . . Waal, you see, he uset to be a rip-snortin' sidewinder. But he's plumb reformed . . . Rimrock" — desperately the sheriff started off on a new tack — "I brung his baby!"

To his dismay he saw that Pard, who should have melted the stoniest heart, had no effect whatsoever upon the banker's.

"Who is this man?" Cold, that query.

Jerry gave up. "Husha . . . I mean, Derringer Reese."

Startlingly Rimrock came to life. His hand shot through the wicket, clamping like a handcuff on Jerry's wrist. A fire kindled in his eyes, leaping into a blue blaze, as he clipped greedily: "Is he here? Near? Quick . . . tell me?"

Appalled by his vindictive spirit, Jerry said bitterly: "He's in Arizony."

33

"But he hasn't reformed?" the man entreated. "Don't tell me that, man."

In proof of it Jerry held out his living testimony.

But impatiently Rimrock waved it aside. "Deuce take the baby! It's Reese I'm asking about."

But the affront to Pard had lit blue blazes in Jerry's eyes, and, putting him on the floor, he lifted an outraged face.

"If it's Derringer Reese," blind to the sheriff's anger, Rimrock raved, "he hasn't reformed . . . it isn't possible! If he has, there's no balm in Gilead . . . no hope anywhere."

Stunned by that speech, Jerry failed to observe Pard toddling to the sunny door to see if Hushaby was out there.

"We need Derringer Reese!" proclaimed Rimrock wildly. "Man, I'll say we do. Go . . . tell him to come to Bear Paw at fast as horseflesh can bring him."

Truth rang in his tone, and Jerry was wild to be on his way right then. But Rimrock struck him as a little too cordial. "You forgive him?" he stopped to ask. "You ain't holdin' Mary's lamb or the flea song ag'in' him?"

Bitter memory darkened the banker's face. "Why bring that up?" he snapped. "There's something bigger at stake. I don't intend to bite off my nose to spite my face."

"You won't have him arrested?" the perplexed old sheriff insisted, sure that there was a string to it now.

"Not if he comes like I say."

"How's he to come?"

"Like he did before." Jerry was knocked cold by that fervent response. "Shooting out the lights! Flooding the town! Raising merry Hades! Only," stipulated Rimrock hastily, "he's to let me alone. That's the only restriction."

"Yeah," Jerry scoffed, in the bitterness of his heart, "an' have that gimlet-eyed, froze-faced ol' sheriff-ess . . ."

"Sir!" Rimrock's mien dropped to subzero again.

Chilled by it, Jerry modified. "That straight-laced ol' hen . . ."

"Missus Rimrock," icily instructed the banker. "Use respect when you speak of my wife. For she is my wife. Yes, sir . . ." — crashing a fist on the counter, with a rapid rise in temperature — "what God has joined together, Derringer Reese . . . the whole county . . . can't put asunder!"

As Jerry listened in horror to this new item in the long list of charges that Bear Paw held against Hushaby, Rimrock continued: "She was content, Paxton, merely to reform me, until he went on that spree. Then I wasn't enough for her . . . she had to go to work on the county. I told her a woman's place was at home . . . and she left me. I tried to show her she wasn't equal to such a job . . . now she won't speak to me. Hasn't spoke to me," said the banker with infinite pathos, "since a year last Tuesday." He sighed and shrugged, continuing plaintively: "Half the husbands in Bear Paw are in the same fix. This town's gone to the dogs. Business is ruined. Everyone who can goes to Red Gulch to trade . . . where a man has some freedom. If this keeps up, my bank will close. Our only hope is to have a real desperado go berserk here, and scare the women back to the kitchens, show them they aren't capable of handling a real situation. And I can think of no man better qualified for that office than Derringer Reese."

Jerry's face was a study. He had a lively sympathy for the male population of Bear Paw, but . . . "I'm a sheriff," he explained miserably. "An' he's reformed. I can't advise him to take up the old ways, even for a noble purpose."

"Those are my terms." The home-hungry banker stood by his guns. "He can take them, or leave them. If he makes Bear Paw look like a tornado hit it, I'll give him his money. If not, I'll sic my wife onto him. I know now that he's in your county. She can extradite him. I tell you, I'm a desperate man."

So, too, was Jerry. Hushaby wouldn't be safe, hereafter, even in Arizona. He'd have thirty cents more on his conscience every day that he lived. And if something wasn't done about Bear Paw *pronto*, the bank would go bust, and Pard's money . . .

Jerry's eyes sought Pard. But, in that square box of a bank, there wasn't a sign of a baby! He dashed to the door, looking upstreet for a pair of pink rompers. But all he saw was a melancholy cowboy sitting with bowed head on the curb before a vacated tobacco store. He swung his eyes downstreet, and panic seized him. Little Pard was paddling right by the jail door. Before Jerry gained the sidewalk, two long blue-serge arms reached out, snatching the infant into the sheriff's lair.

Stricken, Jerry just stood and stared. What could he tell Hushaby? Remorsefully he recalled the look in the big fellow's eyes when he turned Pard over to him, and his own solemn pledge to restore him safely. He would rather face the Old Nick than that woman again! But Hushaby . . . Between the devil and the deep blue sea, Jerry made his choice. His jaw set in determination. Sheer bravado swelled his chest inches beyond its normal expansion. Rimrock's delinquent better half would find that there was a man in Bear Paw.

Taking his courage in both hands and holding onto it hard, he marched to the jail and went right in. It helped his morale that, right at first, she did not see him. She sat at the desk with the bunkhouse baby in her lap, drying his eyes with her own handkerchief, and making little clucking noises to soothe him — but without much success. But merely seeing her employed as he thought a woman should be destroyed most of Jerry's first awe of her, so that he managed to say, quite naturally: "Thanks, ma'am, fer apprehendin' my baby fer me."

He quaked again, as she took cold note of him and said: "Your baby?"

"In my custody," he quavered weakly. "The little rascal made his getaway while I was in the bank."

Rising in all her majesty, she sat the weeping babe on the desk, and placed herself before him protectively. "You didn't have him when you were in here before. I saw you riding into town this morning, and you didn't have a baby."

"N-not the first time." No sheep-killing hound ever looked so guilty as Jerry. "I . . . I went back fer him."

"Back where?"

"W-where I left him." In his extremity, Jerry craned his neck to look behind her, pleading for substantiation. "Didn't I, Pard? Pard, you know me? You know ol' Jerry."

But the two-year-old, sobbing his heart out for Hushaby, wouldn't back him, only wept the louder at the sight of him. Mrs. Rimrock eyed Jerry Paxton in frank suspicion. There was something queer about his actions. He might be impersonating an officer. And with an epidemic of kidnapping sweeping the nation . . .

"You won't get this child," she laid down the law, "unless you prove your claim to him."

"I can prove it!" insisted Jerry. "I can prove it by Rimrock. He seen me have him . . ." His voice faltered as he realized that she would be prejudiced against that witness — a husband that she would not speak to.

But the banker was his only hope, so he rushed from the office and hurried upstreet. He was turning into the bank, when, on his ears — now attuned to Bear Paw's peace — crashed furious hoof beats. With a horrible suspicion, he swung to see, confirming it — a bay horse, tearing madly downstreet, with a wild-eyed, red-shirted buckaroo — Hushaby!

Completely confused by this fatal twist in the awful dilemma, Jerry flew to meet him, babbling, as he seized Hushaby's bridle: "Oh, Jeroosalum, why didn't you stay put? Ain't I already in it up to my neck?"

"Where's Pard?" Hushaby flung out, in terror at Jerry's condition, at not finding Pard with him.

"Safe," the old sheriff had just the wit to assure him, as he pulled Hushaby's horse into a convenient alley, raving chaotically: "But you ain't, by a blamed sight! You ain't heard nothing yet. You got no idea what you done to Bear Paw. You give it a woman sheriff, which ain't only a sheriff but Rimrock's wife, which you alienated . . . you an' a county! An' he's goin' to sic her onto you, if . . . Hushaby, they built a cell fer you special. An' she wants you fer a feather in her cap!"

But Hushaby's mind clung to a single thought. "I knowed something was wrong!" he cried distractedly. "I waited till I couldn't stand it no more, then . . . Where's Pard?"

Faced with the inevitable, Jerry told him: "That ol' she-sheriff nabbed him. An' she won't give him to me, till . . ."

"She'll give him to me," grimly promised Hushaby — no, Derringer Reese. For his eyes blazed with the reckless light of his outlaw days.

Derringer Reese was back in Bear Paw, in the very mood to do all Rimrock asked, and more. Frantically racking his brain for a way to prevent this catastrophe, Jerry talked for time: "See here, don't you go loco. That's just what they want you to do . . . go bad. You'll be twice as bad, if you have a relapse. You'd be locked up fer life, an' shame Pard. What would become of him . . . pore leetle orphan. You'd never see him ag'in . . . they wouldn't let anyone bring him." He had struck the one chord that could touch Hushaby, and he played on it for all it was worth. "No, siree! They wouldn't let a baby inside of a prison. You set tight . . . while I think. We got to git her out of that office without him. Wait!"

A sign on the window of a store, half a block down, caught his eye — gave him his fatal idea.

"I got it, Hushaby." Swiftly he outlined his plan, pointing to the sign. "There's a place what sells fireworks. I jist know they'll be ag'in' the law here. Anyhow, I aim to see. I'll git a bunch an' shoot 'em off in that vacant lot there, while you slip around the block, an' edge up to the jail. She'll come a-rampin' to enforce the law, an' you sneak in, git Pard, an' light out like the Ol' Scratch was after you . . . which it will be. Don't stop this side of the state line. Pard's money ain't no object now. I'll be plenty lucky if I git you two outta Bear Paw!"

Having won the slow-thinking buckaroo to these tactics at last and seen him depart for the jail by a circuitous route, Jerry spurted for the store that sold fireworks. Business being what it was, he got immediate service. And in two minutes he was stationed in the vacant lot, with a box of matches and a big bundle of explosives.

As he struck the first match, he glimpsed Hushaby nearing the jail warily, his big sombrero shielding his face, taxing all his restraint to maintain that inconspicuous pace. Then, steeling himself to do his part, Jerry lit the fuse of a giant cracker, held it until it was spitting sparks almost to the powder.

Bang! Like a cannon it burst on the calm of Bear Paw.

40

Quickly Jerry darted a glance at the jail, in every expectation of seeing a blue gown come flying out. But none came.

Boom! Another cracker burst on the air. Still there was no sign of her. But Hushaby was almost there.

Beside himself now, Jerry set off a whole bunch at a time, then several bunches — *bang, bang, bang!* The only result was to convince him that fireworks were not prohibited, and that it would take something more drastic to jar her out of that office. Forced to it by the sight of Hushaby — who had caught little Pard's heartbroken wails — breaking into a run, Jerry pulled out his gun and emptied it in the air. He heard glass crash, as he made a bull's-eye on a street lamp, and realized with numbing horror that he, Sheriff Jerry Paxton, was shooting up a town.

Then something happened — he never knew what. Maybe it was just his reaction to Bear Paw, maybe something snapped. Anyhow, he was seized by an uncontrollable desire to do it up brown. Something ought to be done about Bear Paw. Even Rimrock, its first citizen, said so. And he would sure cure the town of what ailed it, if the she-sheriff didn't come.

Grimly reloading his gun, he banged away at every inanimate thing in range. Windows suffered in vacant stores, more lamps came down, and Jerry noted, with fiendish glee, that Bear Paw was beginning to look more like it had the first time he saw it — more like a regular town. He saw that others were being drawn by the uproar, if Sheriff Mrs. Rimrock was not. The two or three solitary men on the block had bunched, and after the first awed, open-mouthed moment, overcome by more excitement than they had seen in months, gave signs of still possessing the instincts of he-men.

"Atta-boy, pop!" yelled one, heaving a rock at the poor fish on the poster in front of the theater — star of this week's uplifting offering. While another defiantly waved a plug of bootlegged tobacco on high, with the stirring war cry: "Liberty or death!"

It was with no intent of heading an insurrection that Jerry raced for the fire hydrant that inspiringly loomed in his vision, but with the memory of how advantageously Derringer Reese had used this instrument in getting the sheriff after him. He also realized that Hushaby had vanished inside the jail, and that he, Jerry, must roust the woman sheriff out of there before she discovered who Hushaby was and arrested him.

So with this much method in his madness, he bore down on the hydrant. After him came the long-suffering populace, shouting the battle cry of freedom. Jerry grappled with the hydrant, gave it a hard twist — and a mighty river sprang forth, sweeping his followers back before it.

Sighting a second hydrant, he sprinted for it and was getting a good grip on the plug, when a hand fell on his shoulder — a hand as white as a snowflake, and as light. The berserk old sheriff looked up at the prettiest girl he had seen in his life.

"You must come with me," she lisped — actually! "I'm the city marshal. And I have to arrest you for your disorderly conduct, sir."

Dumbly Jerry stared at her. He had planned to make a break the instant the sheriff of Bear Paw rushed out of the jail, and wait for Pard and Hushaby on the trail. But this turn of events upset his plan, left him with none, held him helpless, while sanity rushed back to him. He saw the size of the crime he had committed for Hushaby. Also, the penalty. But he couldn't see himself facing it — letting a baby-face like this arrest him.

"I'm sure," she said, with sweet severity, "you are too much of a gentleman to make trouble for me."

Handcuffs could not have been more effective. Jerry went with her like a gentleman, and meekly sloshed after her across the street, wondering if he would share a cell with Hushaby.

But when he was led into the jail, he was dumbfounded to see that Hushaby was still free. Not only that, he and the sheriff were engaged in earnest, almost tearful, converse. With Pard jumping for joy in his arms, and his plain face lit up by the lamp of love, Hushaby was telling his troubles to Mrs. Rimrock, a heap too interested to see Jerry. But she saw him.

"Lock him up, Daisy," she said briefly, turning right back to Hushaby. "Now, my good man, go on with your story."

While the big buckaroo touchingly told how Pard had redeemed him, and the men of Bear Paw slumped back into virtue for lack of a leader, the sheriff of Pima County was locked in the good, strong cell built for Derringer Reese.

Up the corridor, through the bars, drifted Hushaby's voice: "When I first got him, I aimed to lay up thirty cents for him every day outta my pay. But somethin' allus come up to take it. Orange juice, ma'am, an' fresh hen eggs . . . baby chuck like that costs a heap in a cow country. An' his leetle clo'es cost most as much as a man's. An' his doctor bill when he had the mumps . . . ma'am, I can't risk goin' in debt to him deeper. I owe him more'n two hundred bucks as it is. But I'll scrimp the rest of my life to pay that, if you an' Rimrock will only give me his money an' let me go back home."

Mrs. Rimrock's voice reached Jerry, too — but so sweet and low and womanly that he hardly knew it. "Mister Reese, I never heard anything so affecting. And the reunion between you two . . . Nobody can tell me you were ever an outlaw at heart. And I believe the law is intended for the uses of justice . . . not for revenge, or persecution. One sinner that repents gives me more joy than a hundred who have never transgressed. Come with me to the bank" — now the voice sounded more like Mrs. Rimrock's — "I'll see that you get your money."

From his cell window, Jerry saw the three wending upstreet, while he . . . As usual, when he tried to help Triangle Z, he was the goat. Jerry's thoughts were blue. He could be sent to the penitentiary for what he had done for Hushaby. And, even if he got off scot-free, it would all come out at the trial, and his political goose would be cooked. Nobody would vote to re-elect a sheriff who had shot up a town in his term of office. A woman's town, too! He would be laughed out of the county. Jerry cussed and choked impotently. When the little Daisy who had locked him there appeared at the bars, plaintively requesting him please to be still and not make her head ache, Jerry was even too far gone to act like a gentleman.

Rimrock had been surprised when he heard that the "tornado" hit Bear Paw. He had thought it fast action, even for Derringer Reese — who he had been told was in Arizona. But it could not be any too fast for the homesick man. Nervous lest the outlaw forget the one restriction imposed on him, he had hidden away in the strongest vault, there listening with timorous pleasure to the muted sounds of the blows being struck for his home, Bear Paw at large, and business in general. He did not emerge until moments after the old hush fell back on the town.

Tiptoeing then to the window to have a peek at the ruin that was to prove to the women their incapability of handling a real situation, he saw — his wife and the terrible outlaw. Being of a jealous disposition, he lost all concern for trade and Bear Paw in his selfish and natural ire at beholding his wife strolling up, on obviously warm and intimate terms, with the man who had caused the original trouble.

"Mister Reese" — fuel to the listener's flames was Mrs. Rimrock's intense sincerity — "you are one of nature's own noblemen."

"Ma'am," fiercely Hushaby's fervency fanned the fire, "you're an angel outta heaven."

Rimrock seethed inwardly. But the green-eyed monster had not yet blunted his reason to the exclusion of self-preservation. He ducked back behind the partition, presenting a hostile face — the only vulnerable part of his body — to Derringer Reese, as they came up to the window, with, he now saw, a baby between them.

Oblivious to her husband's flaming condition, Mrs. Rimrock viewed him as impersonally as though he were one of the fixtures, when, for the first time in a year, she spoke to him: "This gentleman," she said, inferring, by her inflection, that Hushaby was the only person present who could possibly answer to that description, "had an order to enter the safety deposit box of Tim Casey. Also, the key. Attend to him, please."

This was too much. "I'll attend to him!" Rimrock stormed. "Desperado or not, he can't 'angel' my wife." He flew out of his coop to where his wife stood, blushing like a peony, with Hushaby, who was helpless with shock that such an interpretation should be put on his simple expression of gratitude, while little Pard, big-eyed with fright, backed up to Hushaby for protection.

"Why, George," Mrs. Rimrock was startled out of her official poise, "I believe you're jealous!"

He did not deny it. "Nature's nobleman!" he rasped. "Angel! Who wouldn't be?" He put up his fists in a way that meant business and warned Hushaby to defend himself.

With a woman's instinct to protect the helpless, Mrs. Rimrock snatched Pard out of harm's way. Her swift action diverted the gaze of her husband. He looked at her, and what he saw robbed him of all desire for violence. For he saw her — as he had not seen her in

46

years — with a warm, maternal glow in her eyes and a baby in her arms.

The banker put his hands to his face, crying: "Molly, you look just like you did when . . . He looks like . . . Tad. You and him . . . Molly!"

A lovely light broke over her face — lovely, in its tragic joy and pain at what had been. And she whispered as slowly she moved toward him: "You remember . . . Tad?"

Rimrock moaned: "Remember him?"

Then they were in each other's arms. While the big buckaroo stood first on one foot, then on the other, feeling mighty unnecessary, and wishing they would hurry up and give him Pard's money, so he could go at once and find Jerry.

When they did come to their senses, perfectly reconciled, Hushaby had to be told all about Tad — their only child, who had died — whom Pard looked like. Then Rimrock had to hear Hushaby's story. After which, Rimrock apologized to Hushaby, and, before he knew it, Hushaby was doing what he had asked Jerry to come two hundred miles to do for him — begging Rimrock's pardon for the scandalous way he had treated him. The banker was giving it to him with thanks, when, all excited, the pretty marshal of Bear Paw burst into the bank, breathlessly crying to Bear Paw's sheriff: "Oh, Molly, that prisoner . . . He won't be good! I can't do a thing with him. He says we can't hold him without preferring charges, that he knows his rights and insists on them. He's awful! I can't handle him."

"I will," said the valiant sheriff of Bear Paw.

"I'll go with you," offered her husband. "You may need my help. A man . . ."

"Thanks," she declined, "but I won't need any help. I'm quite equal to the situation."

Remembering that this was the rock that had wrecked their matrimonial bark, Rimrock wisely did not insist.

"I won't be gone long," she promised, leaving with Daisy. "And . . . oh, yes, George . . . give Mister Reese his money."

She was back at her desk, her stern self again, when old Jerry Paxton stamped in under guard, raving: "I got my rights, ma'am, an' I know 'em! What's more, I'm a-standing on 'em! I'm jist one of the paltry ninety-nine, but I got as much right to a hearin' as any sinner. An' if you think I'm a-goin' to shut up without a hearin', you got another think a-comin'!"

With admirable poise, Mrs. Rimrock ignored him. "Daisy," she asked calmly, "what are the charges against this man?"

Daisy was stumped for an answer. "There're so many," she lisped. "He mussed the streets with a lot of glass, for one thing. And he muddied them . . . turning the water on. And . . . I can't think of all the things he did. But he . . . swore at me!"

Surveying her palpitating prisoner, the sheriff summed up her honest opinion of him in a word: "Hardened." Then she announced her decision: "We'll lock him up, Daisy, without bail, for breaking the peace, until we can investigate his claims of being an Arizona sheriff. If he is, it will go hard with him, for conduct so unbecoming to an officer. But I've a notion that you'll find you have captured a notorious criminal."

"Investigate his claim" — that was all Jerry heard. Spread his shame on his home range. Tear his reputation to rags, while he was locked up in Hushaby's cell unable to say a word for himself. Where was Hushaby? Why didn't he come and say something, when he had a stand-in with the sheriff?

There was Hushaby, coming in the door with the baby. Surprise and horror were in his eyes, as they rested on Jerry, and on his tongue — which wouldn't work — the whole story. Jerry suddenly, desperately, did not want that story told. It might hurt Hushaby's cause, and it could not help his, would even make it worse — proving that he had committed his crime with malice aforethought. Then, again, something snapped.

For, in that second, while Hushaby strove to unclamp his tongue, and Mrs. Rimrock — excusably off guard, considering the emotional scene she had just been through — held out her arms for Pard, Jerry made a break, ran . . .

He burst out the open door, and made long tracks for his roan in front of the bank, carrying an indelible impression of the startled faces he had left. He saw no more, for, galloping out of Bear Paw, he was too intent on getting ahead to look behind. He raced for dear freedom's sake toward the Arizona state line, nor did he stop until he was several yards west of it.

★ ★ ★

Here, in their camp under the piñons — packed to travel, and pacing belligerently in the wild wish that the Bear Paw sheriff would rampage over the line after him so he could show his authority — Hushaby found him.

"Now, by hickory," Jerry burst out on the big buckaroo and the little one, when they rode in, "I'm a sheriff ag'in! An' I'm goin' to work at it! The nex' yahoo what comes to me with a pitiful tale is a-goin' to git kicked out on his ear. Savvy? The only person I'm goin' to pity from now on is me, number one, Jerry."

With which he mounted his roan, and pointed the little cavalcade down the west slope of Lost Burro Range. He had gone a mile homeward, before he broke out again. "Soft-hearted, heck. I'm soft in the head. What do I git for my pains? Here you are, now, ace-high in Bear Paw. Here I am, a fugitive . . . outlawed thar . . . liable to arrest any minute, fer that woman will sure extradite me."

"No, she won't, Jerry," said Hushaby, with some diffidence. "She's a angel, if ever there was . . ." Jerry's glare silenced him.

"Don't 'angel' that female to me!" stormed the official shock-absorber for Triangle Z. "I got eyes to see, an' ears to hear, an' I seen an' heard plenty! Likewise, I got feelin's . . . an' she plumb cauterized 'em."

But loyal as Hushaby was to Jerry, he had to defend the lady who had helped him. "So would you cauterize a *hombre* what done to Gunsight what you done to

50

Bear Paw. She told me . . . her an' Daisy. An' she was pretty mad at you, Jerry. But when I told her how you was jist tryin' to help me, she said she wouldn't prosecute you at all, if . . . if . . ."

"Shoot," Jerry commanded. "Reckon, now, I can stand anything."

"If you stayed outta Bear Paw."

"Which," feelingly snorted the old sheriff, "I sure aim to. I lived twenty years in that town today. An' if I never go back, it's soon enough."

"But you can go back real soon, if you want to, Jerry," promised Hushaby eagerly. "You see, Rimrock an' his missus made up, an' she's goin' to resign in favor of a man. She never liked sheriffin', she said . . . just wanted to show him she could. Daisy's goin' to quit if Missus Rimrock does. Men's comin' back in Bear Paw."

Great news for Jerry. He knew where he stood with the Bear Paw men, after what he had done for them. But it took a mile or two more of Arizona air to cool him down.

"This here leetle man" — Hushaby surveyed Pard proudly — "saved the day fer everybody. If he hadn't 'a' looked like the Rimrock baby, they mightn't 'a' been reconciled, an' I wouldn't 'a' got his money. Everything wouldn't 'a' turned out so happy."

Jerry turned to look at little Pard, who merrily laughed back at him, and he quit sulking to drop back companionably with Hushaby, and chuck the bunkhouse baby under the chin.

"You fat little rascal!" he reproved Pard with a chuckle. "You wouldn't own me. You know me, now. Ought to . . . ol' Jerry shot up a town fer you."

So, happily, they followed the westering sun to Pima County and Triangle Z.

The Drought

DOROTHY SCARBOROUGH

At the Writer's Club at Columbia University, Edna Ferber mentioned to Dorothy Scarborough that she felt nervous and jittery. Scarborough, who had invited Ferber to speak at the meeting, suggested it might be the wind and then went on to explain the effects of the wind and dry conditions on people, particularly women, and of her intention to tell such a story; she did in THE WIND (1925), her pessimistic and most well-known novel. The theme of the novel had already been touched on in this short story, "The Drought", which was published in *Century Magazine* in the May, 1920 issue.

⸎⸎⸎

Bessie Hickson gazed in despair at her little vegetable garden, which the drought had killed. She and Ed had planted it with eager pride in the early Texas spring, thinking that it would furnish their living through most of the summer, and that they could sell enough extra vegetables from it to provide for their other necessities until autumn. Ed would have no money coming in till he had sold his cotton in the autumn, for he was a tenant farmer, working a few acres on shares, planting only cotton and wholly dependent on the success of that single crop.

The garden had flourished flamboyantly at first, she and Ed tending it with the enthusiasm of very young and newly married folk who adore their first garden, and with the anxiety of those who realize that much depends upon its growth. But the drought had come with its hot days and dewless nights, and now the gay, green plants were shriveled and dead, the cornstalks standing like skeletons that rattled in the wind, the withered beans trailing from their rude sticks in disarray, and all the carefully tended beds full of dead leaves and sifting, powdery dust.

As the young wife sat by the window of her house, looking at the ruined garden and the cotton field behind it, she permitted herself for the first time to face her situation squarely. Until now she had hidden the facts behind her, trusting with the unreasoning optimism of youth to some illogical reversal of events that would make her life again the easy, pleasant thing it had always been until recently. But now she took her thoughts out as from some dark closet into the light of day and considered them. She needed money desperately, and none was available. In September there would be a baby, and she must make its tiny clothes. She had already delayed too long, but now at last something must be done.

"What am I going to *do*?" she asked herself querulously. "I don't see any way out . . . unless . . ."

54

She shrank from that "unless." She wouldn't face that yet; perhaps there would be some other way.

The house, a mere shanty set on the edge of the cotton field, warped by sun and rain, its paint washed away save for a few cracked flakes, its porch lurching forward, and its shed-kitchen dragging back like a slattern's skirt that is hitched up in front and trailing in the rear, was obviously a house that had given up hope.

She could see Ed in the field, chopping cotton, his body, clad in faded blue overalls, bent over the hoe as he patiently cut the weeds from the rows, a red bandanna handkerchief about his neck, and his serious young face shaded by a Mexican straw hat, with broad brim and peaked crown. The sturdy young cotton plants, not yet hurt by the drought that had killed less hardy growths, lifted proud leaves to the light, as in defiance of inimical forces of nature, as if daring the drought to touch that field. Surely rain would come before the cotton crop was ruined, Bess Hickson told herself. The autumn would bring them money, but she could not wait till then.

"It's middle o' June now," she whispered. "I can't wait no longer. There ain't nothing I can do . . . unless . . . unless I wrote to ask Pappy for money. I'd rather die than do that."

Her mind fled from its dreary present to the past, so recent, yet so remote! Until a few months before, Bessie had shaken a gay head with its crinkly red-brown hair as defiantly as a frisky colt at anything that did not please her, and had twinkled her amber-colored eyes at

55

tiresome duties. Country neighbors had said her father spoiled her, but Jeff Holcomb had been wont to laugh gruffly and say: "Well, ef Bess an' I suit each other, nobody else has any kick comin'."

She had not heard from or written to him since her elopement the autumn before. With a shiver she remembered his cold fury when she told him of her marriage. She had followed him out to the cow pen to keep him company while he did the milking, as she often used to do, for they had been fast cronies, she and this hard man who had loved nobody in the world but his motherless daughter.

"Pappy, Ed Hickson and I got married today . . . ," she had faltered as he straightened up to rest a moment from his task.

When, in answer to his look of dazed astonishment, she repeated her frightened avowal, he had lunged to his feet, hurling over the pail of milk beside him.

"Damnation! Then git your duds an' git out of my house . . . quick!"

"But, Pappy," she had cried in alarm, "you'll *like* Ed when you know him better!"

"Like him! He ain't got no more backbone than a twine string. I wouldn't give the scrapin's off my boot heel for him . . . an' you've married him!" His wrath seemed about to choke him.

She had laid importunate hands on his arm, only to be shaken off.

"But listen, Pappy! He's just a boy, only twenty-one. He hasn't had a chance yet."

"I reckon he thinks he'll get his chance by settin' up here to be supported by me ... but he's missed his guess," was the grim rejoinder

"No, Pappy," she had interposed eagerly, "he's rented a piece of land across the Brazos, about forty miles off, an' he's goin' to farm it. We'll live there."

"A pore tenant farmer, scratchin' somebody else's land to raise a bale or two of cotton! An' to think you've thrown yourself away on this *nothin'*, you fool, when I'd 'a' done anything in the world for you!"

She had shrunk in terror from this thick-voiced, furious man, this stranger to her.

"But, Pappy, I wouldn't 'a' thought you'd treat me like this!" Her voice had broken on a sob.

His clenched fists and rigid veins accused her.

"Go, I tell you, damn you! I don't want ever to see you or hear from you again. An' don't come crawlin' to me when he starves you, as he'll sure do."

She had whirled from him, sobbing — "*I won't!*" — with something of his own fierce pride in her voice.

Until now she had kept her word about seeing him or writing to him. She had meant to write, of course, for she loved him. She had meant to send him a loving letter, not to ask any favor, but to tell when she could that he had been mistaken, that Ed was doing well, and that she was happy. She had waited till she might be able to tell him that.

All through the winter she had waited in the rickety house through which the searching northers crept. She had thought of the comfortable living room at home, with its roaring open fire, of her own chamber, furnished girlishly, as she and Ed had huddled over the stove in their front room, or eaten their meager meals from the table in the shed-kitchen. Those two rooms were all they had. She had thought to write in the spring, as soon as Ed had gotten his crop started promisingly, so that she could speak with optimism; but since the drought had ruined their vegetable garden and was threatening to damage their cotton, the prospect was not one to boast of.

She could scarcely bear to think of going on forever like this, in a tenant farmer's struggle between the elements and debt. To farm land on shares meant mortgaging all one's hopes of a crop in the stores to pay for supplies through the year, so that if the cotton failed, one was swamped under hopeless obligations. Already Ed looked dejected when she told him of any household need, so that she had reduced her requests to the lowest possible limit.

At the thought of the future, she was sick with apprehension. Her undernourished body felt a physical fear of what lay before her, and her spirit cowered at the idea of their cruel poverty.

"I wouldn't ask Pappy for nothin' for myself," she muttered. "I'd starve an' freeze an' go naked, as I've pretty near done a'ready, before I'd call on him, after what he said. But baby's got to have some clothes, an' Ed needs proper food to do his work on . . . an' there ain't no other way as I can see."

And so presently she wrote:

Dear Pappy:

I've been meaning to write you for a long time, but I haven't had much news to tell you. I think about you lots, and I wish I could see you. I love you just like I used to, Pappy, and more, because I reckon I've got more sense now than when I treated you like I did.

Ed's mighty good to me, Pappy. He ain't never spoke a cross word to me yet, and he does the best he can. But he's had a run of bad luck lately, it looks like. The drought killed our truck garden, and we are out of money. Won't you let us have enough to make out on till our cotton's sold? We need money for groceries, and I want some for something special besides. There ain't nobody else to give it to me, Pappy, but you. I'll tell you later what I'm going to do with part of it.

When Ed gets on better, I'm coming home to see you. You'll let me, won't you?

Your girl,
Bessie

"If the baby's a boy, I'll name him for his grandpa," she said, with an old-time lift of her head, and a sparkle coming into her amber-colored eyes. "I know Pappy ain't held spite against me for eight months, but he's been waiting for me to write. Pappy was always bitter proud when he got his back up about anything."

She estimated that she could get an answer to her letter by Friday, and she could scarcely control her impatience during the intervening time. Now that the struggle involved in making her decision was over, she realized as she had not before what wretchedness she had endured — needlessly, as she now told herself. Why hadn't she written long before?

On Friday morning she threw her apron over her head and ran down the road to wait for the rural postman, glad that Ed was working in the far end of the field, so that he could not see her. She would tell him about it in good time, and she pictured the relief that would come to his sober young face.

The sun beat fiercely down upon her as she waited. Far down the road came a whirl of yellow-gray dust that might conceal the carrier and his cart. Why didn't he hurry and bring her letter from Pappy? As she stood there, her memory drew pictures of her father, a man passionate in his love for her, passionate in his angers. She could see his big frame stoop as he folded her in his arms, his brown eyes alight with devotion. Other people feared the frown he wore, but for her his mouth and eyes had always smiled till that last day. She was beginning to realize what a parent's love for a child is, and she groped toward understanding of how her unconsidered action had wounded him. Wasn't his fury merely from thwarted hopes for her, from jealousy of a husband who could not make her life what his father heart had dreamed of for her?

She leaned tremulously against the barbed-wire fence, her gaze sweeping the little farm in its pitiful details, the small house forlorn of paint, the few chickens scratching drearily about the steps, the bare yard, the cotton field where Ed was toiling away. She

60

closed her eyes for an instant to vision another farm in the Brazos bottom, a rich, well-cared-for place, with its white house and cluster of outbuildings set among blackberry trees. She saw a graying, middle-aged man going about his chores, milking in the cow pen with no daughter to companion him with her chatter, sitting alone on the porch at evening, always solitary, missing his girl every hour.

"A girl don't never have but one Pappy," she murmured.

The carrier halted his fat, wheezy horse and leaned from his cart.

"Well, I got a letter for you this morning," he said sociably.

Trembling, she took the envelope addressed in the sprawling hand she well knew. She felt unable for the moment to open it, for her heart seemed determined to bound out of her body; but her eyes caressed the name his hand had penned. How strange it must have felt for Pappy to write that new name: Mrs. Ed Hickson! She held the letter in her hand and watched the postman jog along the road till his cart was again obscured in the cloud of dust.

Her quivering fingers tore off the end of the envelope, and drew out a folded sheet from which fluttered a blue slip of paper, a postal order for fifty dollars.

"Oh, Pappy!" she cried ecstatically.

And so he loved her, as always! And so, as always, he delighted to give her without demur what she asked!

She held the letter against her leaping heart before she read it.

And so you think you can come it over me so easy, do you? Treat me like dirt, send me nary a word for eight months, and never give me a thought till you need money. *Well, you can't!* That fine husband of yours can support his wife. The only use you can put my money to is to buy yourself decent clothes to leave him in. I hope you're ready to do that.

If you're willing to cut loose from him, you come on home, and I'll do for you same as ever. I want you back, as you might know. But I want my girl back, not Ed Hickson's wife! Unless you've changed mightily, I know you'll act honest in this.

Jeff Holcomb

When she had read the letter twice over, and realized that it said what it did, a faintness swept over her, and she clutched the barbed-wire fence for support, as the cotton rows overran one another and blurred before her anguished eyes. *Pappy!*

Staggeringly she crept back into the house, to fall on the bed and lie there, shaken by tearless shudders, till it was time to get Ed's noonday dinner ready. She mustn't let Ed know!

The next morning she gathered together the coarse sacks in which flour and cornmeal and sugar had come, and boiled them for a long time on the stove, and then hung them in the sun to bleach. She had never been taught to sew, and, when she set about her task, without any patterns to guide her, her unaccustomed fingers were very clumsy. She wept as the rough cloth scratched her hands, and she thought how harsh it would be for tender baby skin. How had life so incomprehensibly trapped her at eighteen!

At first she was fearful lest Ed might notice that something troubled her, and then she felt hurt that he did not. She told herself that he was only a boy, and that he didn't realize what she was going through, and that he had his own worries. The drought was beginning seriously to menace the cotton, and his gaze was ever on the fields, as if by taking thought he might call down the saving rain. The graceful, upstanding plants were still green, and opening great white blossoms like hibiscus or mallows. Bess had always loved the cotton blooms, but now she felt terror at thinking how her fate hung on them. The flowers that last such a brief time, changing from milky pearl as they first opened to a soft rose, and then to lavender as they died, were such lovely things, if only they didn't have such tyrannic power over man!

"The cotton's stood up pretty well so far, but the drought's beginning to hurt it," Ed commented forebodingly one day. He had laid down a pallet, a quilt spread out on the porch floor, so that he might rest during the worst of the noonday heat.

A lizard darted across the porch, panting with heat, its bright, beady eyes winking ironically at him. A

63

scissortail balanced himself on the barbed-wire fence, and from somewhere a jay sent a jeering cry.

"A farmer shore has a tough time of it," Ed went on moodily. "No matter how hard he works, the weather can always beat him if it takes a mind. Looks like the weather's got a spite against us sometimes."

"It's awful hard on folks as well as crops," Bessie answered apathetically.

She felt withered from the heat, which daily grew worse, and weak from lack of food. She so dreaded to harass Ed by requests for supplies that she stinted herself in order to give him what he needed, and she was hungry all the time. And their little house in the open field, unshaded by trees, was like an oven, especially when the fire was made in the woodstove for cooking.

Ed worked doggedly in the field as the drought grew more intolerable, pitting his puny strength against an unseen force that menaced and derided him. From her window Bess could watch him toiling at his task, his patient figure comical in its grotesque garb, tragic in the intensity of its struggle against a cruel force of nature. The cotton plants were stunted in their growth and had lost their bright, erect dignity and their shimmer of refreshing green. Their leaves hung limply, covered with a gray dust from the road.

"We won't make *nothing* if this here drought don't break," Ed declared in desperation one day as he pushed his plate from him at the table.

Bessie lifted a drawn and haggard face.

"I think I'll *die* if this keeps up much longer!"

"You got it easier'n I have." His tone sounded harsh. "You can lie around the house, but I got to work in this sun that's hot enough to frizzle the insides of a horned frog!"

Her eyes filled with tears.

"You oughtn't to speak cross to me, though!"

"Lord alive, don't you realize what a feller's up against when he's got to bake his brains in this murderin' heat?" he cried savagely. "An' he don't know whether all his hard knocks is goin' for nothin', after all! A farmer's life is a dog's life, let me tell you, if he's farmin' on shares. This here drought is gettin' on my nerves."

He rose abruptly from the table, rasping his chair against the floor in a way to set her own nerves quivering.

"You don't never think of my feelings!" she cried impetuously. "This sort o' life is mighty hard for me, that ain't never been used to it. I didn't expect . . ."

"Then you oughtn't to married a poor man," he jeered.

"I wish I hadn't," she flung at him, and then shrank back, appalled at the sight of his face. He looked as if someone had stabbed him in the back.

In an instant they were in each other's arms.

"Oh, we don't mean what we're saying!" she cried desperately. "It's this heat that upsets us so. Nothing matters, so long as we've got each other."

She felt his body tremble as he held her close, and saw the tears run down his cheeks.

65

"Yes, this drought tears us all to pieces," he muttered. "We got to stand up against it the best we can, or it'll get us."

Day after day the sky was cloudless and intensely blue. Day after day the sun strode nakedly across the heavens, and sank in many-colored fire in the west at evening. Sometimes the air was still, so that they panted for breath, but more often the hot winds blew across the field, sprinkling over everything fine gray dust like ashes of despair. The baked earth cracked in deep fissures like gaping, bloodless wounds.

One day from curiosity Bess broke an egg on the top of a stone in the sun by her kitchen door, and watched the white cook as in a frying pan.

"Hot enough to fry an egg in the sun!" she cried shrilly, though there was no one to hear her. Afterward she scraped up the egg and ate it, reproaching herself for her wastefulness. Their supplies were running tragically low, and both she and Ed were weakened from lack of food, since Ed hated risking refusal for further credit at the store.

Ed would gaze at his cotton field with a look of desperation in his eyes, and then scan the blue emptiness of sky in search of a cloud, as a shipwrecked mariner on a lonely sea might look for a sail.

"It's enough to drive a feller mad to have to work ag'in' the odds like this," he growled morosely one day. "Looks like the elements was shakin' us like a terrier shakes a rat, an' laughin' at us all the time."

"Don't you reckon it'll rain *soon*?" Bess asked in a parched voice, fanning herself with her apron.

"Don't seem like it'll ever rain again . . . looks like it's forgot how. I'd ruther be that there yellow dog than a tenant farmer!"

He flung his hand out toward an old hound that had stolen in from the road and lay looking forlornly at them, his tongue hanging far out of his mouth, his bony sides quivering. He seemed mutely to entreat some reason for this suffering he had to endure. The half dozen chickens, huddled in the shade of the house, drooped miserably, their wings spread fanwise in the effort to cool their bodies.

Bess lay wilted on the bed much of the time now, though the bed itself was uncomfortably hot to the touch. She conjured up images of the cool, shaded rooms in her father's house, of the protecting trees, of the creek that ran back of the house, but chiefly of the plentiful things to eat. Home! If only she could open the refrigerator there and eat her fill for once, and drink deep drafts of ice-cold milk! She and Ed never had any ice or milk, or, in fact, anything that they could possibly do without. Day by day there was less to eat; the cupboard was almost empty, and the fevered chickens were dying of starvation and heat.

There is something about intense heat that devitalizes body and spirit far more than bitter cold can do. One perishes inwardly under it; one surrenders hope, and yet has not strength enough for active despair.

"Maybe Pappy would have wrote different, if he had known I was hungry," Bess whispered to herself one day. She talked more to herself when Ed was in the field than she did to him when he was present, for she could not share her poignant thoughts with him, lest she add to his suffering and anxiety. "Shorely Pappy would have wrote different, if he had known about the baby!"

She sat huddled on the edge of the bed for a long time, and then she crept over to the door, to stand leaning against it, looking up at the sky. The sun, high in the afternoon heavens, shook insolent spears of light at her, and the fleckless blue was a mirror of despair.

Presently she walked to the dresser, where under a concealing sheet of newspaper her father's letter lay. The cracked mirror gave her back a face she scarcely recognized, it was so drawn, discolored, ravaged by anxiety, and thin from hunger.

She held the blue slip in her shaking fingers for a long moment. "If I could only cash this and get enough to eat . . . for the baby's sake!" Her fingers closed over it with resolve, her body thrilling at the thought of food; she would call Ed quickly and send him for supplies.

Then the memory of those last terrible moments with her father in the cow pen swept over her. She heard again his searing words: "I don't want ever to see you or hear from you again! And don't you come crawling to me when he starves you, as he'll sure do!" She heard her sobbing vow: "I won't!"

Could she take his help now, like a shamed and beaten thing begging for food? If he knew her plight, wouldn't his hatred and contempt for Ed be ten-fold worse than before? How could she put such humiliation upon Ed, poor Ed, who worked so hard and did his pitiful best for her?

If she used this money now, Pappy would think Ed responsible for it, would misjudge him further. He was a hard man, but he had always been rigidly honest, and she was his daughter. She saw again the words of his letter: Unless you've changed mightily, I know you'll act honest in this.

She had changed mightily — Oh, Pappy, yes! — but she would act honest.

Her weak, relaxing fingers put the blue slip back in its hiding place, and she turned away.

But the thought of the baby was with her all the time now, a sense of her responsibility pressing down upon her heart like clods upon a coffin. She and Ed would scan the sky countless times a day, to find nothing more hopeful than vaporous wisps of cloud that vanished tantalizingly while they gazed, or else a blue dome of nothingness.

One night while Ed slept restlessly beside her, she lay and gazed at the pallid and starveling new moon that looked at her from between the branches of a tree whose leaves had fallen in mid-summer. She shook as she muttered: "It's the worst kind of luck to see the new moon for the first time through brush." She thought of a sermon she had once heard an evangelist preach from the text: "I will arise and go to my father." She pictured herself as returning to the old home, and thrilled at thought of Pappy's fierce, undemonstrative affection that would receive her back if she met his requirements and came to stay. She could see Pappy sitting on the porch at evening, no longer lonely, with a little child in his arms.

But what of Ed? She thought of the boyish face now seamed with lines no young face ought to have to wear, of the sweet temper sharpened by suspense and want, of the pleasant, drawling voice that now was harsh. Tragedy looked at her out of the gray eyes that had wooed her with smiles a year ago. How could she desert him now when they loved each other through it all? She and Ed were *married*, and Pappy nor nobody else had a right to try to separate them. Well, it was up to her to decide.

"I can't noways leave him when he's having such a hard time," she whispered to her hot pillow. "Everything an' everybody has turned against him, looks like, and his wife ought t'stand by him. I'll stick!"

When Bessie started to get breakfast, she realized that there was nothing in the cupboard but a little flour, enough perhaps to make biscuit a couple of times. She had avoided telling Ed just how things were, but now the pinch of hunger was acute.

She watched him till he had scraped the syrup from his plate with the last morsel of biscuit, and then she faltered: "We . . . we haven't got anything to eat, Eddie. Hadn't you better go to town an' get some groceries today?"

A tormented look came into his eyes. "I ain't got the face to ask Bill Adams for no more credit."

She held one hand on the edge of the table to steady herself as the heat waves danced and blurred before her eyes. "But . . . we *got* to have something to eat!" she cried. "Think of the baby!"

He threw his hands up passionately. "Ain't I thinkin' about it all the time? Ain't I fair' driv crazy thinkin' about it? Thoughts don't get you nowhere if you haven't got no money!"

Nevertheless, he rose and made ready to walk the five miles to town.

"Maybe you can get a lift part ways, coming or going," she drearily encouraged him as he stooped to kiss her.

"Maybe."

She sat on the edge of the bed waiting his return. The pillow was too hot for her to rest her cheek against it, so she slumped forward, swaying from weakness, losing all sense of time. She watched the road, but there was little passing. It was as if life had been suspended for a time because of the heat.

It was mid-afternoon when she saw Ed come dragging up the road as if he could hardly lift one foot ahead of the other, his head sunk forward, his arms hanging limply. His hands were empty!

"You so tired, honey?" she murmured, laying her tear-wet cheek against his as he came in.

"Dog tired," he panted, sinking into a chair. "My head hurts," he went on, putting his hands to his temples. "Feel funny, like an iron kettle full o' live coals."

"This heat has been too much for you." She passed caressing fingers across his burning forehead. "And you . . . didn't . . . get anything?"

71

"No." He shook his head as if the effort were an agony, and his voice was thick and lifeless, as though a corpse were speaking. "Bill Adams said he'd be ruint, with all he'd let out to farmers, if cotton didn't make. Said, if it went on like this a couple of days longer, nobody'd make anything. Said to come back if it rained in a couple o' days. But it ain't ever goin' to rain no more!"

She stood beside him, helpless for a moment, unable to speak; but at thought of his need she roused herself.

"Come on back an' sit in the kitchen with me, honey, while I get you some supper." She felt a need to have him near her, and her love reached out pitiful hands to his in the face of menacing future.

He staggered after her into the shed-kitchen.

"I'll make the fire for you," he said, picking up a stick of wood, but holding it in uncertain hands.

Bessie shook the last flour from the bag into the pan and began making up biscuit dough, working it with her fingers.

"Maybe you can get something tomorrow from one o' the other stores," she suggested, with an effort at an encouraging smile.

His look contradicted her. "I tried 'em. They're all in the same box. I dunno what we're goin' to do!" His voice rose sharply, and his eyes were unnatural in their stare.

Bess looked at him through a veil of tears. She had never loved him so much as at that moment, so pitifully young he was, so helpless, so desperate! Her young eyes gazed at him with more than wifely love; with maternal consecration, with a look such as his own mother might have turned on him as she died. She was his wife; she would die beside him, if need be, with no word of complaint.

And then she seemed to hear from some far distance a little child crying, its thin, poignant wail piercing her soul. Some force seemed to tear her heart out of her body, crush it with iron force, and then thrust it back.

"Ed," she cried, with heartbreak in her voice, "oh, Ed, I guess I'd better go back to Pappy, darling!"

"He wouldn't let you."

Tears were rolling down her cheeks. "Yes, he wrote for me to come."

He lifted his head with a jerk. "When'd you hear from him?"

"Some time back. I didn't say anything to you about it, because I didn't want to go." She looked at him fearfully, to see how he would take it.

He sat in silence for a moment, as if his disturbed brain was attempting to comprehend this new thought, his nervous fingers balancing the stick of wood. Finally he dragged out his words.

"Maybe it would be better for you to go home for a little visit, to pick up an' get strong. I can come for you after cotton pickin', an' maybe we can find a new place an' start over again. Surely there won't be a drought next year, and we can get on better. I'd feel easier to have you taken right care of in September."

She held clenched hands on the rim of the bread pan. How unselfish he was in his thought for her, and how she loved him! But she couldn't lie to him just as she was leaving him.

"No, Ed, honey!" she cried piercingly. "Pappy said I couldn't come 'less it was to stay."

His bloodshot eyes held a bewildered look. "But he don't want me to stay there?"

"No." Her whole body trembled, as if her joints were water. "He says . . . if I come . . . I've got to leave you!"

His look of bewilderment deepened. "Leave me, Bess girl? Why, we're married!"

"Yes, that's what I say. It's near 'bout killing me to even think of it!" Her tears dripped down on her hands.

"You wouldn't leave me?" His voice had an acute ring like that of a child who sees his mother abandoning him. She gave a great sob.

"What can I do, Ed, darling? I'm half-starved, though I wouldn't mind that for myself. I'd honestly rather die than be separated from you . . . but the baby, Eddie . . ."

"You'd leave me when I'm havin' such a hard deal from all creation? You'd turn your back on me when it looks like God and man has forsaken me, an' the elements was makin' sport of me?" His eyes were wild.

She leaned against the table, sobbing convulsively. "Oh, God, why is life so hard for us? There ain't nobody nigh for me to turn to, forty miles away from all the folks I ever knew! I've got to leave you, Eddie, when I'd rather be cut into little bits an' burned in the fire!"

"When you aimin' to go?" His tone was deadly still.

"The sooner the better, I reckon, if it's got to be."

He laughed queerly. "You can't go. You ain't got any money."

She nodded her wretched head. "Yes, Pappy sent me the money for my ticket."

"How much?" he demanded.

"Fifty dollars."

"When?" He sprang to his feet.

"Some time back," she faltered.

"And so you've had money all this time when I was eatin' my soul out! When I couldn't sleep nights for thinkin' how I could get somethin' for you to eat, you had fifty dollars hid away! So that's the kind of wife you are, is it?"

His face was livid, and his eyes glared like a madman's.

Bess shrank from him in terror. "Oh, Ed, you don't understand!"

He came a step nearer her, his muscles tense.

"By God, you think you'll leave me to live as if you'd never known me! No, damn you, I'll kill you first!"

She saw the leaping light of madness in his eyes, and knew that the heat and his distress had crazed him.

He lunged forward, the stick of wood lifted in his grasp.

"Oh, Eddie, don't! don't!" she cried, stumbling backward and around the table, her hands thrown out in appeal.

As he sprang after her, she jerked the table between them, the dishes crashing to the floor.

"Oh, Ed, don't hit me!" she shrieked, and crumpled to the floor.

Even while they had talked, a wisp of cloud as filmy as raveled cotton-wool had floated idly up the sky. Other wisps had stolen from nowhere to join it, till it had hung like a great open cotton boll high in the blue. Presently darker clouds had piled themselves on the horizon, massed and ponderous, like bales of cotton in their brown wrappings. A jagged streak of lightning had slit the face of the sky like a cruel smile.

In a little while a few hesitant drops came down, then more scurried faster from the clouds, until a slow and searching downpour followed. At last the sheeted rain fell like a drop-curtain before the landscape, fell on the cracked earth, which drank it thirstily, on the wilted cotton plants, which lifted grateful leaves, on the roof of the little house on the edge of the field. But the two in the shed-kitchen paid no heed to it.

Until the gathering dusk Ed crouched beside the still figure on the floor. His hands frantically chafed her wrists, his kisses rained on her white face, and his cries implored her to speak to him.

"Oh, Bess girl! I didn't mean it! I wasn't myself!"

When he strained his ears to listen for an answer, he heard only the rain.

Suddenly the wind shifted, bringing a swirl of rain through the window upon that quiet form and unresponsive face. With a swift impulse to shield her, Ed put his arms about the helpless body and dragged it to one side. As he did so, her eyes opened and looked into his, with dazed questioning at first and then with leaping fear.

When Ed saw his wife look at him in terror, he struck his hands against his head, with one wordless cry.

The sight of his anguish swept the fear from her eyes, and only love was left. Her weak hands groped toward him, to draw his head against her breast, to hold it there with tenderness, before she gathered strength to speak.

"I'm not hurt, Eddie darling. I understand. And, see, it's raining!"

WILDERNESS ROAD

JANICE HOLT GILES

Janice Holt Giles is perhaps loved most for her books about her adopted state of Kentucky. Over a twenty-five year period of writing, she produced twenty-four works, both fiction and non-fiction, including a richly detailed multi-volume historical saga which traces the opening of new American frontiers from Kentucky to Oregon. "I wanted to deal with the opening of the West in such a way as to make it vivid, real, dramatic and so authentic it could be taught as history," she once wrote. Additionally, Giles wrote articles and stories for magazines such as *Good Housekeeping*, *Woman's Day*, and *McCall's*. "Wilderness Road", which appeared in WELLSPRING (1975), tells of Daniel Boone and his family's move to Kentucky, and illustrates Giles's talent for imbuing her writing with a distinctive voice true to the period, the setting, and the characters, a voice convincingly real.

"Pa says there's not room for e'er other thing. I don't know if we can get your feather bolster loaded on."

"The feather bolster will not take such a heap of room, James. Make a place for it."

Rebecca Boone knew it was not Daniel who had objected to the feather bolster. James had been strung as tight as a fiddle string since the day his father had named his intention of taking them to Kentucky, and now that the time had come to leave he couldn't hide his pleasure to be going at last, or his impatience at the tedium of loading the pack animals. Give James his way and he would have ridden off with nothing but a horse and a gun, no bothering with women-folks and young ones and house furnishings.

Like father, like son, she reckoned, remembering the times without end Daniel had so ridden off. In a way it was a pity that James had been too little to go along on most of Daniel's great specks, and that this, his own first great speck, had to be cluttered with women and children. A man liked the unhampered speculation. It was a pity for James, but it had been a great comfort to her. It was bad enough to have Daniel away in the woods for months on end without one of the boys being gone with him.

She went about quietly, packing a slat basket with food left from their last home-cooked meal. It wouldn't last long, but it would be a waste not to take it, and she had never had rations enough to waste anything.

From the corner of her eye she watched James struggling with the feather bolster. She knew what he was thinking by the way he tugged and jerked at it.

79

Feather bolster! Feather bolsters in Kentucky, where a man would have all he could do to stand off the Shawnees with one hand and clear him a piece of ground with the other! It went the foolishest, the things women had to have. He laid the bolster on the floor and folded it over three times, but before he could tie it into a neat, compact bundle it escaped him into fat, puffy sausages of air and feathers. He grunted and mumbled down in his throat and grumbled. More so than need be, Rebecca thought, and she paid him no mind.

It was not seemly for a woman to look with favorance on any one of her young ones over the rest, but she misdoubted there was a mother living but had a special tenderness for her oldest son, her first-born. Time and again as the lad was growing up, he had twisted her heart until it was hard to be stern with him. He had been so clever and quick, and so given to lightheartedness. Daniel's sandy hair and her own black, combined, had turned out a sort of goldy-red in James. It had always pleasured her to look on that bright head. But she knew well enough that did she ever allow him to take an inch he would take a mile, so risky were all young ones, so she had oftentimes steeled herself against him. And he need not think, sixteen though he was now, that she could be talked out of taking her feather bolster to Kentucky, either.

Daniel's shadow darkened the door. "You about ready?"

She folded a linen square over the basket and slung it on her arm. "Soon as James gets my feather bolster tied on. Seems it would have been a heap easier to tie it on back somewhere so's one of the last ones could ride on it."

"You want it should get tore into bits by the briars and thorns?" His frustration made James speak scornfully of her woman's lack of knowledge.

Undisturbed either by his scorn or by her lack of knowledge, she followed Daniel out into the early sun, speaking softly to her son in passing. "No, I shouldn't want it to get tore into bits by briars or thorns, or e'er thing else. See it's packed good so's it won't be, if there is aught to be uneasy of."

James would learn in good time that while women might lack the kind of knowledge men had, they had a kind of knowledge of their own, which men, for the most part, made a poor shift of doing without. She knew what would be required of her in the wilderness, and she knew to what uses the feather bolster might be put to ease those requirements. But no need to say. The young had to do their own learning.

The train of pack horses strung out along the trail, each animal loaded heavily. It was a good train, well disposed and well loaded. Daniel had seen to that. There was a place on a good, steady horse for each of the least ones to ride, and a place for her handy to them. The men, Daniel and James, would walk and lead the train. The oldest of the younger ones would drive the milch cows and the three hogs. Daniel pulled her horse around for her and helped her to mount. She arranged her skirts and steadied the basket in her lap.

She was taller than common, Rebecca Boone. She could look Daniel straight in the eye, and though Daniel wasn't extra-heighted, it made of her a tall woman. She was not a woman often given to laughter or to gaiety of spirit, but she had the name among the settlements on the Holston of being steady and sure in her ways, quiet in her speech and high-hearted in bad times. She was stout and skilled in all the ways a woman in the western country had need of being skilled.

She could shoot, though not as well as Daniel, for once, when she was aiming at a deer, she had misfired and killed her own riding mare. They had laughed at her over that, down on the Yadkin, but they did not forget either that the same winter, because of Daniel's being gone on a long hunt for skins, she had killed and dressed out enough meat to feed her family well and have some left over to serve Daniel when he came home in the spring.

She had always made out better than most women when her man was away. She asked no help in tending her crops, but set to and tended them herself, plowing and planting and gathering, all. Whatever she turned her hand to, man's work or woman's, she did well. That is what people on the Yadkin said of Rebecca Boone.

James came out of the cabin with the feather bolster tied into a roll and, peering around it, made his way clumsily down the slope of the yard.

"Go back and pull the door to," Rebecca called to him.

In disgust James flung the bolster on the ground and turned back.

Daniel chuckled mildly. "What difference, Rebecca? You are leaving this place for good and all. What difference whether the door is shut or not?"

"I wouldn't like to think of the weather blowing in and making a ruin of the house," she replied quietly.

She looked down at the string of pack horses. Eight of them, there were. Daniel had done well in his trading for the animals. They were smaller than most men would have wanted, but Daniel said you needed small, fast, sure-footed animals on the trail going into the Kentucky country, and he had reason to know, the times he had been there. She wished, though, there had been a way to take more of the house-plunder. Not that she questioned Daniel was right. The trace was no more than a path, and steep and ledgy in places. No wagon could go over the trace, he had said. Still and all, it was a wrench to leave her beds and her tables, her chairs, and the dish dresser Daniel had made for her. It came hard to leave them, but the worst was having to leave her loom. How she was going to manage without it, she had no notion. Likely Daniel would get around to building her another one, but, knowing Daniel, she knew it would be a time and a time before he got to it. She sighed, but not in real distress. It was mostly a sigh of habit. In twenty years of being married to Daniel Boone she had sighed and given up many things, but mostly without too much regret.

It was what a woman had to expect if she married up with a restless, wandering man. And most men in this western country were what you would call wandering. Wasn't much to be done about it. You married your man, had his children for him, fed him, made his clothes and oftentimes his crops, tended his home when he had one, worried over him when he was gone, which he mostly was, never knowing whether he would come home dead or alive, or even if he'd come home at all. You made out, one way or another. And when he got restless and began looking past the corn rows toward the woods and mountains, you sold out and crawled on the back of a pack horse and went toward the west with him, for it was always the west that pulled him. To the east were people, and comforts, and an easy way of life. All the women in the western country thought with longing of the east. But they never looked in that direction, for they knew better. No man who ever got as far west as the under-mountain country turned his eyes east again.

"Well, it's shut, for all the good it'll do," James told her, coming up the near horse and laying the feather bolster across its back. "It's closed and bolted. I took the trouble, seeing you wanted it shut."

"Yes," Rebecca said. "You done good."

The lad took thongs and cinched the bolster down tight, making certain, for all his impatience with his mother for taking it, that it would be safe on the trail. She watched him, thinking how well Daniel had taught him. It pleasured Daniel for James to be so near grown now. He had been, you might say, waiting for it a long time. So they could be men-folks together. A man set such a heap of store by his sons.

Daniel took his place at the head of the train of animals. He looked back. "All set?"

James sent a proprietary glance down the line. "All set!" he called; then he stepped up and took his place by his father, topping him by a good inch. They turned their faces up the trail, and the horses fell into line behind them.

Rebecca did not mean to look back. It did no good, she had found. In spite of her intentions, she found herself twisting her body around to take one more, long look at this last home she was leaving. Men, she thought, hadn't the feeling for places a woman had. A man wouldn't likely know what she meant when she said she left a little piece of herself behind each time she moved away from a house that had sheltered her and her brood, but there wasn't ever a woman who had left a place that wouldn't know. Whatever of yourself you had put into a place, you generally left behind you with it, so that no matter how puny a place it was, there was a sadness when it came time to turn your back on it. Likely it was but natural for a woman to want to stay put, to build fences and set out an apple tree and a rose bush . . . to know that the sun of an evening was going to set over the same place it had risen of a morning. A woman was so natured she liked a sameness. She felt better when she knew she could gather the corn in the fall she had planted in the spring. With a man it was different. Men were poured from a different mold. Ever moving, they were, like water seeking the sea.

She had known this time was coming almost from the day she had married Daniel Boone, for even then,

85

as long ago as twenty years, he had talked of little but the land over the mountains, the Kentucky land. It was during Braddock's War, in 1755, before ever they were wed, that he had met up with John Finley who had been a trader among the Indians on the Ohio. When Daniel was home from the war and they were wed, he had remembered all the things John Finley had said, and he had told her, it was untelling the times: "It must be a fine country, Rebecca. John says there is an abundance of game of every kind. He told of seeing buffalo in such herds as to be uncounted, coming down to the salt licks. And deer and elk and bear. Pigeons and turkeys so thick they make a cloud over the sun. And the land. He told how the land was richer than any he'd ever seen, good land, well watered and prime. I have a great desire to see that land, Rebecca."

Mile by slow mile he had moved them toward it, each new shift and change taking them ever westward. He had seen the country, too, for he had gone hunting there, and when he had come home in the spring of 1776, after two eternally long years spent hunting out skins for his stake, when she had not known from one good day to the next but what he was scalped and his bones left bleaching in the elements — when he had come home, she had known the time had come. "I've got my stake," he told her, "and there's forts there now, Rebecca. There is other folks."

He had been gathering together the families to go with him to make a stand in Kentucky. Forty head of folks all told. In a way, she thought, easing the leg thrown over the saddle horn, it was a relief to have it

86

over and done with, to be shut of it, all the talk and the speculation, and to be leaving out.

They made slow time to the Powell Valley, but if it fashed Daniel she couldn't tell. Driving milch cows and hogs on the trail was a tedious thing, although the children did as well as could be expected of them. They just naturally dallied and had to be put up with. It seemed like the horses were always rubbing the packs loose against things, too — rocks, or limbs or stumps, and time was lost having to stop and straighten them. Making camp of an evening took time, too, with the young ones to see to and the cooking to do. Even so, they reached the meeting place where they were all to come together in plenty of time.

It was a good thing to see the other women-folk and to hear woman-talk again. Some took it in good part, this moving to Kentucky with their men, but some took it ill. "We'll never see our homes again," mourned old Mrs. Donohue, watching the sun set that evening behind the craggy cliffs that marked the gap to Kentucky. "We'll all be killed by them heathen varmints. I misdoubt we'll ever see the land itself. They'll be laying in wait for us ere we step foot on it. You mark my words!"

"The way I see it," a younger woman said, shielding her face from the heat of the fire with her arm crooked over her eyes. "Indian trouble is Indian trouble where'er it is. We've had it in good measure on the Holston. Don't see as it could be much different in Kentucky."

"My John says," another spoke up, "the land is worth the trouble. He says if enough of us go and stick together we can stand off the Indians." She was a bride and she blushed as she spoke of her John.

"What do you say, Rebecca?" they asked, turning to the wife of their leader.

She turned the browned hoecakes out onto a flat shingle of bark. "Why, what's there to say? If your man has got to see what's on the other side of the mountain, he's got to see, is all."

"And you think it's right for them to go dragging us women and young ones out there so far from home?"

Rebecca Boone's dark eyes were steady on the woman who asked. "Where is home," she said, "except where your man is?"

They took a few days to get the cumbersome and now fully assembled train repacked and loaded, places and duties assigned, livestock rounded up and belled, last-minute preparations done and last-minute ructions and misgivings settled. Daniel checked and rechecked their own provisions. "I wish I'd brung along that least anvil I left at Billy Russell's," he grumbled. "And I'd like it a heap better if we had more flour and salt. Be a time till we get more out there."

Colonel Russell's station was the last place one could buy such necessities. They had passed it two days before. "Well, it's too late now, Dan'l," Rebecca said sensibly.

"Yes. We'd best be moving. The season's getting late."

It was September, and the nights were already chill. They had to get where they were going and make some sort of provision for the winter before cold weather set in. They had taken what care they could, and there was nothing for it now but to move on out beyond, break the last ties that bound them to the settlements, and go it on their own hook. They left at sunup the next morning, well ordered and well organized, guarded front, flank, and rear by Daniel's own picked riflemen, as safe as caution and experience could make them.

The first day was bound to be slow, Daniel told them when they camped that night a bare twelve miles from where they had started. They would get the hang of it in a day or two, he said. "Make camp and get your rest tonight whilst it's still safe."

He couldn't get to sleep himself, however. Rebecca felt him turning and twisting beside her. "You wearied, Dan'l?"

"No. But I'm going to send James back to Billy Russell's for that anvil tomorrow. I know in reason there'll be need of it, and I can't rest for thinking of it. I'll have Billy send some more flour and salt, too."

"You aiming on waiting here?"

"No, we'll move on. He can catch us up easy, him alone that way and us moving slow."

His mind made up, he slept. It was Rebecca who was restless now. She wished Daniel would wait for the boy, but doubtless it wouldn't be fair to the others. And James was good at taking care. She had to stop thinking of him as a little fellow. He could do his part the same as the rest. It would pleasure him to be sent on an errand . . . make him feel big to be so trusted. She composed her thoughts and finally slept.

The next morning she saw to it that the boy had a good breakfast while Daniel explained what it was he wanted him to do. "Take the little sorrel mare," he concluded. "She's fast. And don't tarry. Don't lose no time. You'd ought to catch us up the day after tomorrow."

After he was mounted Rebecca walked toward the boy. Impatiently he pulled up the mare and waited. She had it on the tip of her tongue to tell him to mind out and take care, but she bit the words off. It would shame him in front of the others to be so cautioned. "Best get me another little awl," she said instead. He nodded and gave the mare her head. Rebecca watched him until he was out of sight back down the trail, the mare traveling swiftly, James's goldy-red hair bent over her neck.

The party moved slowly on westward, ever nearer the overhanging cliffs and the dark breastwork of the mountains. On the evening of the third day Rebecca caught her self listening and looking back. He ought to be turning up any time now, she thought.

When he had not come by the time they camped, she felt a deep uneasiness, which she tried to hide, going about her cooking quietly as usual. The stock tethered and guards set, Daniel came up to eat his meal. "Doubtless," he told Rebecca as he ate, "Billy Russell has furnished him a heavier load than I thought, and he's made slower time. He'll be up with us in the morning."

90

"Yes," she said. No need dwelling on it, but Daniel had not dispelled the uneasiness.

Camp had been broken the next morning and the animals loaded when Billy Russell himself rode up, his horse lathered and breathing hard, and Billy as distraught as a man can be and still talk sense. Throwing himself off his horse, he yelled for Daniel. "Daniel! Daniel Boone!"

Daniel came running.

"Daniel, a terrible thing has happened! Your boy, and mine . . . ambushed last night! They're killed. Indians! Shawnees! A big party of them!"

"Your boy?"

"I sent him along with James, and two workmen. One of the workmen just got back from Williamsburg with a load of powder and I thought you'd welcome some extra. I came on behind and just overtook them . . . what's left of 'em. I made sure they would catch up your party yesterday, or I would never have . . ."

"Where?"

"Back down the trail. Not more than five miles. They must've camped there last night." Colonel Russell groaned. "Dan'l, they tortured 'em. Pulled out their fingernails. Stuck splinters in 'em and burned 'em and slashed 'em. Skulped 'em. They're burnt and cut till a body . . ." He broke off, his face twisted and white.

It was too late. Rebecca had come up and heard. A slow shudder, beginning in her stomach, ran over her body and ended in a weakening of her knees till she could barely stand. She felt as if her breath was being choked off in her throat. Last night, while they slept unawares, James was being hurt so . . . Her hand reached up and pushed at the knot lumping in her throat. But her voice came clearly. "They are dead now?"

The colonel swept off his hat. "Yes, ma'am." His mouth trembled and his voice shook. "I am sorry, Miz Boone."

Daniel turned quickly, his jaw tight. "There are these to think of!"

Indians! Indians! The word swept like a flame over the people and set them shaking. Daniel gave hurried orders, and the party scattered down the narrow ravine in which they were camped. The women and children were herded under an overhanging bank where the roots of giant trees had hollowed out a shelter. "Stay here," they were told. "Don't move, no matter what."

They were barely hidden when shots back down the trail told that the attack had begun. Daniel gathered his men and posted them at the mouth of the ravine. "Wait till they come nigh," he warned them, "and make sure you've got a good shot. Make ever' one count."

There was no time to see to the cattle and the horses, and they were immediately stampeded, crashing off into the woods in all directions. Soon the ravine was filled with the hideous yells of the Indians and the clatter and crash of gunfire. It was made more awful by the crying and moaning of the women and children. Rebecca went about among them. "Hush, now," she soothed. "Hush. It does no good to cry. Feed the least ones these hoecakes, and you girls . . . that gravelly bank looks like there was a spring underneath. Dig there and see. We'll be thirsty ere long."

She went about among them fearlessly because there was nothing in her to feel fear. There was only a deadness that hung like a heavy weight about her neck. Nothing was real to her, not the gunfire, nor the savage yells, nor the babies crying. All that was real to her now was the thought of James, lying yonder stiffened and still, his bright head shorn, his hands gashed and cut, and his tormented body mutilated. She soothed the babies and encouraged the frightened women, and there was no break nor tremor in her voice, because she did not know what she was doing or saying. Habit was serving her, for inside her heart was squeezed and bleeding, crying over and over: "My son . . . my son."

The day, in all its fear and awfulness, wore on. The Shawnees did not keep up a sustained attack. After the first great, almost overpowering, surge they fell back; then slowly they vanished into the woods, taking cover behind the trees and bushes and logs, firing from hidden places that were hard for Daniel's men to discover.

Fearing to be surrounded and besieged in the narrow cove, Daniel fanned out his men, thinning them along the front but covering the sides and rear. The men hid as best they could, behind rocks, a bank of earth, a felled tree, and they fired at the smoke of the Indians' guns. That a shot told now and then was evident when a painted Shawnee fell, twisting, from behind a tree, his last scream drawn harshly and quaveringly from his throat.

There would be periods of silence, lasting sometimes an hour or more, silence so complete as to make the men wonder if the Shawnees had crept off. But if a man grew careless, or restless, a shot rang out, echoing down the ravine, bouncing off the rocky ledges, and dying out in a fading rumble. There would be other times when it seemed as if every Indian fired on signal, and the woods rang with the noise and filled the ravine heavily with sound and smoke. From one moment to the next, it was impossible to know what to expect.

When she had done what she could for the women and children, Rebecca went to stand where she could see. So it happened she was watching when a bullet glanced Daniel's skull and sent him reeling. She was beside him in a moment, her hands feeling, his blood staining her arms and the front of her dress. "It's but a scratch, Dan'l," she told him then, tearing at the hem of her dress. "I'll bind it so's the blood won't blind you."

"Knocked me down," Daniel said, "but it don't hurt much."

"No. Did you see where the shot came from?"

He shook his head. "I was loading."

Rebecca's hands finished with the bandage. "He's up there behind that biggest beech tree. Near the rim of the hollow."

"I'll get him."

But, when he reached for his gun, he staggered. Rebecca took it from him. "You set here a minute. I'll shoot for you till you feel able again."

He allowed her to take the gun. "I come over dizzy all at once."

94

"Yes."

Slowly she lifted the gun and rested it, readied it for firing. Daniel coached her. "Wait until he shows hisself. He'll not be able to keep from looking out to see. He'll edge hisself out a mite. Wait till there's enough of him to kill, then fire."

Rebecca nodded, laid her cheek along the walnut stock, and waited patiently.

First she saw the smallest movement along the tree trunk, no more than a shadow darkening the far side. Then she saw a shoulder bulge a little larger. Her finger tightened. Boldly, then, the Indian peered out, and, as he did, something swung loose from his chest and hung, swaying, glinting goldy-red in a shaft of bright sunlight. Rebecca's thigh quivered. She made the new scalp her target and squeezed the trigger. She saw the Indian spin and stagger, heard him yell, watched him fall heavily to the ground. She handed the gun to Daniel, and vomited sickly at his feet.

Daniel watched her, puzzled. When she lifted her head, he said: "You got him."

She nodded. "He had James's scalp on him."

She walked slowly back to the cave-like shelter of the women and children and sat down on a rock. Little by little the nausea, the oily bile of her sickness, passed. She kept seeing the goldy-red of the scalp, swaying with the movement of the Indian, and an ague took her, shaking her achingly for a moment. That, too, passed, and, when one of the least ones came up whimpering for comfort, she took it on her lap, cradling it gently.

"There, now. It's all right. Hush, now, there's nothing to harm you."

Toward the middle of the afternoon the firing became desultory, and then it stopped entirely. The men waited. An hour passed. The men grew restless, and then one deliberately poked his hat on a long stick up above a log. It drew no fire. "They've left out," Daniel said. "They've headed for the Ohio."

Cautiously the men reconnoitered, but there was not an Indian to be found. As suddenly as they had come, they had gone, stealthily taking their wounded and dead with them. Slowly the people gathered in the mouth of the ravine and the women and children, freed, formed knots about their men-folk.

The party was not without its casualties. Isaac Cooper was bad hurt, a shot through his stomach. He would die within a matter of hours. James Goodwin was also badly hurt, his leg being broken, but he had a chance to live. Robert Whitney had a flesh wound in his shoulder, and Daniel had his skull creased. Only one man had been killed outright. They had been lucky, they felt. It could have been so much worse.

As the tension of the fighting eased and the talk grew louder, however, there were hysterical overtones in the women's voices. "Lord have mercy," they wept, "but it was terrible."

"We'll have to turn back now. We can't go on. We're too bad hurt."

"This is just the beginning . . . this near the settlements, too. We'd best turn back while we can."

And higher and more hysterical than all the others was old Mrs. Donohue's voice. "I said it! I warned you! I said they'd lay for us. It's going against the will of the Lord to go on, I tell you! I'm crossing no mountains! I'm going back to my home!"

Apart from them sat the young bride, a widow now, the dazed tears making pools on her round young face, John Steever's head pillowed on her lap. "You'd best tell her," Daniel said to Rebecca, "that we've got to bury him now."

Rebecca went to her, spoke gently, lifted her up, and held her while the men carried off the man who had said so surely the land was worth fighting for. Someone else would get the worth of it, for John Steever would never see it now.

When the men returned, Rebecca went up to Daniel. "Can we have a fire, Dan'l? These need something hot to eat and drink. They will calm down quicker with hot vittles inside of them."

He nodded. "No harm. There's ne'er an Indian within miles of us, nor won't be again."

While the woman cooked, the men rounded up what was left of the livestock and tethered the animals. More than half of them were gone. Many of the pack horses, including four of Daniel's, were missing. The provisions and packs were scattered and burst, and no one could yet tell how much was lost. The people were bewildered by the attack. It was not to be expected so near the settlements. They were frightened, and their courage had drained away. As they ate, they muttered among themselves. They wanted to start back at once. No use

97

waiting till another day. "We want to turn back now, Daniel. This is the Lord's hand pointing the way."

"Yes, God knows, it was not meant to be."

"We want to go home, and we aim to leave out ere night falls."

Daniel raised his hand, and they quieted. "We knew," he said, "when we left the settlements, there would be Indians to contend with. It wasn't likely they'd start pestering so soon, and it was bad luck that a war party of Shawnees should be crossing just now. But they have cleared out. They've took what they wanted of the stock and have made tracks for the Ohio. Like we can finish the journey without more trouble. We are a strong party. We can send back for more provisions, and we can go on."

"No!"

"Don't listen to him!"

"I'm turning back, now!"

"It's not you," a woman's voice cried, "that lost your man today . . ." Then, remembering John Steever's widow, put her hand over her mouth and shrank back into the crowd.

"We'll decide in order," Daniel said. "We'll take a vote." He pointed to a tall man up front. "How do you vote, Jonathan Derwent?"

"I say go back!"

"Benjamin Graham?"

"Go back!"

"Abraham Lyne?"

"I'm turning back."

The voting went on. Not a voice was lifted in favor of going on. Rebecca sat by the fire and waited, her least ones about her knees. Maybe Daniel would go back, too. Maybe now that he knew no one would go on, he would turn back his own head. Maybe now that his whole party favored turning back, he would forget that other land and take her home again and they would live peaceably in the settlements and raise up these least ones decent and God-fearing as young ones were meant to be raised up. It was too late for James, but these others . . .

She looked about her strange surroundings. Back home the late sun would be shining softly on the shingle-boards of the cabin roof. The rail fence would be warm from its heat, and the apple tree at the corner of the house would be throwing a long shadow across the stepping-stones. Back home it was almost time to cut the corn and gather the pumpkins and pick off the gourds from the vine on the woodshed. Back home these least ones would be safe.

She lifted her eyes and looked at the craggy mountains that barred the road to the west. The rock cliffs were already shadowed, and they looked broody and dark and forbidding. That way lay the wilderness road — a weary and blood-stained road. She shivered slightly and wished she might not have to travel it.

At last the voting ended, and the question she had been waiting for was put. "What do you aim to do, Daniel? What are your intentions?"

She saw the sandy head go up, saw the thin mouth firm, saw the faded, squint-wrinkled eyes turn toward the mountains. Before he spoke, she knew what he was going to say. His face had been turned westward too long. "I aim to go on. My intentions are just what they was in the beginning. They've not changed."

There was a clamor of voices. "Alone? You'll never make it!"

"By yourself?"

"On your own hook? Man, you're crazy!"

Stubbornly he insisted. "The danger is over, I tell you. There will not be another Indian betwixt here and the forts."

They shook their heads, not willing to believe, and then they crowded around Rebecca. "Come back with us, Rebecca."

"You can stay with us till Dan'l makes a place for you."

"Bring your least ones and go with us."

"He can come for you next year."

She looked at Daniel and saw that he was watching her. Her hand touched the soft hair of the child leaning against her knees. Daniel nodded at her. "I can come for you next season, Rebecca."

Quietly she stroked the child's hair. James's had been just as soft. Then she looked slowly around at the people clustered about. "I thank you," she said, relinquishing the home, the Yadkin, the peace, the safety, "but I reckon I'd best go with Daniel."

In goodness of heart the people shared with them, then. "Take my big bay, Dan'l. He'll carry a right smart load."

"Take this flour. We can get more in the settlements."

"You can have this bar of lead, Dan'l. I'll not be needing it now."

"Here, Rebecca, is my Rose of Sharon quilt."

They accepted the things offered, setting them quietly aside, then they helped the people make up their dwindled packs. At the last there were a few tears, a few shamed looks among the men, and then they were gone, back down the trail over which, only yesterday, they had come.

Daniel slid wearily to a log. Rebecca handed him a bowl of food, and he looked up at her, his eyes unseeing what it was she was handing him. They had a burned look, as if they had been turned in on themselves and glazed by what they had seen. Her heart lunged and tightened within her. A man set such a heap of store by his sons. In all their days together she had never seen Daniel look like this. He was hurting fearfully inside. He had been hurting like this all the time, but now he could let it show. "Here," she told him, "eat now."

Methodically he obeyed her, eating all that was in the bowl. When he had finished, he put the bowl down beside the log and went to catch up one of the horses. "Before it's dark," he said, "I'm going to bury him."

"Yes," she said. "Wait."

She went to one of the packs. Her roughened hands fumbled with the knots. He had tied them so good . . . James. For all his scorn of women's ways, he had made sure that nothing would happen to it. Patiently she raveled each knot to its end and pulled loose the feather bolster. She carried it to Daniel. "Here. I'd like him to lay easy, Dan'l."

101

His tormented eyes met hers. "Rebecca, they . . . Rebecca!"

She did not fail him. Never in her life had she failed him, and she did not now. She would have time to grieve later. She would have all her life to grieve. Now she must comfort this man who had lost his son, who was tormented because it was through him that he had been lost, but who even yet could not give up the dream that had driven him to the loss. "There, Dan'l. There. It's all over for him, and he is at peace."

"Yes. I'll be back."

He settled the feather bolster in front of the saddle and rode off down the trail. Rebecca watched him out of sight. Then she turned and laid down the Rose of Sharon quilt for a bed for her least ones.

Brother Shotgun

JEANNE WILLIAMS

Jeanne Williams is held in high esteem for her historical novels set in the West for which she has won four Spur Awards from the Western Writers of America. She got her start writing Western stories for the pulp Western magazines in the 1950s. Over a twenty year period Williams published more than seventy Western, fantasy, and women's stories in pulp and slick magazines. Her Western stories appeared in *Ranch Romances*, *Thrilling Ranch Stories*, and *Real Western Romances*. In many of these stories Williams displayed a sensitivity to women's concerns and social issues. It was this interest in presenting a female point of view as the focus of her stories that led her in the direction of the historical novel, although she was met with resistance from publishers until the highly successful publication of A LADY BOUGHT WITH RIFLES (1976). "Brother Shotgun," which appeared in *Ranch Romances* (2nd June Number: 14/6/57), is one of Williams's own personal favorites.

His name was still Johnny Chaudoin when he hitched his gray nag in front of the two-story frame building. It was the only house in this town that both showed a light and looked as if it might have room for a stranger. A day's ride in the raw March wind had made his bad leg so stiff it didn't want to hold him up. He cussed it in French, Spanish, and English. He would've cussed it in Cherokee, too, if there'd been swear words in that language. His Indian grandmother claimed there weren't. He stamped till the blood came alive beneath the knee a Minié ball had smashed and went on to the house. It wasn't till he'd climbed the steps that he could make out the lettering on an old card tacked to the door.

ROOM AND BOARD
INQUIRE WITHIN

The board probably wouldn't amount to much, the way this part of West Virginia had been raided and counter-raided in the war, but, as far as Johnny was concerned, he wouldn't enjoy a man's meal anyway till he was settled down to a rib of freshly killed buffalo. Buffalo — a sea on the plains, huge-shouldered, small-flanked, with enormous heads bent to crop the sweet, curled grass. How many nights in camp with the 8th Kansas had he chewed on corn bread and cow peas and closed his eyes, trying, if only for a flash, to see the herd and sniff the wind with them? The Reb Minié ball had put an end to that. Johnny had been able to earn a stake working in a coal mine — they were glad to get even kids and cripples this fourth year of the war — but his soldiering days were finished. Now he was going home.

He knocked, his chapped knuckles cracking against the splintered door. Laughter came from inside, then there was scurrying and the impact of bodies hitting the panel. He had time to think — *Sounds as if all the boarders have ten kids apiece* — and then the door swung inward. Johnny stood looking at more children than he'd seen since he ran away from home and his own ten brothers and sisters, forty years ago. Or at least it seemed that way. The boy in the door was red-headed. Above his blazing thatch leaned a black-eyed girl with the copper skin of an Indian. A blonde baby had pushed under the boy's arm and was staring up at Johnny with a finger in her mouth. Behind these three others crowded — all ages, all sizes.

Johnny, in spite of an addiction to minding his own business, wondered what the parents of this bunch could look like. He was a mixture himself, with a French-Spanish father, an Irish-Cherokee mother, but at least he and his ten siblings had all possessed black hair and eyes. Anyway, they used to have. His hair was streaking now, and he guessed his two older brothers would be white headed — if they were still alive.

There was a flutter. A tall girl had come up, gathering the kids back, effectively yet without fuss. She looked at Johnny half smilingly, half questioningly, and he saw that her eyes were the gray silver of the underside of a cottonwood leaf. She had funny colored hair, too. It reminded Johnny of the shine of yellow

105

moonlight off an aspen — almost white but warmed with gold. You could say she was towheaded, but Johnny had lived with Indians and did not lump shadings as white men did.

He took off his hat. "I wonder, ma'am, if I could put up here for a day or two?"

Quite frankly she looked him over. He was in his buckskins. There was no way for her to know which Army, if any, he had fought for. Was she for the Union, or did she believe in the Confederacy as many people did in the young State of West Virginia?

Her question startled him. "Can you pay in greenbacks?"

Johnny blinked. With Yankee money almost ten times as valuable as Confederate that was a sound question. Yet — well, he had her mixed up with moonlight and cottonwoods in his mind. "I can pay greenbacks," he said, and reached for his money pouch.

She flushed. Her eyes flickered down a second before they came back to his. She said in a distinct tone: "If my husband's alive, he's in a Yank prison. But it takes money . . . real money . . . to buy shoes and food. Come on in, mister. We've just sat down to the table."

Johnny looked at the kids. The Indian-looking girl was in her teens. The girl with the gray eyes could not possibly be the mother of all the others — but, if you don't ask questions, folks'll tell you more than if you do, Johnny believed, so he bowed and backed out the door. "I'll join you directly, ma'am, but first I have to take care of my horse. Is there any hay in that stable out back?"

106

"There hasn't been for the past three years, but my neighbor, Eli Stricker, who sells me milk, keeps cows. I don't imagine he'd mind selling you some of their hay." She turned to the redhead. "Timmy, run over to Mister Stricker and ask him if he'll fork some hay over in the lot for this gentleman's horse, please."

The boy ducked past Johnny, making for the house to the right, and the girl's lips curved in either amusement or contempt. "No use asking Eli to *give* anything. I pay for milk and get blue-john. You can come in the back way when your horse is tended to."

She swept the children in front of her, back to the lamp-lit kitchen. Johnny unhitched the gray and rode it around to the fenced lot surrounding the stable. A stocky red-faced man was already levering a pitchfork of hay over into the lot. Johnny met his curious stare.

"I guess you're Stricker."

"You'd guess right." Stricker twitched up another forkful, making sure all the clinging wisps fell off before he tossed the central mass over in the lot. "Danged raiders burned off most of my field last fall. I hardly had enough to help my own stock through the winter. Afraid I'm going to have to charge you a Yank dollar for this fodder."

Johnny, lifting off his cobbled saddle, rubbed the gray's sweaty back and withers with the saddle blanket. It was an old horse with its teeth worn off smooth from years of grinding, but it was about the only four-legged critter Johnny had been able to find after the surgeon decided Johnny was through soldiering. At first, remembering fast Indian ponies, untiring hounders of the buffalo, Johnny had been wild at this beast's shambling gait, but days before he had reached the mine where he'd worked out his stake his impatience had turned into a feeling of kinship. He was getting old, too. Some days he felt nearer seventy than fifty. *I want just one more hunt*, he thought. *One more season.*

He led the horse over to the trough that the spring spilled into and left it drinking while he moved back clumsily — for the day's ride had left his leg still numbed — to Stricker. "I figure on resting up here for a couple of days. Fork over hay for my horse in the morning, and the next day, too, and you're welcome to the dollar."

Starting to protest, Stricker's gaze tangled with Johnny's and fell. He tossed over another forkful of hay then put down the fork with the air of a job well done. "All right, stranger. I'll do it as a favor to Luanne, to keep her from losing a boarder. You're the first paying guest she's had in three months."

Baffled though he was at the set-up, Johnny didn't care to hear this man talk about the girl. But neither did he want to rile her neighbors, causing her unpleasantness that would linger after he was gone. He nodded to Stricker. "I'm much obliged for the fodder, mister. Guess I'll go up to the house and get me some food, too."

Stricker's voice floated after him. "Better hurry or the orphanage will have gobbled it all."

Orphanage? Johnny shunted his saddle into the stable, first untying the tarp that held his extra socks and camp stuff, and taking his shotgun out of the

108

scabbard. There was an Indian flute in the trap, carried through all the war and these last months at the mine. Johnny wondered if the kids and Luanne might like to hear him play it. He would kind of like to do that — leave them a song before he went West to the buffalo. Mingled shrill voices, the sound of chairs scooting back, and the rich smell of stew hit him all together as he stood at the back stoop a minute, listening, before he opened the door.

The stew was tasty, even though it was short on meat, and there was pan bread. Except for the three youngest children, none of them over two, everyone drank sassafras tea. Johnny had dreamed about coffee, but sassafras tea was better than some of the roasted acorn brew you got nowadays. Johnny squinted at the milk in the three babies' cups. It was thin, a transparent blue around the edges. He said to Luanne, who had properly introduced herself by now as Mrs. Benton: "Ma'am, that milk sure looks as if it had been skimmed. Good cow's milk is bad enough, but that's sickening."

"Eli has the only cow's milk left in town," she said wearily. "He scrapes off the cream and sells it to people who can afford it. Anyway, what do you mean 'good cow's milk is bad enough'?"

"Goat's milk is 'way ahead, ma'am," said Johnny, expounding his pet theory. "What can you expect from folks who eat hogs and sheep and chickens, who drink milk from critters that're so dumb they have to be fed and sheltered through the winter?" Johnny thumped down his fist. "It stands to reason that what you eat

109

makes up your body. If you eat helpless, stupid, feckless critters, it'll affect your nature, too."

Luanne smiled. "I think we're safe, Mister Chaudoin. Raiders have pretty well gotten off with all those animals. The meat in our stew was from a squirrel Timmy killed today with his slingshot."

"Squirrel's good meat," Johnny approved. "They's smart creatures. They store up food against the winter and live free in the woods." Timmy glowed as Johnny nodded at him, then listened with his thin face pushed forward as Johnny went on. "A man who lives on wild game has to be quick and silent and has to depend on himself. He eats venison from swift deer and the tongues of buffalo who can scent a storm coming. Bear makes him strong, and he gets speed from the antelope, and cunning from the sage rabbit. Freedom is in all of them, in their flesh, to thrive again in his flesh. The Comanches know this. They won't eat a turkey unless they're mighty hungry. They figure the meat will give them chicken hearts so they'll run from danger."

"Are you telling the plain truth, mister?" squeaked Timmy, his blue eyes sparkling.

"So help me," Johnny affirmed. He leaned over and roughed up the boy's carrot-colored hair before he turned to Luanne. "Goat's milk would be the thing for these youngsters, ma'am. It'll make 'em quick, sure-footed, and independent."

A smile teased at Luanne's mouth. From the way it settled into natural lines, he could tell she'd never lost the grace of humor in spite of the war, and whatever had happened to her husband, and Stricker's blue-john.

110

"Even if it wouldn't do all those things, Mister Chaudoin, it'd be nourishment. But we might as well as pine for strawberries in cream."

"Seems it'd cost less to buy a goat than to pay for milk."

"I don't pay in cash." When Johnny frowned, Luanne explained. "This was my parents' home, and mother had some lovely furniture . . . a chair from France, a pianoforte, marble tables, that sort of thing. Eli's wife has always wanted to be a social leader. By owning my mother's things, she must hope to acquire mother's character."

"You traded that furniture for milk?"

Luanne shrugged. "My parents are dead. They won't feel any grief over it. And you can't eat marble and wood."

"Then why in Sam Hill didn't you trade the stuff for a cow?"

"Eli wouldn't agree to that. He says the cows furnish his living. No one, in these days, is going to trade a milk animal for furniture. Eli's wife, fortunately, wants the things enough to barter milk for them."

Johnny's mind hummed with questions. She ran a boarding house. Didn't she get any money from it? Where did the kids come from? Was she paid for their care? Would they be on her hands till they grew up? What would happen when the furniture was traded off? Johnny coughed and pushed back from the table.

He was on his way home. This was none of his business. It was three years since he had crept up on a buffalo, careful of the wind, wrapped in a hide. It was three years since he feasted on hump rib and lay in his blankets, settling into that deep, sensuous sleep that came as the rich flesh was absorbed into his own blood and bone and muscle. He thought: *Just one more season, God . . . one good hunt.* It was the prayer that had sustained him through the war and the Minié ball and the weeks in the coal mine. He had hated the mine. It wasn't right that a mine should be down deep, with no sun or wind. He didn't want to be buried underground even. When he thought of it, he hoped his bones would bleach out pale in the prairie grass, with the wind over them and the buffalo sniffing all around.

A hand on his knee brought him back to West Virginia. The blonde baby girl had come up to him. Rosy mouth puckered over her finger, she watched him with calm interest.

"Mustn't suck your finger," Johnny said, bending down and lifting her to his good knee. "It'll make your teeth grow crooked, missy."

She giggled, and he saw her teeth. They were the shade of the transparent edge of blue-john. And her body on his lap seemed to weigh no more than a huddle of bones with the marrow gone. Oh, hell! Ought to be able to get some kind of milk critter without blowing too much from his stake. Of course, he'd wanted to buy a rifle. You had to get up too close with a shotgun, and many a hunter had been gored to death by the buffalo he was trying to kill. He'd need another horse, too. Even if the gray could stand the trip to the plains, it sure couldn't chase a herd. But the little girl was so danged scrawny!

Johnny said to Timmy: "Suppose you dig into that tarp of mine and fetch me the flute."

He played them songs and then let the Indian-looking girl try to make tunes, while he sang "Las Mañanitas," "Green Grow the Rushes, Oh!," a chant his grandmother told him the Cherokees used to sing, and "Frère Jacques" to commemorate his French blood. But Timmy didn't know French.

"Frère Shotgun!" he cried. "By grannies, I finally puzzled out a word from those *dor-may-vooz* and *sona-lay matinas.*"

"Hold on," Johnny said. "That just means Brother John."

"Well, your name is John, and you have a shotgun, too," Timmy said. "The song's about you. Teach it to us!"

Johnny did, while Luanne smiled, and the black-eyed girl fluted. Even the baby girl caught the spirit and tried to sing. By the time Johnny went to bed, his name was Shotgun.

Next morning Johnny found out a lot. While he searched the town and visited a few farms, he let it be known he was boarding at Luanne's. At that nearly everyone he met burst out talking. Although he hadn't been able to abide the hypocritical concern of Eli Stricker, Johnny listened to these others. He had to know the answer to the questions that had pestered him last night, the answer to Timmy, and the baby, and the Indian-looking girl, and the other five children. Johnny talked mostly to old men and women.

The providers, the earners, the young men, were nearly all off to war, some for the Union and some for the South. Johnny saw that what Luanne had said about raiders looting the country was true. Fields lay charred and black from being burned the summer before. Poverty crushed hard on nearly all the people, although a few had chickens or a cow or a pig. The Strickers were probably more prosperous than anyone in the little village. The one store didn't have much merchandise. The owner had been killed by marauders, and his widow either couldn't or wouldn't stock even staples. Luxuries nested beside tallow and flour and maybe what you wanted was there, and maybe not.

"Luanne's a fine girl," the widow told Johnny as he paid for the candy sticks he was getting for the kids. "But she got in over her head, taking in those youngsters. She can't buy food for 'em much less shoes. Her father . . . he was a doctor . . . left her the house but precious little cash. And the last she heard from her husband, he was a prisoner up north among those damyankees."

A girl, with her parents dead and her husband gone to war, had decided to run a boarding house to bring in cash and keep herself from sinking into self-pitying uselessness. And then, instead of paying guests, the place had filled up with children. Timmy, a cousin of her husband's, had been beaten savagely by his stepfather and had run away from him. Sara, the dark girl, who was sure enough half Indian, had lived off in the brush with her crazed father till his death a year

114

ago. Luanne, gathering berries in the woods, had found the girl and brought her home.

The blonde baby girl with the bluish teeth had been left, along with an older sister, by a young couple who had stopped at the boarding house last spring. The man and woman had fussed a good deal, and they seemed worried. It turned out later that the man had deserted from the army, and the sooner he could get to California, the better he'd like it. The woman had seemed to love her children, but she was the kind who is plain crazy over her man, worthless and mean as he may be. Luanne woke up one morning to hear the babies crying and to find the parents were gone. The woman left a note and a little money she must have begged from the man. She said he wouldn't fool with the children and that she couldn't live without her husband. Luanne was so kind, wouldn't she take care of them and not let them know what kind of a woman their mother had been? She'd try to send money. But she never had.

And the other four children? Oh, a young farmer got killed in the war, and his wife sickened and died that same winter. The wife had no close kin, and her husband's folks wouldn't have the kids because their father had fought on the Union side. How had Luanne managed to get by? Well, she still had an occasional boarder, although she had surely finished what money her father, the doctor, had left. She was a marvel with knitting and made sweaters for a shop in Charleston. When they could, people helped with what they had — a few eggs, cast-off clothing, fruit, and vegetables. In summer Luanne and the children made a big garden. But it got a little harder all the time to stretch her tiny resources. She was just doing the best she could, trying not to think about the morrow, hoping the war would end and her husband would come home.

Johnny pieced it together. When he had, he knew he had to get a goat, or at least a cow. He had no luck that morning. But after more stew for dinner, Johnny went forth again, riding his horse because his leg was paining him, and he figured he might have to cover a lot of ground. It was at a cabin back on a wagon road that he found the goats. After some argument, and the production of his greenbacks, Johnny persuaded the old man who owned them that the kids of one nanny could be weaned or bottle-fed with the milk of the other "fresh" female. Poorer by fifteen dollars (which was two dollars more than he'd been paid for a month's service in the Army), Johnny led the goat home.

Luanne protested. But Johnny, fixing up a milking block in the stable, finally turned to her and said grimly: "Look, ma'am, I want to go West and enjoy my hunt. I couldn't do it if I left these youngsters drinking that blue-john."

"But you . . ."

"I'm crippled some," Johnny finished for her. "I'm not so young, either. I fought for the Union . . . on the opposite side from your husband. But you see, I'm a man. And a man's supposed to help feed children."

Her eyes had grown cold when he named his Army. "Are you trying to salve your conscience?"

He thought of the buffalo and the rest of his greenbacks. "Maybe, but not the way you mean. I never could relish the idea of any man's belonging to another. That's why I fought."

She looked at him, and he looked back, and after a few moments the tenseness left her muscles. "Well, you must take your board and room free, then, as long as you stay. I thank you for the goat, Shotgun."

He grinned and went back to his work. "She'll be thrifty, ma'am, and will forage for herself. Her milk'll make the babies strong and able to walk the edge of a cliff without falling over. And, see, with this block you can milk her and not have to bend to the ground."

"I'll learn to milk," Timmy said, "if you'll teach me, Shotgun."

Shotgun rumpled the red hair. "Sure. Sure, I will."

What were a few more days of staying here? The horse could use the rest. But the few days became a week. The stable, now it had an occupant, needed patching up, the fence had to be mended, and a heavy storm caused leaks in the roof. Johnny spent several more dollars on these repairs. It seemed ornery not to attend to them when, while they didn't cost a lot, it was more money than Luanne could scrape up. Tim could milk Nanny now as if he'd been doing it all his life, and Sara was getting to play a smart tune on the flute. The kids could chant in Cherokee and sing snatches of French and Spanish. Johnny felt kind of pleased. It was a strange new feeling to know that after he'd gone on, and maybe even after he was dead, these kids would sing the songs he'd taught them and teach them to their children. Johnny had always passed through life as traceless as the wind, except perhaps for the bones of animals he'd killed and the ashes of his fires. He had never left his trace on human hearts. Now he was leaving his songs in the minds of these children and rich milk in their stomachs.

But it was a long way West, and the buffalo were sniffing some Kansas breeze. He was old. It was time to be going. Early one morning he put his things in the tarp. The flute he held a minute, then laid aside. It had been his grandmother's. Now it would be for Sara who played it with love. He counted his money. Each bill represented hours in the black earth and the pain in his leg. The bills had been earned to get him home and to buy the rifle, a horse, and supplies for that hunt, which had to be good since it might be the last. But now the bills took a different shape — shoes for the baby, a pair of whole pants for Timmy, bright red cotton for Sara, medicine if a child fell ill and coughed till its life was rasping out, an easing of the worry lines in Luanne's face. The buffalo wouldn't be at their best now anyway. They would be scabby and mosquito-bitten and muddy from their wallows. He wouldn't relish the meat at all. Of course, he wouldn't. Funny it should be so hard to leave the money there on the bureau.

He went back to the mines without telling Luanne or the kids good bye, except in the note he left instructing Luanne how to use the money. If it had been hard in the mines before, it was twice as bad now. Starting all over for the second time, the day when he'd have enough scraped together to leave seemed mighty far

118

off. His leg raised the devil with him till he could hardly sleep at night, and his dreams were full of buffalo, spread out over the plains for miles. He kept track of the time by thinking what the herd would be doing now.

April. May. June. Little yellow calves were dropped and ran beside their mothers. Buffalo rubbed themselves raw trying to get away from the flies and the gnats. Johnny began to have a funny feeling in his heart sometimes as if a hand had lifted it and held it high and pulseless for a second before dropping it back in place.

July. August. September. Bulls fought and took the cows. By now Johnny was sure there was something the matter with his heart. He wondered what would happen when the hand kept hold of it and didn't let it slip free.

In October he left the mines. His home-stake was meager, but he guessed he'd better head West while he still had a hope of seeing the plains again. The gray horse had aged even in these months, and Johnny rode slowly. The hand squeezed his heart now. Sometimes it hurt so bad he thought the blood must be plumb wrung out. It bothered him especially when he climbed up or down from the saddle. Still, he felt glad to see how much better the children looked. When he stopped in front of the boarding house, as he had done seven months ago, Timmy was chopping wood.

He dropped the axe, yelling: "Shotgun's back! Luanne, Sara, it's Shotgun!"

They all came out, the little blonde baby girl hugging his knees, Sara waving the flute, saying: "I play it so well now, Shotgun, you must hear!" The other kids hung onto his sleeves while he led the horse out back to be sheltered and fed.

He lifted the baby — she weighed a good bit now — and was swept into the house. There were beans with ham hock and dried peach pie for supper. The milk in the children's cups was rich and white. When the children were shooed off to bed, Luanne came over to Johnny.

"I just don't know how to thank you," she said. "The money you left bought clothes and shoes for the children who needed them most, and, when Timmy had pneumonia, it paid for his medicine. It got wool so I could make more sweaters for sale, and . . . Shotgun, I was at the end of my rope last spring. But we didn't know where you'd gone, and I was afraid you'd given up all your savings. You did, didn't you? . . . or else you'd be chasing buffalo right now?"

"No matter," Johnny said. "I have another home-stake, and I'm purely glad you're doing better. Don't the baby's teeth look nice? Don't you fret, Luanne. I'm going home. Glad I could help you on my way."

She wasn't the crying kind of woman, but the gray eyes were extra bright as she went over and brought a red bundle from a shelf. She shook it out. Johnny got the scent of the rose leaves she must have put in it to keep the bugs out, and then he stared at the long-sleeved, hooded red sweater. It was made with a black stripe at hip level and two others at the chest. It was knitted of warm yarn.

"It's yours," she said. "And I made you a pair of black socks and a pair of red. I thought surely someday I'd learn where to send them."

Blindly Johnny took the sweater and pressed it with his callused hands. No one, no woman, had made him such a garment, sewn with love, since he was a child. He said: "Why, it's the fairest thing I ever saw."

When he went up to bed, he had to stop on the stairs twice as the hand clutched at his heart, but he held the red wool as if it were medicine, and the spells passed. Johnny was tired, but it was only for the gray's sake that he stayed at the house four days. If you had time, this was good — singing with the kids, holding the baby, watching Luanne looking brighter than he had ever seen her. But Johnny had no time.

With the instincts of the beasts he had lived among and hunted, he felt death in his flesh and bone. He felt it in his heart. If he wanted to see buffalo again, he must travel fast. This was the best time of the year, the time it would be when he got home, late in November. The calves would be fat and brown, and the insects would trouble the herd no more. It was the fat time of the buffalo, the rich time for hunters. He had to go. His tired horse, ruined knee, bad heart wouldn't get better. If they were to carry him home, they had to do it now.

He packed his tarp on the morning of the fifth day and put on the red wool sweater. He went down the stairs to find Luanne crying in the kitchen. She couldn't stop even when she saw him. He thought at once, her husband. "What's wrong, Luanne?"

She said: "Shotgun, my husband got exchanged, but he was so sick in prison, they're going to let him come home. But he hasn't any money and can't get paid, and you know they don't get good care in Army hospitals." She shook her head back and forth as if she were driven wild. "If I could go take care of him, bring him home . . . ! If he dies now . . . !"

Johnny said, with a great tiredness and a great peace settling on his soul: "There's no need for crying. I can lend you the money, Luanne."

She gazed at him. "Your stake?"

"No," he lied. "I can give you the money and still have enough to get out West."

"Are you sure?"

"Of course I am!"

She put her face against his shoulder and cried. "Here," said Johnny, patting her arm, "you'd better get ready to go to your man."

When she was gone on the train, Johnny told Sara, who was to care for the children, good bye, and he told Timmy and the others not to forget the Cherokee prayer or "Green Grow the Rushes, Oh!" or "Las Mañanitas."

Timmy said: "We'll remember 'Frère Jacques,' too, Shotgun. Send me some buffalo horns, will you?"

"If I don't," said Johnny, touching the boy's head, "you go out in a few years and get your own. Sara, mind you play that flute pretty."

He mounted up, with the hand on his heart clutching. He waved with his hat as he rode off, and the baby girl ran after him crying, till Sara caught her.

122

For a good way Johnny could hear them calling: "Shotgun! Shotgun! Good bye, Shotgun! Shotgu-u-un!" He waved again, at the edge of town, and turned his face West.

He was in pain now. The hand gripped. But he sat as straight as he could and directed his intention and his will. If he was going West with all his desire, might not his spirit keep on after his body stopped? Might not his direction be so strong that the flesh couldn't stop it? If he fixed his mind on the buffalo — was that drumming their hoofs? Was that their dust obscuring the way in front of him? He strained to see. But the soft hills were falling away, slipping back. The hand lifted his heart and squeezed and squeezed and squeezed. He was slipping. He felt the earth. Then there was the sound of a great herd. He was running after them, West, to the prairies — West, to the hunt. The meat would be good and the sleep sweet.

The Widow's Stallion

PHYLLIS DE LA GARZA

Born and raised in Illinois, Phyllis de la Garza moved West in the 1960s. Between 1971 and 1980 she and her husband, a retired Mexican cavalry officer, owned an international riding school in San Miguel de Allende, Guanajuato, Mexico. While in Mexico, de la Garza began writing articles and short stories as a creative outlet for her interest in horses and the old West. Over the years more than fifty pieces have appeared in magazines, including *Horse & Rider*, *Western Horseman*, *Seasons*, and *Sombrero*. Subsequent work has included a biography of the Apache Kid and two novels, CHACHO (1990) and BOUNTY HUNTER'S DAUGHTER (1998). "The Widow's Stallion" first appeared *Western Digest* (11-12/99).

⚜

The bad news came Thursday morning — the message was brief. Sheriff Cochran was killed taking a prisoner to the hanging at Salt Creek. Cochran's horse had been returned last Monday to Hipshot, and was at the town stable. Could his widow get the horse? Board was a dollar a day. If she did not appear by Friday, the horse would be auctioned on Saturday morning.

After reading the message, Patsy Anne crumpled the paper into a wad. She looked up at the messenger, Willy Blue. He rode a feral-looking little horse of mustang descent named Mouse, because of its color.

"My husband is dead," she told Willy.

"Yes, ma'am. We knew it since Monday when a deputy from Salt Creek brought Sheriff Ned's horse back. Deputy Ahrens is the new sheriff until elections in the fall."

"You knew my husband was dead since Monday? That's four days ago."

Willy flushed red with embarrassment. "I only carry messages . . . I do what I'm told. You coming to pick up the stallion, or what?" Unable to look her in the eye, he stared at the ground, nervously flipping the extra bridle rein back and forth across his saddle horn. "I always liked Sheriff Ned. He busted the nose of Rattler Pete for shooting the tail off my dog."

Patsy Ann walked into the house and closed the door. She sat stiffly at the table knowing Willy was still out there waiting for her answer. He worked as a swamper at the stable in town — a teenage orphan. Lanky, blond, and round-shouldered, he was a pest who did not impress anybody as being too bright. Right now she wanted to slap him.

"You going to send a message back?" Willy yelled from his horse.

"No." She sat with her fists on her knees, staring at the solid wooden door. Her husband, Ned Cochran, had made the door himself. Ned, who had planned to quit his lawman job the end of this term. Ned, who had wanted to raise cows and a family.

Patsy Ann finally heard Willy Blue's horse amble away. She trembled; fear and anger gripped her. Ned murdered five days ago and they were just now letting her know? And only because she owed a board bill in town on Ned's horse? She thought of the town busybodies rubbing their hands together, waiting to see what she would do next.

Patsy Ann. Ex-saloon girl turned wife and homesteader. Patsy Ann, married to the sheriff less than one year, a marriage predicted not to last. Well, it turned out they were right. The whole town had gossiped its jaws off the past twelve months, so much so Patsy Ann hardly ever went there.

Ned had faced everybody down. They did not dare make comments in his presence. He was respected and good with a gun. He said everybody had something in their past they were not proud of, but most people deserved a second chance. He had told Patsy Ann to hold her chin high and go about her business, they'd leave her alone sooner or later.

She figured it would be later. Somehow going to town lost its charm anyway. Everything she wanted was right here — the house, the garden, the small herd of cows expecting new calves. It was the beginning of Ned's herd. And there were six Quarter Horse mares heavy in foal bred to the stallion. Malachi. Patsy Ann laughed thinking about it. Malachi, a big red and white, bald-faced pinto. The horse had glass-blue eyes, and feet the size of pie tins. Malachi, with his Roman nose and long ears. But Ned only scoffed at suggestions that Malachi was not exactly thoroughbred stock. He said Malachi's high withers and big flat knees, short back, deep girth, long neck, and quiet disposition more than made up for anything the horse lacked in fancy. Ned said he chose a horse like he did a wife — smart and tractable, something he could depend on. Ned did not care who laughed behind his back; he knew what he wanted.

Patsy Ann put her face in her hands and cried, letting it out. Might as well get it over with . . . there was a lot of work to be done, and she would have no more time for tears. While wiping her nose with the corner of her apron, she looked around the kitchen and made up her mind. She would hitch up one of the mares and drive to town. No way Malachi would be auctioned off to the highest bidder.

Patsy Ann's first stop in town was the bank. If she had a board bill to pay, she needed money. Ned did the shopping. Ned paid the bills. She never thought about money. She let Ned handle their finances. She did not have five dollars cash money to her name.

She pushed open the bank door and felt a rush of coolness. A teller looked at her from behind his barred window, then quickly dropped his gaze. She inquired about Mr. Sherwood, was he in?

The teller merely nodded, then strode to the back office door and knocked rapidly. "Sheriff Cochran's wife is here," he said.

Mr. Sherwood came out almost immediately, rubbing his nervous hands together. His suit was black and neatly pressed. He had a habit of clearing his throat just before he spoke. "Come in," he beckoned, leading her inside his office.

She sat in front of the desk, heart racing. "I need some money. Ned has our savings here."

He pulled open a drawer, shuffled through a stack of papers, then drew out a ledger. "Yes. Five hundred and sixty-five dollars and twenty-two cents."

"Five hundred dollars?" She felt a flood of relief. She had been struggling with fear all the way to town. She worried about how she was going to make it until spring when the new calves would be saleable, when the new foals would be on the ground, when she would have something to sell. She had to hold things together. There was a baby coming in the spring, too . . . and she strangled back a sob, thinking Ned died without knowing. She had been saving the news for him until she was sure . . . she planned to tell him after he got home from this trip to Salt Creek. Now it was too late.

"Can I have some of the money today?" she asked. "Not all, of course, just enough to get Malachi for now. I need five dollars."

He looked at the papers before clearing his throat. "Well, er, I'm afraid that's not possible."

"What? You just said I have five *hundred* dollars."

"Ned had the money in his name, with you as beneficiary. That is, if he dies, it goes to you. But the account is not in both of your names. So it will have to go through probate . . . that will take a couple of months. And, of course, there will be court costs, so you won't exactly be getting the whole five hundred."

"A couple of months!"

"The circuit judge will be here in September. That's only three months away."

"Three months away! Meanwhile, how can I get Ned's horse?"

He twisted the ends of his mustache. "It seems to me you have more trouble than a horse, Missus Cochran. I know the ranch is in both your names. I was there when the title was drawn up. I can pay you eight hundred dollars in cash for the place. What do you say? That ought to get you a far piece from Hipshot."

"I don't want to go a far piece from Hipshot." She felt her neck getting hot under her collar.

"But . . . Missus Cochran, what else are you to do?"

She did not answer right away. His snide smile caused her to cringe. She remembered he was a regular visitor at Maude's Palace. And now he acted like he knew something she ought to be ashamed of, when it was really the other way around.

"The ranch is not for sale," she blurted.

"Well, all right, then. One thousand dollars. But that's as high as I can go. And that includes the equipment, cattle, horses, the milk cow, everything."

"Ned paid two thousand dollars for the land before we built the house."

He cleared his throat again. "Well, land prices have not gone up that much around here. You're in a pinch. You better take what you can get."

She stood up. "The only thing I need is five dollars. Can't you loan me five dollars? I'll pay you back as soon as the circuit judge does his probating."

He smiled at her. "Oh, no. I'm afraid I can't make a loan. The only way I can help you is to buy the whole ranch. One thousand dollars. Cash."

She turned and left the office. She stomped across the street to the sheriff's office where Deputy Syd Ahrens lounged in the doorway, picking his teeth. "I've come for Malachi and Ned's gun and saddle," she said.

Shrugging, he walked inside and sat behind his desk. He did not offer her a chair. "Ned's gun is here. The saddle and bridle are over at the livery stable." He opened a desk drawer and lifted out Ned's gun, rolled inside the gun belt. "The sheriff over at Salt Creek sent this back, but the killers robbed Ned of whatever money he might have been carrying, and his watch."

She reached for the gun, touching the leather holster but keeping her hands off the pistol grip. It was too painful for her to handle Ned's belongings. She fought tears thinking of him. The way he handled his guns . . . the way he walked . . . the way he put on his hat . . . his slow grin.

"How did it happen?" she whispered.

"Ambushed. Friends of his prisoner jumped him about a mile out of Salt Creek. Some farmers heard the ruckus and came running, but it was too late."

"Ned? He's buried at Salt Creek?"

"Yep. Since he worked for the taxpayers, the county took care of it."

"His body won't be sent back here?"

"Well, no . . . with this heat and all . . ."

"You say Ned's saddle is at the stable? Can I get it?"

"Yep. But you'll need five dollars to pay the board on Malachi," Ahrens said.

"I don't have the money right now. Mister Sherwood said it will take some time for probating. I don't suppose you could loan me five dollars? I'll pay you back in September."

"September! Three months away? Hell, I could be dead and buried myself by September. The life of a lawman don't come with guarantees. Here one day, gone the next."

She looked at him sharply, amazed that he would say something so unkind. "I'll pay you back."

His glance was shrewd. "Tell you what, I'll give you five dollars for Ned's gun . . . and that includes the holster . . . and the bullets."

"Five dollars for Ned's gun? I couldn't sell Ned's gun for five dollars."

"Well, make up your mind, girl. It's the gun or the horse."

He would not have called her "girl" if Ned was still alive. Suddenly she had become Patsy Ann from Maude's Palace again. Ned was no longer her protector. She took the gun and gun belt and tucked it under her arm. "Thank you, Deputy Ahrens," she said, turning to go. *Five dollars for Ned's gun!* Her husband's reputation as one of the finest lawmen in the territory made the gun valuable as a collector's piece, if nothing else. *Five dollars!*

Ahrens hurried around his desk and blocked her path. "Let me tell you something, Patsy Ann. Your acting uppity around here will get you nowhere. Ned's gone now. I'm the new sheriff. And a saloon gal belongs inside a saloon. I said I'd give you five dollars for the gun. Take it or leave it."

She squinted at him. "I'll tell you what, Deputy Ahrens. I'll trade you Malachi for the gun."

"What? I don't own Malachi. He'll be auctioned on Saturday, if you can't come up with the money."

"So buy him at the auction, and I'll trade you for the gun."

"I ain't got no use for that walleyed plug," Ahrens said. "That spavined clang never could get out of his own dust."

"Buy him and I'll trade." She walked out the door.

She went to the stable where she met Jake Ormsby sweeping down the barn aisle with a well-used broom. "Jake? I understand my husband's saddle is here. I've come to claim it."

"You picking up Malachi, too?" He rested the broom against the wall before tucking his thumbs behind his braces.

"I don't have five dollars to pay Malachi's board. I don't suppose you'd lend me the money? I'll pay you back in September when the circuit judge comes to do probating."

He had a way of raising his eyebrows so his hat jerked up and down on his head. "By golly, Miz

132

Cochran, I ain't in the habit of loaning money to folks who can't pay their bills. Business is business." He scratched his chin while ideas flitted back and forth beneath his pale eyes. "But tell you what, I'll give you five dollars for Ned's saddle . . . if you throw in the blanket and bridle."

"That saddle is almost new, Jake. Ned bought it last year. His old one got the horn shot off in that running gunfight he had with the Brewster bunch. And that bridle has a silver inlaid bit made special for Ned down in old Mexico. It even has his initials on the shank. I expect it would be something nice for you to own now. I mean, think of the advertising. People would stop here from miles around just to have a look at Ned Cochran's saddle and bridle."

Jake Ormsby blushed. His hat was still jerking up and down on his head. "Well, I don't know nothing about advertising, Miz Cochran. I just offered you five dollars for the rig. Take it or leave it."

She walked into the tack room and lifted the saddle, blanket, and bridle from the rack. "I'll trade you Malachi for the outfit, Jake."

"What are you talking about? Malachi ain't mine to trade. He's going to be auctioned on Saturday if you don't pay the bill."

She hefted the saddle in her arms and made for the door. "Buy him in the auction, and I'll trade you this gear."

She drove the buggy slowly down the street. Preacher Mondale and his wife lived in a white frame house next door to the church. Honeysuckle clung in profusion to the fence beside the gate. After tying the mare to the hitching post, Patsy Ann bolstered her nerve and stamped up the walk.

Mrs. Mondale answered the door and gave Patsy Ann a weak smile. Before Patsy Ann could state her business, Mrs. Mondale called her husband from a room at the back of the house.

Reverend Mondale came to the door. "Missus Cochran! What a surprise." He stepped out on the porch and closed the door.

"I've come to town to pick up my husband's belongings."

"Yes, I was sorry to hear about Ned. How can I help?"

Patsy Ann sat on the porch swing. He had not invited her to sit down, but she felt a sudden dizziness and knew it was that time of the morning to experience a queasy spell. It would pass. "Reverend Mondale, Malachi is being held at the stable. If his board bill is not paid, he will be auctioned on Saturday. I have money in the bank, but Mister Sherwood said I can't have it until the circuit judge does probating in September. I wonder if you could loan me five dollars. You know I'll pay you back."

"Me? Loan money? This is highly irregular. If a church were to loan money to people, how could we survive? I mean, the church needs money!"

She looked him in the eye. "Remember the day you married us? You charged Ned fifty dollars to perform the ceremony. That was forty more than you charge

134

anybody else. On account of I was a saloon girl, you put the screws to Ned that day."

"I beg your pardon, young lady! What do you mean coming here with language like that!" He paced back and forth on the porch while his lion eyes searched her person. He knew she was right.

"I'm in a tight spot now, and I thought you'd help me out with five dollars. I'll pay it back," she repeated.

He looked at her buggy. "What will you do now that your husband is dead?" His question was blunt, but then he did not respect her enough to worry about protocol.

"I've had an offer on my ranch," she said without lying.

"Ah! Then you will be leaving Hipshot. I think the church can afford to buy that buggy of yours. I'll give you five dollars if you throw in the harness."

"Five dollars! That's a Studebaker buggy. Ned paid twenty-five for it last year. New."

"Well, all right then, seven. But not one cent more."

She stood up. "Tell you what, Reverend Mondale. I'll trade you Malachi for the buggy and harness."

"Trade Malachi? But I don't own Malachi. Besides, it wouldn't be fitting for a minister to drive a . . . piebald!"

"No. But if you buy him in the auction on Saturday, I'll trade you the buggy and harness for him." She stepped off the porch and made her way back down the street to the Hipshot mercantile.

★ ★ ★

Ben Baker ran a well-stocked business, everything from gunpowder to calico was piled from floor to ceiling. The smell of dill pickles and saddle soap greeted customers when they stepped through the door.

Patsy Ann walked right up to the counter.

Ben Baker saw her coming before she crossed the street. "I'm sorry about Ned," he told her.

"Do I owe any money here, Mister Baker?" she asked.

"No, ma'am. Sheriff Cochran always paid cash. The one time he did ask for credit was when you were building fence out there and he needed one more payday to settle his bill. But that was a year ago. He's not owed a cent since."

"I need five dollars to pay the board on Malachi, Mister Baker. Could you loan it to me? I'll have the money in September when the circuit judge comes for probating. I'll pay you back then."

"Five dollars! This is not a lending institution, Missus Cochran. People borrow money at the bank."

"Yes, sir, I understand. I only thought you'd be able to help me out a little since Ned saved your place from being robbed last year. Remember? When the Russell gang rode in that time? Shooting windows out of stores, and killing the barber because he happened to be in the way? Ned stood in your door and shot it out with the robbers before they could get to you . . . hiding behind the counter the way you were. As I recall, Ned took a bullet in the arm that day."

"Now look here, Patsy Ann! Ned was doing his job. Defending lives and property is what he got paid for."

"Yes, sir. I appreciate your reminding me about that." She turned to go.

"Er, wait a minute! You still got that Jersey milk cow? The one Ned bought from Mattie Brunk when she lost her place?"

"Yes, I have Jersey. Ned paid Mattie Brunk thirty dollars for that cow, ten more than anybody else in town would pay. Ned never took advantage of a person."

Baker eyed her. "That cow still giving all that milk?"

"Four gallons a day. More than enough for cheese and butter, and plenty left over to feed the pigs."

"I'll give you five dollars for her so you can get your horse out of hock."

"Tell you what, Mister Baker. I'll trade you the cow for Malachi."

His lips pursed into an astounded "O" before his eyebrows came together. "I don't own Malachi! I have no use for another horse, especially not a pigeon-toed hay burner like that one."

"You buy him Saturday at the auction, and I'll trade you the cow for the horse." She walked out of the store.

Maude sat in front of her dressing table while looking back at Patsy Ann through the mirror. "You come around here now? Wanting five dollars?" She dabbed face powder into the fine wrinkles around her mouth.

"I'll pay you back in September. The judge is coming for probating. I'll have the money then."

"September," Maude scoffed. She drew the tip of a charcoal pencil along the edge of her left eyebrow. The harsh line gave her an unreal look, like the face of a painted doll. Her dyed hair was the color of ripe pumpkins.

Patsy Ann stood in the middle of the room feeling dizzy again. Without being offered a seat, she leaned against Maude's bedpost. She studied Maude's smooth, firm back through the flimsy nightgown. She figured Maude was at least fifty years old, but seemed much younger with the help of make-up and whalebone corsets.

"You look kind of peaked," Maude said, still watching Patsy Ann through the mirror.

"I have not had breakfast today," Patsy Ann said. She hoped Maude would accept that answer. Maude was shrewd, usually seeing right through people. Patsy Ann worked for her less than a year, coming to Hipshot, Arizona after running away from an abusive stepbrother in Texas.

Maude turned in her chair. "Let me get this straight. You want to borrow five dollars to pay the board on Malachi. Otherwise, he will be auctioned on Saturday."

"Yes."

"And you haven't got a lousy five dollars? Anywhere? Not tucked away some place? Inside a cookie jar or something? You harebrain!"

Patsy Ann gulped the dryness from her mouth. Her stomach churned. Her hands felt clammy. "Please, Maude. Just five dollars? I worked hard for you. I did lots of favors, and I always played straight. I never kept any money like some of the girls did. I always accounted for everything."

138

"I'll say you did. You even accounted for my Ned! Ned Cochran was mine before you came along, you little chit! To think my Ned wound up marrying a . . . saloon girl!"

Patsy Ann closed her eyes. "I just want to take his horse home. If Ned ever meant anything to you, then let me do right by him now. You know how much that horse meant to him. I want to take Malachi home where he belongs. I don't want him to fall into the hands of somebody who doesn't care."

"Care!" Maude jumped from her stool. Pacing back and forth, her bare feet made little sticking sounds on the hardwood floor. Her pink silk nightgown was open at the throat, the long see-through sleeves showed her shapely arms. "Tell you what, sis. Come and work a few nights." She threw back her head and hooted. "That ought to be worth five dollars, ain't it?"

Trembling, Patsy Ann tore her eyes from Maude's cruel beauty. "That's not fair, Maude. I gave you notice I was leaving. You can't blame me for falling in love and wanting a better life."

Maude stopped pacing, hands on hips. The heady odor of lavender water permeated the hot still air. "Ned Cochran was mine! One look at you and off he went like a pet squirrel."

"I'm sorry, Maude. I better go. I didn't know you were so resentful."

"Resentful! It was me Ned loved! Don't you remember the way he jumped between me and Rattler Pete who was trying to cut me up? And the time he foiled a robbery in my office when the Paddy brothers broke jail? You think he'd have done that if he didn't care about me? He loved me long before he even knew you existed!"

"I'm sorry I bothered you," Patsy Ann whispered.

"Bother! You'll come crawling back here looking for work one day soon. You'll never hold that ranch together by yourself. There's only one thing you're good for."

"I'll go, Maude." Patsy Ann staggered a little.

"Not so fast. I see you're still wearing my ring."

"It was Ned's mother's ring. He gave it to me for a wedding ring," Patsy Ann gasped.

"What kind of wedding ring is that with rhinestones in a cameo? That's no wedding ring."

"It is as far as I'm concerned."

Maude shook her fist under Patsy Ann's nose. "I wore it till he went off with you that night . . . after jerking the ring from my hand at gun point as I recall!"

"You wouldn't give it to him. He said he wanted me to have something that once belonged to his mother."

"Yeah, well, you got it. Tell you what. I'll give you five dollars for it so you can get your horse. I want my ring back!"

Patsy Ann looked at her. "I'll trade you Malachi for the ring."

"I don't own Malachi. What would I do with that clodhopper?"

"Malachi will be auctioned on Saturday. You buy the horse, and I'll give you the ring for him." Patsy Ann left Maude standing there with her red-painted mouth agape.

★ ★ ★

140

Back at the stable, Patsy Ann asked Jake if she could see Malachi before leaving town. He only shrugged, pointing the way through the stable to the corrals where the horse was in a small pen by himself. There was no hay in the manger, and the water bucket was empty. Malachi stood with his head hanging until he heard Patsy Ann's voice.

"Come on, fella. Here, boy," she crooned.

He came right to her and thrust his big head over the top rail. He pressed his forehead against her chest, searching her fingers with his pink lips for a hand-out.

"Malachi," she laughed, putting her arms around his head, feeling his big warm jaws where the bone joined his throat. She smelled his horse smell: leather and alfalfa. She pressed her forehead against his and began to cry.

"Patsy Ann? Miz Cochran?"

She pulled away from the horse, embarrassed somebody had caught her bawling. Willy wore his ragged straw hat propped to one side of his head. He switched back and forth from one foot to the other like he had to go to the privy.

"I've come to see Malachi," she said.

"Are you taking him home?"

"Not yet. I haven't got the money."

"He's looking kind of poorly," Willy said. "Jake told me not to waste grain on him, but I sneak him a handful morning and night. And I give him hay."

"I see, Willy. Thanks for looking out for him."

"I can loan you the money . . . I got five dollars saved." He shoved a handful of coins and one crumpled

141

bill at her. "I always liked Sheriff Ned. He smashed the nose of Rattler Pete the time Pete shot the tail off my dog."

"Yes, Willy. You told me. But I can't take your money. I bet you've been saving it up for a long time."

"Nearly two years. But I really want you to have it, Miz Cochran. Otherwise, some fellow is liable to buy Malachi and ride him hard on account of some grudge against the sheriff."

"Don't worry, nobody's going to abuse Malachi. I'll see you at the auction Saturday." She patted his arm and walked back through the stable to her buggy.

Deputy Sheriff Syd Ahrens acted as auctioneer. His yodeling was awful. With the crowd of people making so much noise, he had to call out good and loud so everybody could understand.

The first person to bid five dollars was Willy. He poked his hand in the air, and the auction got under way. Right away the bidding went to six dollars, Syd Ahrens himself saying he'd give that much. Somebody from the crowd protested the auctioneer bidding against the crowd. But when Ahrens reminded everybody he was running for sheriff in the fall, no more complaints were heard.

Patsy Ann had been sitting beside her buggy near the auction corral an hour before the bidding got under way. She wore her cleanest calico dress and blue bonnet. She squeezed the reins between her knees, leaving her arms free to rest her elbows against the back of the buggy seat. Even though the baby wasn't showing yet, Patsy Ann's spine felt the stress. The buggy was dusted and polished. The old pregnant mare stood hipshot in the shafts, swishing her tail at flies. The nine-mile trip to town had tuckered her out. Behind the buggy, Jersey was tied, cleaned and brushed, looking around at the crowd. In the back of the buggy was piled Ned's saddle, bridle, and blanket. Patsy Ann had washed her wedding ring in ammonia water so the rhinestones sparkled for all to see.

Mr. Sherwood from the bank strolled around, puffing on a cigar. An eye-watering billow of smoke followed him through the crowd to Patsy Ann's buggy.

"You here to bid on Malachi?" Patsy Ann inquired, although she had not made any offers to him about trading the ranch for the horse. Malachi was one thing, the ranch was another. As much as she wanted to keep the horse, the ranch was security for her and the baby.

Sherwood puffed smoke in her direction. "I never get into a stink contest with a skunk."

"You calling me a skunk?" she could not help asking.

"Let me put it to you this way, Missus Cochran. Everybody around here knows you've put certain conditions on the sale of this horse. People are jabbering like a flock of crows. I expect there will be hurt feelings before this day is over. You've got the whole town fighting over rings and cows and buggies."

"I only want my horse," she said.

"Let me know when you get ready to sell the ranch," he said. "Then we'll talk business. I don't play games." He walked away.

Maude, Ben Baker, Reverend Mondale, and Jake Ormsby circled around. Patsy Ann nodded to them. The bidding was under way. Everybody strained to hear what Syd Ahrens was yelling about.

"Seven, seven . . . who will give me seven dollars? Come on, folks, Ned Cochran's horse is worth much more. The county has five coming, and the rest goes to the poor widow. We owe Ned that much. Who will give ten?" His eyes roved toward the buggy where Patsy Ann had Ned's gun on the buggy seat.

Willy walked back to the buggy and stood beside Patsy Ann. He stuffed the five dollars back into his pocket. "I tried," was all he said. His dog followed him; the black creature's tail stump wiggled oddly to one side.

Patsy Ann fanned herself with one hand. The heat was getting to her. It was that time of the morning when she usually felt faint. Syd Ahrens's voice droned: "Fourteen dollars . . . fourteen . . . fifteen. Sixteen . . . sixteen . . . who will give me sixteen? Sixteen! I have sixteen. Sixteen once? Sixteen twice?"

It was Maude offering sixteen dollars for Malachi, while her greenish eyes slithered toward Patsy Ann's ring.

"Seventeen!" Preacher Mondale shouted. He glanced at the buggy.

"Seventeen . . . who will give me eighteen? Seventeen once, seventeen twice . . ."

"Eighteen!" shouted Ben Baker. He had been running his hands over the back and hips of Jersey, while poking his head under the cow's belly to get a

144

look at her udder. "I'll give you eighteen dollars for this cow!"

"We ain't selling cows today, Mister Baker," Ahrens laughed. He made a big joke out of it until the crowd roared and clapped their hands.

"Now I'll tell you what, folks," Ahrens said. "I myself will give twenty dollars for this horse. Who can top it, eh?" He winked at Patsy Ann after his eyes darted over the gun again.

Jake had been checking Ned's saddle. He raised a finger now, and offered twenty-one dollars.

"Twenty-two!" Maude screamed.

"Twenty-three!" Ben shouted back.

"Twenty-four," the reverend said.

"Twenty-five," Jake roared, matching the preacher's determination.

"Thirty dollars!" Maude cried, sashaying around the crowd. She wore a long green velvet dress with frilly lace collar, and carried a black parasol to protect her face from the sun. "Thirty dollars!" she hawked.

When there was no immediate answer, Syd Ahrens lifted the hammer he used as a gavel, ready to hit the top of the corral post. "Thirty dollars once . . . thirty dollars twice . . . thirty dollars . . ."

"Two hundred dollars!" a man's voice boomed from the back of the crowd. Patsy Ann twisted frantically in the buggy seat to see who it belonged to.

Rattler Pete! Slouched in his saddle, a satisfied look on his bronze face, Rattler Pete waved a fistful of greenbacks. "I bid two hundred dollars for the widow's

145

stallion." His white teeth flashed under a gray mustache.

Syd Ahrens choked.

While shading her eyes with her parasol, Maude put her free hand on her hip. She tipped her head kind of saucy. "Two *hundred* dollars?"

"I'm not bidding against Rattler," the reverend muttered.

"That's too rich for me," Ben Baker said.

"Ain't no saddle or bridle worth tangling with Rattler Pete," Jake announced.

Willy Blue's dog dove underneath Patsy Ann's buggy.

"Two hundred dollars . . . once . . . Two hundred dollars twice . . ." Syd Ahrens's voice was hardly audible. "Sold," he whispered, "to Rattler Pete for two hundred dollars."

Rattler Pete urged his dun horse to the fence where he untied Malachi's halter rope. He handed five dollars to Syd Ahrens. "I'll take my receipt. Wouldn't want no posse chasing me for horse stealing!" His laugh challenged the crowd who had already begun slinking away.

Syd Ahrens scribbled on a piece of paper and handed it to him. "The horse is yours, free and clear."

Rattler Pete reined away from the fence. He directed his horse to Patsy Ann's buggy where he dropped one hundred and ninety-five dollars on her lap. "For you," he said with a grin, then rode away, leading Malachi.

Willy looked like he wanted to cry. "You should've borrowed the five dollars from me," he told Patsy Ann.

She braced herself, disappointed and feeling queasy. The hushed crowd disappeared. Some folks glared at her as if the whole thing was her fault. She looked down at the money. One hundred and ninety-five dollars would see her through until the judge came to do probating.

It turned out clear that night with a moon rising yellow in the blue-black sky. Rattler Pete's camp was on a rise where he could see anybody coming from any direction. He had a small fire snapping — Malachi and the dun were tied to a mesquite bush nearby.

Patsy Ann pulled the buggy to a halt. It had been a long, slow trip what with Jersey pulling back on her halter, and the pregnant mare not wanting to go any faster than she had to.

"Step down, Missus Cochran," Rattler Pete said, sounding bored. "You look like your leather's too tired to squeak."

Patsy Ann clambered stiffly from the buggy seat. She had been on Rattler's trail for nearly six hours, having followed him out of town right after the auction. There was no point going home to unload her buggy or get rid of the cow. She'd have lost Rattler's trail for sure.

She hunkered across from him in front of the fire. "I could use a cup of coffee," she croaked.

He simply handed her his metal cup. "Only got one cup."

She sipped the bitter brew. "I've come to talk business. Been following you all afternoon." She handed his cup back.

147

"Yep. I saw you."

"You did? Why didn't you stop and let me catch up?"

"I figured you'd do less talking if you were out of breath."

She sighed. "I want Malachi."

"How much money you got?"

"One hundred and ninety-five dollars."

"I can get that much in a fast poker game," he said.

"I got this fine Studebaker buggy and harness," she said.

"Do I look like a preacher?" He slurped his coffee. "I don't ride around in buggies."

"I have the mare. She's sound, a Quarter Horse."

"Yeah, well, she looks pregnant to me. I got no time for messing with foals, nor fools, either one."

"There's Ned's saddle and bridle. I'll throw in the blanket," she said, looking into his flat eyes. She could understand why he was called Rattler.

"I got me a good saddle. I only use one at a time."

"There's Ned's gun, and holster."

Rattler Pete let out a snort. "If I'd have killed him for it, that might have meant something. But buying it off his widow is sissy work."

"What about the milk cow?" she asked.

"What am I, a nester?" he rolled his eyes.

She looked down at her hands. "Then I reckon I followed you all this way for nothing."

His gaze settled on her ring. "I remember when Maude wore that ring."

"It was Ned's mother's ring," Patsy Ann said.

He chuckled, flipping the last of his cold coffee into the bushes. "I gave it to Maude. Picked it up off a drummer in Tucson one time. I liked the white cameo face and those hard rhinestone eyes. Reminded me of Maude. I gave it to her."

"What? Ned told me it once belonged to his mother."

"Well, who the hell you think his mother is? Didn't he tell you?"

Patsy Ann stared at him across the fire. "Maude . . . is . . . Ned's . . . mother?"

He reached his hand out to her. "You married into quite a family, Patsy Ann." He threw his head back and laughed until tears ran down the landscape of his face. "Me and Maude go back a long ways. Ned was our son."

She slid the ring off her finger and placed it into the palm of his hand. "Are we even? That's all you want . . . Maude's ring? I can have Malachi?"

He rolled the ring between his fingers as if caressing a small and delicate flower. "This is all I want, Patsy Ann. Take your horse, and go on home."

Callie

CYNTHIA HASELOFF

Cynthia Haseloff's characters embody the fundamental values — honor, duty, courage, and family — that prevailed on the American frontier and were instilled in the young Haseloff by her own "heroes," her mother and her grandmother. Her stories dramatize how these values endure when challenged by the adversities and cruelties of frontier existence. Her talent rests in her ability to tell a story with an economy of words and in the seemingly effortless way she uses language. Her novels include THE CHAINS OF SARAI STONE (1995), MAN WITHOUT MEDICINE (1996), THE KIOWA VERDICT (1997), winner of the WWA Spur Award for Best Western Novel in 1997, and SATANTA'S WOMAN. She once said: "I love the West, perhaps not all of its reality, for much of it was cruel and hard, but certainly its dream and hope, and the damned courage of people trying to live within its demands." "Callie" was written for this collection.

Callie Daniels closed her worn Bible over her fingers and rocked, holding the old book in her lap. Rising, she laid it on the reading table beside her and went to the window to look out into the storm. Rain was a blessing in this dry land, a land that fed her herds of cattle and supported her household. The streaming rivulets of water had long since washed the red dirt off the panes. Now, as she watched, they washed away the years. In the blurred distance beneath the aged pecan tree, she saw the rider again as clearly as she had seen him thirty years before. "And I saw and, behold . . . And there went out another horse that was red, and power was given to him that sat on it to take peace from the earth, and that they should kill one another . . ."

"Oh, Callie, do you see him?" whispered Nell Jack.

"I see him," answered Callie Daniels, looking at the figure sitting above the sight of her rifle.

"Ye cannot shoot him, Cal." Nell caught her arm gently.

"No, I cannot. The sound would give us away. They would find us and the children sure, then."

"Has he seen us, do you think?"

"It may be."

The two women watched the painted Comanche sitting beneath the tree across the rocky creek. When the fighting had begun, when the Indians had come down Elm Creek into the scattered cabins along its banks, they had fled to the hiding place in the undercut bank and pulled the brush over the entrance behind them. It was a place appointed for such needs, for the Indians were plenty and ravenous now that so many fighting men had gone East to wage war with their white brothers.

Callie glanced at the children huddled against the bank. Her oldest, Lud, was just six but a man coming. The Indians would make him a Comanche because he would never cry, and, when he had fought enough, he would listen and learn their ways. Her infant twins, Rafe and Gabe, would never leave the cave alive. Nell, great with child, had no chance. She and Nell would be spared nothing, and in the end they would die before the children's eyes. The Indians would cut the baby from Nell's belly just as they had the Walker woman's last year. Callie made the assessment without emotion. She had been on the frontier long enough to know her enemies' ways.

"Callie." Nell nudged her.

As both women watched, the Comanche slipped from his horse. Callie's fist came to her mouth as her other arm folded across her stomach. The Indian bent to study the ground, then looked up at the embankment as if he saw them.

"I haven't seen any others. Have you seen any others?" Callie asked.

"Just him."

"We must kill him," Callie concluded.

"Oh, Callie, how?"

"Quietly." Callie tugged on Nell's sleeve and eased her farther back into the cave. "Nell, you must stay back with the children. If he comes . . . just cover the little ones like you are alone, by yourself. Don't let on I'm here. I will try to . . . Lud, give me your knife." The

152

child looked up from his whittling, then handed over the pocket knife. Callie touched his hair and smiled softly. "Stay with Nell, Son." Callie saw Nell's small steady intense face, now pale with fear. She patted her friend's shoulder, then moved to the shadowed lip at the front of the cave to wait.

Callie Daniels had survived the rough frontier by facing facts. Her druthers played way behind the needs of her family. She had never tried to kill a man before, had never thought on it. Now she searched her brain for the way to kill the Indian with one unexpected blow. She would get but one chance. She watched him turn away back toward the horse and closed her eyes in gratitude. But he stopped and went to the side, sorting the grass, picking out a small piece of corn bread one of the children had been eating. She saw his mind work through the presence of the still moist bread, the fact that it had not been there long enough to dry out, not long enough for a bird or animal to take it. He started back toward them then, carefully studying the bank, carefully placing one foot, then the other in the water. Callie heard her own blood coursing through her ears as her pale eyes watched through the heavy brush. The man lowered his torso slightly, crouching now, but moving steadily, listening with each step. He reached into his belt and removed the brass tomahawk. Callie drew in her breath. He balanced the glittering heft of it with practiced grace. *One blow*, she thought. She would get only one killing blow.

One of the children made a noise, a fretful baby noise, but the man heard. He did not react, did not

153

change the position of his body or weapon, but Callie saw the hearing in his black eyes. Here, before her, was the consummate hunter, disciplined and worthy in his craft. Sure enough of what his quarry was to be cautious, but not afraid. Sure enough of himself not to have called for the others.

Callie chewed her lip, waiting. *One blow. Just one.* The interval between the hunter and the hunted closed. The time hung suspended, ticking off in eons with each forward step through the water and onto the smooth round rocks and coarse red sand of the bank. *One blow. Just one.*

The man read the earth. Saw the sign they had tried to brush away — little feet, children's footsteps, a woman's.

Come on, thought Callie, struggling with her fear. *One blow. Just one.*

The man's left hand reached out and caught the brush. Almost imperceptibly he tested it. Then the hand closed hard and jerked away the shield of branches.

One blow. Just one.

Nell screamed at the sudden burst of light into the darkness of the cave, at the man blocking the entrance. For a second, the briefest of seconds, he was startled, blinded in the darkness perhaps. Callie drove the pocket knife into the small notch at the base of his throat. He gasped and caught her hand, pushing the knife, twisting the knife. Throwing her aside, his hand went to his throat, grasping to hold the escaping warmth of air and blood. His eyes blazed now in anger

154

as he turned to the woman at his feet. He held the shining hatchet as he wrestled with Callie Daniels, smearing her with his still warm blood. She fought against him, watching the glint of the blade, feeling his knee planted in her stomach, his hand on her throat as he raised the tomahawk.

"No! No!" Callie fought fiercely to free herself. She barely heard the grunt, the deep "uuh" as he released her, and the hatchet tumbled from his hand. He straightened, catching at his back, then sank slowly, revealing Nell, holding his knife wet with his blood in her hand. The Indian watched them with dying eyes as they caught each other and Callie lifted Lud into her arms and turned him away.

Callie heard the front door slam against the storm. "Lud?" she called.

"Yes," the man in the dripping slicker said. "It's me."

"Hang that coat on the porch," Callie Daniels instructed her son. "You're ruining the floor."

"Esperanza can mop it up after she gets my dinner," Lud answered.

Callie came to stand in the doorway. "Out."

"God Almighty, Mama. I got more things on my mind than the damned floor."

"Put the coat on the porch."

Lud opened the outer door and threw the coat onto the painted boards of the porch.

"There."

"Why did you miss dinner, Son?" Callie asked as she preceded Lud into the dining room with its long polished table and refined furnishings. "We had company. You were missed."

Lud sat at the table. "Esperanza! Some business came up."

A Mexican woman appeared in the door.

"Fix me some dinner."

Callie settled into the upholstered armed chair at the head of the table. "Business?"

"That's right." Lud folded his hands on the table as he waited.

Callie watched him with interest. "Newt Parsons said you've caught the cattle rustlers," she said innocently.

"That's right." Lud unfolded his hands from the table and sat back in the straight chair.

"Where are they?"

"The stone jail."

Esperanza brought a plate and glass of milk and set them before the rancher.

"*Gracias*." Lud's attention focused closely on the food. "This is real good. Best beef we've ever raised."

"What are you going to do with them?"

"They are in jail." Lud chewed.

"Yes," said Callie. "That is where they are, but what do you plan to do with them?"

"You don't need to know that, Mama." Lud did not look at his mother. "Well, shoot, we're not going to do anything with them probably. Hold 'em. Try 'em. Send 'em to prison. That's the usual, isn't it?"

Callie's eyes had not left Lud.

156

"That's the law."

"That's right. They stole cattle, Lud, just cattle. We have twenty thousand head."

"We won't if every rustler in Texas thinks he can take what he wants. You're goin' soft, Mama. The point is they took our cattle. If they get away with it, the next guy will think he can, too."

"Newt said Conner Jack was one of them."

"That's right. Our favorite sheriff, Conner Jack, our trusted friend, Conner Jack, your son-in-law, my brother-in-law, Conner Jack." Lud tossed his fork at the table. "He helped us chase the rustlers. No wonder we never caught them. He was killing our cattle, sinking the hides in the Brazos, and selling the meat to the Army. Makes me sick to think of what he's done to us, to Ruby." Lud put his head in his hands.

"Killing him won't help Ruby, Lud. There's no point to make here. Conner's a thief. People know that now. He's made a fool of us. People know that, too. We can take it and much more. There's no point to make with a man's life."

Lud wiped his mouth with the damask napkin. "You're wrong, Mama. Conner has stepped over. He must pay for it. People will say we're letting him off because of Ruby. The other ranchers will never trust us again if we let our own off."

Callie stood up and came to her son. "I want you to think about what you are saying and doing, Lud, and why. I am telling you that there is no point to make here. I'm telling you . . ."

"To let Conner off for Ruby's sake, for the family's sake," interjected Lud, rising to stand above his mother. "No. It's not right. It's not justice."

Callie sat back in the fine chair in her fine dining room as she heard the front door slam shut. Esperanza cleared the remaining meal away without her noticing. In a little while Callie went up the broad curving stairway to her room. She removed her black silk dress and laid it across the bench at the foot of her rosewood bed. Opening the doors of the burled walnut armoire, she selected a riding skirt and short jacket.

The storm had not abated when she entered the barn and saddled her horse. As she rode into town, the lightning danced across the prairie illuminating the small, slicker-clad rider, her horse, and another ponied alongside.

The stone jail was built like the rest of the town from the native limestone. It had two floors with living quarters. Remaining on the little Indian Peak ranch, Conner and Ruby had never lived there. A night watchman-jailer stayed there now. His wife cooked for the prisoners.

Water streaming from the brim of her hat, Callie opened the heavy oak door.

Sim, the deputy, immediately dropped his feet from the desk to the floor and stood up.

"'Evenin', Sim. Quite a night out there. Haven't seen rain like this since . . ." Callie caught herself. Tonight there had been too many memories. People did not care about them because they were not their memories. "What are you still doing here, Sim? Shouldn't you

158

have gone off somewhere by now? They'll be here soon."

"Who?" Sim acted curious.

"No one will ever know for sure. It will be their secret. Their blood bond."

"Now, Missus Daniels, you're not supposed to be here," he stuttered.

Callie Daniels walked to the door leading into the cell corridor and opened it.

"Missus Daniels," protested Sim.

Callie had not been here before. Her sons, the foreman, had recovered the drunken cowboys and identified the thieves for her. Inside, the six rustlers lay face down, tied, hands and feet, on the hall floor. "You do this, Sim?"

"Yes," the jailer said.

Callie turned to face him. "Looks like a real fair fight. Undo it."

Sim hesitated.

"I will wait."

"No, Missus Daniels. I can't do it. This is what the posse's expecting, and, if I don't do it, there will be hell to pay. I need my job. I got kids."

Callie sighed heavily and dropped her head. "Oh, Sim, you could save us so much time."

"No."

Callie Daniels snugged the muzzle of the old Navy Colt against his stomach. "I've killed better men than you, Sim. Now drag these rascals into the cells and cut them loose."

Sims began to drag the men laboriously into the cells as Callie found Conner Jack among them. She stood for a long moment, looking at the betrayer.

"I didn't . . . ," he began.

"Shut up, Conner," Callie said, kneeling to cut the ropes that held his hands behind his back. "Listen to me very carefully. I have brought you a horse."

The rustler smiled as he rubbed his wrists. "I knew, for Ruby's sake, you wouldn't let them hang me."

"Shut up and listen to me, or I'll kill you myself."

The smile left Conner Jack's handsome face.

"I am taking you to your mother. After that, I hope never to see you again. I won't be responsible after that."

"I can get away by myself." Conner worked the knot on the rope holding his feet.

"My sons will catch you and hang you this very night if you try."

Confident in what the woman had said, Conner bent to the knot again.

Callie heard Sim grunting with his exertions behind her and turned to consider his progress. He had cut the last man's hands free. The five rustlers all worked to untie their feet.

"Come out now, Sim," Callie said, going to him. She swung the barred door shut. "Lock it, please." Sims complied. "Thank you. Now be so good as to give me your keys and step in here."

Sims handed over the iron ring and entered the adjoining cell. Callie closed it, locked it behind him.

160

"You're a pistol, Missus Daniels," observed Connor Jack, rising from the floor. "You'll get your rustlers hung, after all."

Callie turned to her son-in-law. "If I let them go tonight, they will be hunted down out there and hanged. It will take a while to get them out of here. Work will spoil the fun and it will be daylight by then. Let's go."

"I'll get the extra key ring." Conner went back into the office. As he lifted the keys from the back of the drawer, his hand also closed over the grip of a pistol.

"Leave the gun, Conner. You will not kill my sons as they will not kill you."

Conner considered the woman and left the revolver.

It was thirty miles to Nell Jack's house, thirty miles across open country, thirty miles across time and memory. Callie and Conner cantered at first. The rain washed their tracks away as swiftly as they passed.

"Are you up to this, Missus Daniels?" asked Conner, observing his companion. Conner had never seen her on a horse before. Tonight in the driving rain she looked very small.

"You'd better hope I am," answered Callie, and that was the last they spoke until they crossed the overlook that revealed — in a flash of lightning — the stone corral fences of the ranch headquarters.

Away from the main house, closer to the river, he saw a light burning in the bungalow where Ruby waited.

"Say good bye, Conner."

"You mean to break me up from Ruby?" the man asked.

"That's Ruby's decision," Callie answered.

The handsome sheriff felt a strange lump in his throat, a pain for sweet Ruby. "I'm sorry, Missus Daniels."

"Yes, you are, Conner. But you have a good mother. And I have three fine sons who have not yet killed their sister's husband." Callie turned her horse off the rise and rode on.

They paced the horses walking and trotting, occasionally cantering across the open country that paralleled the Brazos. The rain remained their steady companion, furious and violent at first, but tapering off as the miles passed. By the time it had rained itself out, a full moon came out revealing the land. Callie breathed deeply as she walked her horse, appraising the night and the land.

"It's still a beautiful country."

"Beauty's in the eye of the beholder," Conner replied. "I'll be glad to be shut of it. Nothing here but snakes and scorpions."

"No Indians any more, though," observed Callie as she dismounted and led her horse.

Conner swung down to walk beside her.

"We used to call that a Comanche moon, and it wasn't a bit romantic. Our walls were three feet thick, and the shutters had shooting slots. A repeating rifle was the finest comfort a person could have. You ever see a scalped person, Conner?"

The rustler shook his head. "I heard about it."

"That's the trouble with life, Conner. People just hear about things. They don't know about them. Can't feel the sickness in their stomachs. Can't taste the tears. Can't see the families and know their grief because it is yours, too, by turn. Life has become a hearsay thing, lacking vitality." Callie mounted again after a while and took up a trot toward the thread of coming daylight.

Conner followed after a quick look at the back trail. He saw no riders coming hard after them.

The miles passed as the daylight grew. They let the horses drink from the fresh puddles that followed the storm. Callie handed Conner a sack of jerky and a canteen, then watched him drink deeply.

"Why'd you steal my cows?"

"I needed the money." The rustler wiped his mouth with the back of his hand.

"We're rich people, Conner."

"That's right, Missus Daniels, you are rich people . . . you, not me. I don't like to be beholden to no man, let alone a woman."

"You are a self-righteous ass," concluded Callie, tossing the last of a stringy bit of jerky on the ground. "You're too proud to accept your place at our table, but not too good to steal our beeves. The problem with your generation is you've never had a problem . . . not a real live or die problem, just a little money problem or a little social problem. There is considerable difference in worrying about how you part your hair and how you keep your scalp. You could use a problem."

"Well," observed Conner Jack, "I've got one now."

Callie followed his eyes to the horizon. A speck of a rider was coming hard, towing a spare pony. "I'll be damned," she blurted. "He's doing that old Indian trick of switching from a tired horse to a fresh horse at a gallop. He sure does want to kill you, Conner."

"Let him try," swore Conner Jack.

"No, I won't," said Callie. "I love my son, and I will not let him kill a man for nothing."

"He thinks it is something."

"He's wrong. Let's go. This is getting interesting."

"We can't make it to Ma's place."

"Sure we can. I know a short cut across the Brazos."

"You're crazy. That river's in flood."

"A lot of good men have drowned in Texas, Conner. Come on, it's five miles to the old crossing. We'll see how she looks, and you can decide whether you'd rather take a chance on the river or let Lud kill you for sure."

The two set off then with more speed and urgency of purpose than they had had before. On the high places Conner turned his head to look back.

"He's there," assured Callie as she pushed over the rise and began a light lope toward the swollen river.

They drew up on the bank and watched the red tormented water dashing itself in frothy patches against the trees and rocks. Flotsam bobbed over and under the surface, leaving débris in the trees.

"Well, that's bad," Callie agreed with herself as she studied the situation. Callie talked as she thought. "I remember Doctor Herman . . . brilliant man with a wonderful classical education . . . got swept away and drowned on the Trinity. Horse panicked. True enough horses are strong swimmers. But a horse can drown you if it panics. Right there between the trees is the ford. Good bottom there, but there must be four or five feet of water over it now. Well, hell." Callie moved her horse off upstream, searching the shore. "You coming, Conner?"

The man hesitated as he watched the woman pick a spot on the bank to enter the water. He glanced back at the hill, back in the direction they had come, the direction that Lud Daniels was coming now. "We can't make it!" he shouted above the sound of water as he rode up to Callie.

"I'm willing to try to get you safe to your mother and to save my son. I can ride out of here right now and leave you in such a bad shape Lud will have to stop to take care of you."

"You'll have to catch me."

Callie eased her horse toward the red water. "Be easy." She talked softly as calmly as if she were in her own parlor. "That's it now."

For the first time, Conner realized that Callie Daniels was not just his wife's mother, not just the matriarch of the ranching clan. She was more than the handsome little woman who ate and drank from bone china and attended the governor's ball by invitation. Callie Daniels had come from somewhere — a tough and real somewhere, a place that demanded strength and skill not to mention guts. Conner understood this was not Callie's first perilous ride. She was, in fact, a seasoned horsewoman. Her horse moved into the

165

current slowly and then began to swim with neck stretched forward. Callie held on, but released the reins. The red water stained her white shirt, soaked her clothes. Once she disappeared beneath the water, bobbed again to the surface, still holding to the horse, as her hat raced away on the current. But her trajectory was right. Her horse swam until it found its footing again and began to climb out on the far side of the ford. Riding onto the bank, she wiped the hair and water from her eyes with her arm, then motioned to the young outlaw to follow.

Conner Jack swore as he turned his horse once more to look back at the hill, at Lud Daniels, before following Callie into the river, before crossing to the other side.

Nell Jack's ranch had changed little in the years since she and Callie Daniels had neighbored on the Brazos. Her husband and a child were buried now on the small hill to the west, but the buildings were the same. The stone house sat low on the land, cooled in summer by the thick walls and breezes off the river. She was feeding her chickens when she saw the riders coming out of the distance. For a moment, Nell thought to get the gun as she had during the Indian wars. For a moment she cursed her carelessness in letting them get so close without seeing them. She raised her hand against the sun, then, scattering the last of the corn quickly, she returned to the porch to watch.

"Hallo, the house!" a distant voice called out.

"I'll swear," murmured Nell to herself. "That's Callie Daniels." Nell waved her apron and beckoned the rider.

166

Then she waited, until she could wait no more, and went out to meet her friend.

Callie dismounted into her embrace.

"Oh, Callie, Callie, I've missed you so."

Callie held her friend tightly, catching and holding the times that bound them tighter than sisters. "Nell," she whispered against her friend's cheek, "I've brought you your son."

Nell released Callie far enough to look into her eyes. They were young women, then, standing on the sand of the red Brazos de Dios when the Comanches and Kiowas had ravaged the land. Nell saw the cave, the dead Indian. She nodded with tears in her eyes. Then, she put her arm around her friend's waist and led her into the old house.

Callie inhaled deeply. Nell's house was as familiar as her own.

"You'll find dry clothes in the bedroom," she said. "I'll make us something to eat. Conner bring in some cool water from the spring."

"Ma," Conner began, "I did something wrong. I don't want Callie to tell you about it."

"Callie would never tell me, Son. She'd think that was between us. We'll talk on it after our company goes home."

Conner Jack stood for a long moment looking at his mother. "She's different than I thought. Maybe things are different than I thought."

When Lud arrived late in the afternoon, the two women sat quietly rocking in the fresh breeze on the

167

He walked with his swinging long gait, leading .orse played out from the river and run. The animal w. , tired, but would recover.

Callie smiled. She'd taught her boys to take care of their animals. Lud was just following his raising. The horse carried no saddle and no rifle because he had discarded all weight in making his run to catch Conner Jack. Callie glanced to see if he wore a gun. He did not.

Lud Daniels removed his hat as he stepped onto Nell Jack's porch.

"You must be hungry, Lud," she said, rising. "There's plenty left. I'll fix you a plate."

"Thank you, Missus Jack," Lud said, sitting in the empty rocker beside his mother as Nell went inside. "You crossed that river."

"That's how you get to the other side."

"That was crazy."

"That's the same thing Conner said."

"Where is Conner?"

"Gone, I guess." Callie rocked, looking at the land. "Gone."

"Where's your gun, Lud?"

"Gone, I guess."

"And the sword in your heart."

"Gone, too. I thought about what you said. I was going to kill Conner because . . . It wasn't the cattle he took. I thought it was, but it wasn't. Well, he sure made a fool out of me."

"At least you didn't make one out of yourself. I'm proud of you, Son."

168

Lud lay back against the rocker. "Mama, don't do this again. All you had to do was remind me. I've ridden through a storm and a river on the bareback spines of four horses to tell you I'd remember your debt. I know Missus Jack once saved your life. I know you want to give her Conner."

Callie turned to Lud and studied his care-worn face. "Is that what you think, Son? It wasn't my life, Lud. It was yours. You'd come to help me, and the Indian was about to kill you when Nell killed him." Callie returned to rocking. "You see one time on the Brazos, Nell Jack gave me back my son. Giving her back hers was the least we could do."

Sidesaddle

RITA CLEARY

Rita Cleary was born in New York City. Some of her ancestors were pioneers in the frontier West. At an early age she learned to ride horses, an interest that continues. SORREL (1993) was her first Western novel and was voted a Spur finalist that year by the Western Writers of America. It was followed by GOLD TOWN (1996), a novel set in the mining camp of Varina, based closely on Virginia City, Montana. Always having had a profound interest in history, and Western American history in particular, Cleary is a member of the Lewis and Clark Trail Heritage Foundation, the Montana Historical Society, the Missouri Historical Society, and the New York Historical Society. RIVER WALK (2000) was the first entry in her saga about the Lewis and Clark expedition. This is the first appearance of "Sidesaddle".

"I'll take a hickory stick to your backsides!" Sarah Wheelock screamed.

The boys knew it was a vain threat. "You'll have to catch us first!" The boys were gone, kicking and galloping over the bench. Sarah's humiliation was complete.

The boys had little patience with a girl riding sidesaddle, driving cattle. They'd sassed her unmercifully, but she'd whipped old Dolly to keep up with them, nose to nose, through thorn and over rocks, until the bulls clashed on the way to the high pasture, knocking the cows off the side hill into the thick chaparral. There was no skin left on her right knee where it rubbed against the saddle, and her right foot, hanging loose, was numb. Her left foot was the only thing between her and the hard, dry earth. It ached where it braced against the stirrup. Pain shot like a bullet up her thigh into her lower back.

When she and the boys arrived, there should only have been one bull at the base of the draw, and one harem of cows. There were two. The second bull and his twenty yearling heifers should have been ten miles away.

The two bulls had already clashed horns before Sarah and her two younger brothers rode down off the bench. "Brothers!" She wanted to curse the devils. They hooted at her and the cows, at the sharp horns and stiff hoofs that could gore and trample. They raced about, charging at the cows and scattering them carelessly, dangerously, in every direction.

171

She'd shouted again: "Settle the cows! Don't run the calves! Ride easy! Don't make them spook!" But the boys paid no attention. They charged in close, teasing, harassing, deliberately baiting their big sister and taunting the cows.

Sarah screamed louder. "You'd better start them up the trail before Grandmother rides over the bench! The bulls will follow!" The boys were hollering, but they heard the threat, and they did get a bunch moving up onto the bench. It was so easy for the boys, riding across the side hill and up the steep trail. It was not easy for Sarah. In a normal saddle with one leg on each side of a horse, she would have kept up with them. But now her saddle slipped with each lunge of the horse, pulled by gravity to the downside of the hill.

The bulls were moving now. One had pushed his way into the lead. The cows followed docilely. The other bull hung behind the lumbering bunch of cows. Suddenly the lead bull turned, bellowed once, and charged his challenger in the rear. He ran headlong at his opponent, back down through the bunched cows, knocking and smashing into them. They scrambled frantically to avoid his horns and crashing weight. Some lost their footing, fell, and rolled down the mountain's flank until a tangle of thorns stopped their slide. Sarah and the old horse, Dolly, were caught in the middle. Dolly bolted with the cows to avoid the onrushing horns. Somehow the mare lunged out of the way. Sarah almost fell off. She grabbed the mane, bounced wildly, and barely held on. Then she heard the boys, laughing and riding away, and burning anger welled up in her face.

When she used to ride astride, she always outrode the boys, until Ma died, Pa sickened, and Grandmother Wheelock arrived and decreed that only Indians, Mexicans, and bawdy women separated their legs, one on each side of a horse. No acceptable suitor would possibly consider a girl who stooped so low as to spread her legs. What amazed Sarah was that her father had agreed. He was too sick or too spineless to contest his own mother.

She thought back to the days when she used to ride the younger horses. Wonderful rides! The younger horses sprang lightly off the ground. Sport was her favorite. He was an eager gray, one whole hand taller than Dolly, with long legs and flexible pasterns that absorbed the shock of hoof on rough ground. Sarah had exulted in the sway of her own body to his graceful movements. There were no stiff-legged, jarring bumps, no slapping her bottom against the hard cantle, no raw, skinned patches on her legs. She'd ride over the bench where no one else could see, and play tag, horseback, with her brothers.

Dolly tripped suddenly. Sarah felt the jerk in the small of her back. She steadied the horse, then urged Dolly on. Dolly's step was uneven; her rhythm was off. But Sarah bounced on, swallowing her anger, stuffing her frustration like a towel in a tight-necked bottle. She whisked away a tear and dried her wet hand on the old mare's mane. The tears kept coming, and she wiped her face on her skirt. The dusty cotton left a muddy smudge. She could imagine what her face must look like, layered in dust, like her clothes, like the horse, only worse because the tears had streaked dirt into every pore.

It wasn't Dolly's fault. She reached down and petted the poor horse. Half-inch thorns had dug furrows in the old mare's legs, just as they had snagged Sarah's sleeves and shredded her skirt. Worst of all, blood was seeping through her skirt where the cracked old leather had rubbed the skin from her knee. The sidesaddle was dry and hard as stone, but Grandmother didn't care. She would scold her unlady-like granddaughter who could not keep her clothing clean, and Sarah would have to scrub her knuckles raw to get the bloodstains out. She tried to raise the bloodied leg now to ease the pain, but the folds of her skirt pinned it tightly in place.

"Miz, if I was you, I'd walk that horse."

Startled, Sarah turned. The jolt of her hand brought the tired horse to a halt. There stood a good-looking young man on a handsome bay horse jogging up beside her. She recognized him as Bob Farrow's son, Clyde.

Sarah put up her hands to hide her tear-stained face. When she looked over the tops of her fingers, Clyde Farrow had dismounted and was waiting patiently to help her down.

"You done a man's work on an old ladies' horse, miz, that's all." His voice was deep-throated and kind. Sarah looked away, mortified.

"Beg pardon, miz, but why you herdin' cattle in skirts?

"How'd you know I was herding cattle?"

"The boys, I passed 'em on the road. I told 'em to slow down, cool their horses. They were braggin' how they'd outrun their big sister."

Clyde Farrow waited until she turned back to face him. "If you get down, rest, stretch, you'll feel better, an' I can check the mare."

"I can check her myself, thank you." Sarah kicked her left foot out of the stirrup and slid down. Her knees trembled unsteadily, but she smoothed her skirts and bent over to feel Dolly's leg. The horse stamped. The hoof came down on a torn piece of skirt, pinning Sarah to the ground.

Clyde Farrow snickered.

Sarah's temper rose, and she slammed her knuckles into the barrel of the horse. Dolly jumped sideways, and Sarah fell suddenly backwards on her rump.

Clyde Farrow laughed harder.

"Stop that!" She was angry now, and there was an edge to her voice.

"I'm sorry, miz, but you do look funny. I didn't mean to rile you." Clyde Farrow bit his tongue. He tried a compliment to redeem himself. "You're still pretty underneath all that dirt, an' you didn't land in the prickly pear." But he was more at ease talking about the horse.

He picked up the rein of the injured horse, then ran his big palm down the cannon bone. "There's heat in 'er leg. Good you stopped. How long you been ridin'?" He offered a hand to help her up.

"Thank you," she huffed and stood up painfully. "We started at noon."

175

"Four hours on that old plug! You need a better mount, you gonna stay out that long."

Sarah frowned indignantly now. "Dolly is not a plug. She taught us all to ride."

"Then you need a better saddle."

"Tell that to my grandmother."

"I'll do that, miz, an' I'll tell your pa. It ain't safe, you chasin' around after bulls in a broken rocking chair, half on an' half off. You want to ride my Pal, I'll walk, miz, an' lead your Dolly home. I don't trust that old nag to carry you one step more."

Sarah was breathing easier now. "Could we just rest here for a minute?"

"Long as you want, miz. I'll just loosen cinches an' give my Pal an' your Dolly a blow."

Sarah sank down gratefully on a flat rock at the side of the trail. She stretched her right leg out full length, rubbed it, and felt the circulation return. When she arched her back and flexed her shoulders, her taut muscles relaxed. She lay back flat upon the rock, resting her head against the unforgiving granite and gazing up at the snowy clouds in the expanse of sky.

Clyde loosened Pal's cinch and approached old Dolly. As he jerked the old strap loose, Dolly cringed. "This horse looks sore in the shoulder, miz. I can get a better look and feel if I unload this contraption completely."

Sarah heard him but didn't react immediately. She lay motionless, staring up into the great blue depth of space. It absorbed and enveloped her and diminished all the petty earthbound conventions. The sky was

176

clean, open, free from pain and restraint, empty of anger and resentment. It imposed its own wide reality on the earth and all its creatures, on the cows and horses, on Grandmother Wheelock and Pa and Clyde Farrow, and on her.

She answered finally: "Yes, take off the saddle . . . Bury it, burn it, throw it in the creek!" She flung her daring words at the canopy of space. She didn't turn her face toward him or compel her tired body to sit up.

Clyde Farrow straightened in confusion and shock. He lifted the saddle from the horse's back and lowered it to the ground. It toppled awkwardly into the sage. Twice he tried to set it right, but it wouldn't stand on its lopsided tree. He let the saddle fall one last time and stood speechless, staring keenly at her lithe, seductive body stretched out upon the rock, at the pinch of her waist, the mounds of her breasts, and the long, lean lines of her legs beneath their drapery of skirt.

He held his face expressionless and his voice flat. "We'd best be goin', miz."

"Can I have a drink of water first?"

"Of course, miz." He reached slowly for the canteen on his saddle, turned, and unscrewed the top. His knuckles were white. His hands were shaking. He gripped the canteen nervously, like a beggar grips his last coin, and he swallowed hard before speaking. "You'll have to sit up, miz, if you want a drink."

"In a minute." She gazed harder at the boundless blue heaven, rolled her face east to the incipient dusk, then west to the pink blaze of setting sun. When she pulled herself up to a sitting position, she reached for the canteen and took a long, slow drink. She wet a strip of her skirt and mopped her face and pushed back the strands of her hair. "Thank you. I feel better now."

He repeated: "We'd best be goin', miz. Evenin's comin' on. You want to ride or you want to walk?" He motioned toward Pal.

"I'll walk, thank you." She hated the thought of sitting in a saddle again on the piled pleats of her petticoats. She stood up and reached for Dolly's reins. The sky, the water, the freedom of movement had revived her, or was it Clyde Farrow's simple kindness, the concerned look in his eyes, and the quiet competence and assurance of his manhood?

"It's three mile, uphill, over the bench. You sure you're up to it, miz?"

She squared her shoulders. "It will be a pleasure. Enough of 'miz.' Call me Sarah." She flashed him a brilliant smile.

The blood rushed to his face, but he turned to pick up the reins of his own horse before she could see. "I'll walk with you, Miz Sarah, an' carry your saddle." He bent to pick up the offending saddle.

"No, leave the saddle." And she repeated decisively: "I told you. Burn it . . . bury it . . . throw it in the creek."

He heaved the saddle up onto his back and the fabric of his shirt pulled tautly over his broad shoulders. "You don't mean that, miz."

"Oh, yes, I do. My name is Sarah, and I mean every word of it." She tugged at his arm, and he released the saddle. It crashed down in a cloud of dust. "If you carry

178

it home, I'll hack it to pieces with my father's axe! Leave it . . . please."

Clyde Farrow frowned. It was against every fiber in his thrifty bones to abandon a good, useable saddle. A saddle had value. Even this peculiar old thing could be oiled, restored. Old Mrs. Hammond still used one. He hesitated.

"Clyde Farrow, I swear to you that I shall never ride in that saddle again. Look at me! Look at Dolly! We can hardly walk, the two of us."

It took a moment for the cowboy to acknowledge that what she said was true, and he barely tipped the brim of his hat in agreement. The horse was lame. That was why he had stopped her in the first place, that and the twisted, painful slump of her lithe shoulders. "If you say so, miz."

She smiled at him again, a wide, skyward curve of mouth and crinkle of eyes that smoothed every dust-filled line of her face and made his heart pump. She started walking, and he followed.

"Aren't you going to ride, Clyde Farrow?"

"Not while you're walking, miz. It ain't polite."

She stopped, and he caught up to her.

"My name is Sarah. I told you, call me Sarah."

He had to force himself. "Sarah, I can't ride and let a lady walk. It wouldn't be right."

Sarah mused: "You men are lucky, Clyde Farrow. You can walk or ride, wherever, whenever you choose."

"Whenever and wherever's not now, miz . . . Sarah. It'll be dark soon, an' I intend to walk you home." His left hand held the reins; he offered her his right.

179

She slipped Dolly's reins from her left to her right and placed her free hand in his.

It was almost dark when they arrived. Tug Wheelock, Sarah's sick father, was out of bed, sitting in the old captain's chair and waiting outside the door, waiting for her. He hadn't been out of bed for a week, but he loved his only daughter and had rallied fast when his boys arrived on lathered, winded horses, without their big sister. He personally watched the boys walk the horses to cool them out for half an hour and sent the boys to bed without dinner.

Sarah saw him when they were about a hundred yards away, handed Dolly's reins to Clyde Farrow, and ran to greet him. He looked white and shriveled and pulled a blue knit shawl around his hunched shoulders and the cavity that was his chest. He coughed when he spoke, but he smiled at her. "You all right, girl?"

Sarah bent to hug him. "Yes, Pa." She could hear the labor in his lungs like the rasp of a blade on a whetstone.

"Who's this?" Pa looked at Clyde Farrow who approached shyly with the two horses.

"Clyde Farrow, this is my father, Tug Wheelock. Old Dolly went lame. Clyde found me on the trail and walked me home."

Tug Wheelock straightened his once broad shoulders and scrutinized the young escort of his only living daughter like a hard-nosed horse trader appraising a new purchase. "Farrow . . . Bob Farrow's boy?" Even in

180

his weakness, he made the words sound fearsome, but he stuck out his hand.

"Yes, sir." Clyde Farrow grasped the feeble hand and fell back on his reserves of courage. "Mister Wheelock, Miz Sarah was all alone on the limpin' mare. Your boys shouldn't've rode off an' left her."

Tug Wheelock nodded and focused on the old horse. "What's this? You been herdin' cattle, girl, and you been ridin' bareback on Dolly!"

"In that old sidesaddle, not bareback. Grandmother says I'm too old to be trampin' around in chaps, that I shouldn't be spreading my legs like a tart."

"Grandmother had a maid and a groom and never had to do a man's work." His breath failed him then, and he went into a fit of coughing. Sarah clasped his heaving shoulders, and Grandmother came running. She stiffened in icy silence and arched a suspicious eyebrow when she saw the young cowboy and Sarah's torn dress.

Clyde Farrow didn't wait for an introduction. He picked up the old man, carried him inside, laid him on the bed, and propped him up on pillows. Tug Wheelock's breathing calmed.

"Thank you, son, for helpin' my Sarah on the trail today."

The cowboy fumbled. "She's a fine girl, sir, got spunk . . . I'd like to call on 'er, sir, if you'd permit."

The old man smiled and nodded. "She'd be glad for the company, son."

"Thank you, sir. I'll see to the horses."

Grandmother's hawkish glare made him nervous. She sucked in her lips with offended pride as the cowboy walked out, then turned on Sarah. "What is the meaning of this?"

Sarah protested to her father. "The cows were calm, Pa, until the bulls started fighting and the boys started yelling and running. I couldn't herd the cows and control the boys and ride *that way*."

"What way, girl?"

"Sidesaddle, like Grandmother insisted." She flashed an angry look at the old matriarch and turned her back on her.

Grandmother lashed out: "She's marriageable age, Tug. You can't let her go tearing around like a Bowery brat with the first cowboy happens along!"

"Mother, the Bowery's a thousand miles away!" He took several mercifully even breaths. "An' she wasn't tearin' around. She's the only one can hold this place together and manage those cows until the boys are old enough. You can't do it, not at your age. An' you can't ride like her." He turned to Sarah. "You got it to do, girl." He stopped again to catch his breath, but his grip was firm on Sarah's arm. "That's Bob Farrow's boy. He's growed into a fine man. You like him, girl?"

"Yes, Pa, but we didn't . . . My leg was sore, and Dolly was almost hobbling home on three legs." She felt Grandmother's eyes like needles on her back, but she didn't turn around.

182

Tug Wheelock smiled at his daughter. "I know, girl." He faced his mother. "You're not helpin' me by pinnin' this girl like a filly to a snubbin' post. You hear!"

Grandmother sputtered: "She's a pretty one, Tug. She has no mother. You're her father. You've got to be careful, teach her the rules of propriety."

Clyde Farrow came back in, and Grandmother bridled. "Beg pardon, Miz Sarah, I'll be goin' now. Hope you feel better, Mister Wheelock."

Tug Wheelock pulled himself up on his elbows. "Clyde, wait, boy! Sarah, why don't you ask this nice young man to stay for dinner?"

Sarah glared defiantly at her grandmother and hesitated. Clyde Farrow gawked.

Grandmother Wheelock was the first to speak. Her words were clipped and brief. "I have already eaten. I shall retire early with the boys." She whirled and swept out of the room.

Sarah cooked the dinner, and they ate and conversed, and Clyde helped wash the dishes. He left long after dark. It started to rain as he guided Pal back down the trail to his own home back over the bench. He wrapped his poncho around his shoulders. The moon was nearly full and cast a pale light over the trail where he had walked with Sarah a few hours before.

When he came upon the sidesaddle, it glistened black in the wetness, an incongruous lump protruding from the sage and cactus, near the flat rock where Sarah had gazed at the sky. He dismounted to examine it. The cinch was good and could be used again. The leather could be stripped. The stirrup was solid. He

183

threw it over Pal's rump and carried it in. He had no use for the saddle himself except as a souvenir. It was like saving the ribbon that a sweetheart wore. He couldn't give it away. He set it on a log in the shed, oiled it carefully, and covered it with an old tarp.

The Indian Witch

MARCIA MULLER

Born and raised in Detroit, Michigan, Marcia Muller has been a full-time novelist since 1983. She is the author of thirty crime novels, twenty-two of which feature her much-loved San Francisco investigator, Sharon McCone. Recipient of numerous awards, in 1993 Muller was presented with the Private Eye Writers of America's Life Achievement Award for her contribution to the genre. With her husband, Bill Pronzini, she has co-edited twelve mystery anthologies and 1001 MIDNIGHTS, a guide to mystery and detective fiction. She has also written Western stories, and a collection of them, titled TIME OF THE WOLVES, will be published as a Five Star Western in 2003. Her interest in the Western story stems from her love of history and research. This is the first publication of "The Indian Witch."

MARCIA MULLER

From the Santa Clara, California, *Observer*
January 1, 1900

We called her the Indian Witch, even though her name was really Mrs. Morrissey. Her husband, Thad Morrissey, ran the only saloon in town, and they lived, just the two of them, in a big clapboard house on Second Avenue a few doors down from Main Street. In 1884 Santa Clara was a small town where everybody knew everybody else's business, but no one knew the Morrisseys'.

No one even knew where they had come from. They arrived in town in the fall of 1863: a big, fair-haired, red-faced Irishman and his small, dark Indian wife. Within the week Thad Morrissey bought the saloon and they moved from their rooming house to Second Avenue. Every day at exactly quarter to noon he would walk to the saloon, open up, and spend the hours between then and midnight pouring drinks for loggers who had come into town from the heavily forested ridge that separates Santa Clara from the rugged northern California coastline. He was a genial host, always willing to listen to a man's troubles or extend credit, but he spoke little of himself.

Mrs. Morrissey was even more of a puzzle. From the day she and her husband moved into the house on Second Avenue she never once left it. It was thought she feared shunning from the town-women, as marriages between whites and Indians were generally viewed as repugnant, but that did not explain why she dared not venture so far as her own yard or deep front

186

porch. A servant girl from one of the town's poorer families did her shopping and presumably was paid well enough that she was reluctant to talk about what she saw and heard inside the big, shadowy house. And so the Morrisseys lived for over twenty years.

In 1882 my family moved to the end of Second Avenue, where grassland spread to the eastern hills. Often my younger brothers and I would play with our friends in the vacant lot across from the Morrissey house. We boys would see Thad Morrissey leave for the saloon and the servant girl come and go, but we never set eyes upon Mrs. Morrissey until one hot July day in 1884, when a curtain moved in an upstairs window and a stern, dark face looked down at us. I was close to the house at the time, having run into the street to retrieve a ball my brother had thrown, and, when I looked up, her gaze met mine.

I shall never forget her eyes: black and implacable — although I would not have known what such a word meant at age twelve — with a flatness that bespoke knowledge of many terrible things. They frightened me so badly that I dropped the ball and fled back to the safety of the lot. And on that day we christened Mrs. Morrissey the Indian Witch.

Every day for the rest of July and August we would wait for her to appear in the window. Every day she obliged us on the stroke of three. She would remain there, unmoving, watching us at play for exactly ten minutes. When school began in September, she would watch us as we walked home. By then it seemed to me that I was the object of her gaze.

September passed quickly, and then it was October: lemon-yellow days with a chill on the evening air. But shortly before Halloween, as if nature were angry at the passage of summer, heat enveloped our inland valley. On the coast the dog-hole ports, where logging companies sent their timber down chutes to schooners at anchor in the coves, were unnavigable because of fog, but Santa Carla experienced no such relief. And on one of those still, blazing afternoons Thad Morrissey toppled forward as he reached across his bar to pour whisky for a logger and died at the age of sixty-two.

Word of his death spread quickly through town. We boys gathered at the vacant lot after school to see what would transpire at the Morrissey house. A delegation of men, including Doc Bolton and Mayor Drew, arrived. They were met by the servant girl, who spoke briefly with them. The next day we learned the Indian Witch had sent instructions through her that her husband was to be buried without ceremony in a plot he had purchased in the graveyard. The townsfolk were shocked to hear it was a single plot. Thad Morrissey had made no provision for his wife, and not even a funeral wreath adorned the forbidding house's door. The Indian Witch continued to appear at the upstairs window, but now she seemed to study me more intensely.

The heat wave finally broke, and November turned chilly. Our thoughts moved forward to Thanksgiving and Christmas. One evening nearly three weeks after Thad Morrissey's passing I was walking by his widow's house on the way to visit a friend when a voice spoke to me.

"Young man, come here!"

I stopped, my blood suddenly colder than the air, and peered into the shadows. She was on the porch, wrapped in a black shawl, her hand beckoning to me. My first impulse was to run, but curiosity overcame it and I moved closer.

"Come up on the porch, please."

The voice was refined with scarcely a trace of an accent, not at all as I had imagined it. Or perhaps I had not imagined her as possessing any sort of voice, so stony and silent had she seemed as she stood at the window. I ascended the steps slowly.

The Indian Witch looked me up and down, taking my measure. Then she nodded as if satisfied with what she saw. "I want you to do something for me," she said.

"Ma'am?" The word came out a croak.

She brought out her other hand from beneath the shawl and extended a folded sheet of paper. "I have here a list of things to be purchased. I will reward you for doing so."

"But your girl . . ."

"Martha cannot perform these errands. No one is to know these things are for me. Will you do this?"

I looked into her eyes and saw both pride and pleading. Then I nodded and held out my hand for the paper, which was thick with money tucked into its fold.

"Why did you choose me?" I asked.

"I have watched you. I know you are trustworthy. Bring the things tomorrow night." Then she turned and went into the house.

I forgot about my visit to my friend and ran home, clutching the Indian Witch's list. My brothers were in the bedroom we three shared and my parents in the parlor, so I took the list to the kitchen, where a kerosene lamp burned low, and examined it.

The items puzzled me: a pair of sturdy boots in the smallest available size; heavy socks; a warm jacket; a small pack; dried meat, and other portable foodstuffs. It appeared to me as if she were about to embark upon a long hike, except in those days respectable matrons of our town did not walk great distances (and, so far as I know, still do not).

I saved my errands for late the next afternoon, as I was sure they would attract notice and I wanted my father to return from his work at the grain mill before anyone could question him about his son's unusual purchases. By the time he heard about them, the deed would be done, and I would have quite a story to tell. My father loved nothing more than a good story.

By suppertime my shopping was completed and the bundles, along with some extra money, stowed behind our outhouse. I could barely taste my food for my excitement. As soon as I could, I slipped out, retrieved the bundles, and carried them to the Indian Witch's house. She was waiting on the porch, wearing the same black shawl, but on this night she beckoned me inside.

To my surprise, the house was quite ordinary, not much different from my own. She motioned for me to deposit the bundles beside the front door, then bent to look through them. When she straightened, she had the extra money in her hand.

"Yes, I was right about your trustworthiness," she said. "I always could judge a good man."

A good *man*. My heart swelled at the compliment.

She handed me the money. "I want you to have this."

My reward! I had thought perhaps a piece of pie or cake. But this was too much money, five dollars.

"I cannot accept . . ."

"You can and you will. Come into the parlor, please."

I followed, clutching the money, wondering what else she had in store for me.

A fire burned on the hearth, strong and steady. She had laid and lighted it herself, which impressed me, as my father always proclaimed women incapable of such acts. The Indian Witch motioned me toward a large chair that must have been Thad Morrissey's, and claimed a cushioned rocker for herself. She gripped its arms with long-fingered hands, and, when she looked into my eyes, the firelight made hers glitter fiercely.

She said: "I know what you call me, you and your friends. 'The Indian Witch.' "

I gulped and could say nothing.

"It is because I am different. You need to put a name to that difference, so you imagine I have evil powers."

"Ma'am . . ."

"Be quiet! I have decided to tell you my story. Perhaps it will teach you not to judge others until you know the reasons behind their differences. But first you must promise to tell no one."

"I . . ."

"Promise!"

I promised. And then she began.

My story begins in the winter of Eighteen Fifty-Six. My tribe . . . I am Pomo . . . had always lived on Cape Perdido, at the northwestern boundary of this county. The rains were bad for two years, the sea worse. Fish and game were scarce, the wild plants even more so. My father could not feed our family.

There was a man who ran a saloon in the logging town on the ridge who was known to be charitable. My father went to ask his help, taking me along. My father was proud, he did not want to beg, and the man knew that. So he bargained. He would give food in exchange for me, Wonena. I was fourteen years of age, the man thirty-four. His name was Thaddeus Morrissey.

My father had no choice but to agree to this proposition. The family would have starved otherwise. For myself, I was not afraid to stay. As I said before, I could always judge a good man. A lesser man than Thaddeus Morrissey would have made me his slave and turned me out when he tired of me. But instead he married me and gave me my Christian name, Emma. He moved me into his rooms above the saloon, asked a neighbor woman to teach me to cook and bake bread and keep house. In the mornings, before he went downstairs, my husband taught me English. He laughed at my mistakes, but gently. He in turn learned words

192

and phrases from my language. In time I came to love him, and he to love me. I think perhaps he had loved me from the first, although we never spoke of it. I became more white than Indian.

In Eighteen Sixty-One we began to hear rumors. A white man had discovered oil on my tribe's land on Cape Perdido. Now the big companies wanted to drill wells there, but the tribal council said they would never permit it. Those lands were their hunting and gathering grounds. Their ancestors' spirits dwelled there. Cape Perdido was sacred to them.

The government, of course, was on the side of the big companies. They sent troops to force the Pomos off their land. This, of course, was happening to Indians everywhere when valuable things were found on their lands, and some fought back. My tribe decided to fight back, also.

Do you know Perdido means something not easily tamed? In those days it was even more rugged and wild than now. The Pomos knew that cape, but the government soldiers did not. For over a year they stumbled into the ravines and got lost in the forests and fell from the steep cliffs, while the Pomos hid in natural shelters and moved invisibly across the land, killing the intruders one by one.

Finally the government agreed to peace talks with the Pomo leaders. They were three . . . my uncle, my cousin, and my brother. I remembered my uncle and cousin as violent men, my brother as easily led by them.

The Army officers had heard of me, Emma Morrissey, who used to be Wonena. They knew I could speak both English and my own language, and that these leaders were my people. The officers conscripted me to accompany them to the talks.

My husband was against my going. He feared my tribesmen would harm me, or the officers abandon me should trouble arise. But the officers were insistent, and I wanted to help bring about peace. As I said before, I had become more white than Indian.

At dawn on the day of the talks my husband and I met the officers at a stage stop at the foot of the ridge. They also were three . . . General Shelby, Commander Bramwell, Indian Agent Avery. My husband cautioned them to protect me. He said he would wait at the stage stop for no more than four hours and then follow us. General Shelby said we would return long before then.

We set out for the meeting place, an ancient clearing in the forest that was sacred to the tribe. There, three boulders stood in a row, as if cast down by the heavens, as no rocks similar to them existed for miles. I rode astride my horse, trying to remember the faces of my brother, uncle, and cousin, but it had been too many years since I had parted from them. All I could see was stone. Three great stones, hiding three stone faces. And with that vision, the knowledge of what was to happen grew upon me.

I reined in my horse, called for the others to halt. I told them that, if they went to the clearing, they would surely be killed. They scoffed at the notion, refused to believe me. The Pomos had given their word to the government, the general said. They would not dare break it. I pleaded with the men, told them of my

194

vision. I wept. Nothing I could do or say would stay them. We rode on.

When we arrived, the clearing was empty. The boulders stood before us . . . massive, gray, misshapen. All around us redwood trees towered, the sun shining through their misted branches. Nothing moved or breathed. The clearing no longer felt sacred, because death waited behind those boulders.

General Shelby was angry. "These savages have no timepieces," he complained. He dismounted, began pacing about.

It was then I saw the barrel of the rifle move from behind the boulder nearest us. It was then I shouted.

The shot boomed, and a bullet pierced General Shelby's chest. Blood stained his uniform.

As the general fell, Commander Bramwell wheeled his horse and galloped from the clearing. He was abandoning me, as my husband had feared the soldiers would.

Indian Agent Avery was confused. A second bullet from behind a second boulder brought him down before he could take shelter or flee.

From behind the third boulder my brother, Kientok, stepped. He aimed his rifle at me, but he did not fire. After a moment he lowered it and said in our language: "Another day, Wonena." Then all three were gone into the forest.

Weak and weeping, I made my way back to the stage stop where my husband waited. When I told him what had happened, his lips went white, but he said nothing, simply took the reins of my horse and led me home. By the next afternoon he had sold the saloon and loaded all our belongings into our wagon. We journeyed inland, and, when we moved into this house, I found that I could not leave it. If my whereabouts were discovered, soldiers would come for me. Surely Commander Bramwell would want to destroy an Indian woman who could brand him a coward. Men from my tribe might come to exact retribution. I believed that so long as I remained indoors with my loaded pistol at hand I would be safe. But I was not safe from the fear. It became my constant companion. It ate at our lives, as did my husband's knowledge of what I would surely do after his passing.

Shortly after my husband and I came to Santa Carla my tribe was defeated. My uncle and cousin, upon the testimony of Commander Bramwell, were hanged for the murders of General Shelby and Indian Agent Avery. My brother and a number of other men escaped to the ridge, but most of the tribe was removed by the government to a reserve in Oregon. The oil companies drilled their wells on Cape Perdido. Like the wells at Petrolia in Humboldt County, they soon went dry. Oilville, the town that had grown around them, fell into ruins.

Few of the Pomos returned to their lands after they were abandoned by the white man. The Oregon reserve had become home to them. My brother and his renegade band dwell on the cape, however, and now, my duty to my husband fulfilled, I must return to them and take up the threads of my life. My husband knew I would do so, and this is why he made no provision for my burial at Santa Carla.

This, young man, is the story of Emma Morrissey. Now the story of Wonena will begin.

After I left Emma Morrissey's house that November night, I waited, cold and cramped, behind a manzanita bush in the vacant lot. I was aware that by now my parents had discovered my absence and would punish me upon my return, but it seemed small price to pay to view the conclusion of Mrs. Morrissey's story.

I was rewarded when, at half past midnight, a small, shadowy figure emerged from the house and moved down the porch steps. It wore a warm jacket and sturdy boots and carried a small pack that I knew to be filled with provisions for a long journey. Emma Morrissey did not look back at the place that had been her prison for the past twenty years, but merely slipped down the street and disappeared into the darkness as invisibly as her tribesmen had moved across Cape Perdido over two decades before.

I remained where I was, shivering and wondering if Mrs. Morrissey believed the lies she had told me. Her self-imposed confinement to the house had not been out of fear, but in penance for betraying her own people. And she was not making her journey to Cape Perdido to take up the threads of her former life. Instead, this woman who had become more white than Indian would return to face the retribution that her brother, Kientok, had promised with his final words to her: "Another day, Wonena."

★ ★ ★

The boy to whom Emma Morrissey told her story is, of course, I, Phineas Garry, editor of this newspaper. You know me as a serious, middle-aged man of many words and opinions, most of which have inflamed the more conservative elements of our population. For nearly a decade, outraged readers have asked me why I espouse certain causes, particularly those I support of the rights of our natives.

I have chosen the dawning of this new century to break my long-kept promise and tell the tale that has shaped my life, in order that Wonena should not have lived — and died — in vain.

Saddle Pals

PATTI HUDSON

Patti Hudson grew up in Texas and now lives with her husband in a cabin they built in the Blue Mountains of eastern Oregon. Ten miles from the nearest neighbor, they generate their own electricity and share their remote acreage with two cow dogs, three Quarter horses, and an abundance of wildlife. Since moving to Oregon in the early 1970s, Hudson has worked as an architectural designer, surveyor, buckaroo, and freelance writer. "Saddle Pals" grew out of her experiences as a day rider and the bonds she has developed over the years with horses and humans alike. She has completed a novel about a woman's struggle to save a doomed horse and find her place in the changing West.

ॐ๏෴

I didn't know it would be the last time we trailed cattle together, that winter Jake called and said the Bar J needed us. We had been saddle pals for so long neither he nor I could remember exactly how or where we met.

199

But like most horsemen, we could clearly recall the animals we were riding at the time. (I was just starting a conscientious young filly that would die too soon, and Jake was on an ornery old buckskin that would live into his twenties and still be bucking people off.) By this measure, we had climbed the spruce-blued mountains, loped across grassy meadows, picked our way through the rocks and gray-green sagebrush of eastern Oregon in every season, on good horses and bad, for more than twenty years. We knew the John Day, the Powder, the Snake, how each of their tributaries ran and where to look for cattle the way a Portlander can sniff out the nearest Starbucks.

We were "day riders," hired by ranchers whenever they needed help gathering and moving cattle from one range to another. Over the years it came to be expected if one of us was called to ride, it meant he or she would bring the other. We always rode as a pair and got paid to do what either of us would have done for free, if not for professional pride. We weren't wannabes, like the recreational riders and town-dwellers who sometimes tagged along to play cowboy for a day, taking off from their regular jobs and riding for no pay.

Jake and I were not hobby horsemen. We were buckaroos, worth $50 to $75 a day in the Northwest, perhaps as much as $100 in California if we'd had any desire to live in such an over-regulated, overpopulated place. We did once talk about Texas: what it would be like to wear shirt sleeves in January, watch our horse graze on year-'round pastures, and not have to pitch hay and chip ice off the water troughs to keep them alive. Then I met my first Texan. It was it at the Pendleton Roundup, and we were dancing close. He asked what I did for a living, and I said I was a buckaroo. "Sounds sort of Howdy Doody-ish," he said.

I stepped back and puffed up with self-importance and told him how in the Great Basin it was an honor to be called a buckaroo. It meant you were a specialist and above any work that couldn't be done horseback. Aside from a high level of prestige that came with being labeled a buckaroo, I pointed out that the term was without gender bias and had been that way long before political correctness started neutering the language. Not that I minded being called a cowgirl, it just wasn't necessary to separate the boys from the girls, since once we're horseback with 1,200 pounds of muscle between our legs we're all pretty much equal.

I was still half mad later when I bumped into Jake at the Rainbow Room and told him about the Howdy Doody comment. He bought me a beer and said Texas was out. "I sure as hell don't want to go anywhere I might get thought of as a puppet. Believe I'll just stay right here in the Big Empty where nobody's pulling my strings."

We both were fairly independent and liked working freelance in a part of the country that still valued a well-educated horse and an able rider. But every now and then one of us would get to thinking we needed more stability in our lives and sign up for a full-time ranch job. The sort that came with a house, a pickup, and a small but steady pay check. For this bit of security you got to fix fence, maintain irrigation ditches, run heavy equipment, and toil at any number of other tasks in which you were not allowed to utilize your skills with horse or rope. Still, there were some opportunities to ride, and, when it came time to gather cows, to move them or sort or ship or brand, whichever one of us had the job always called the other to come help.

Jake tended to take these seven-days-a-week nightmares more frequently than I did. But they rarely lasted long. As soon as he felt there was even the slightest possibility someone might try to pull his strings, he was out of there and back, like me, trying to find affordable housing far enough away from traffic noise and city lights to still be able to hear the coyotes and see stars at night.

Ranch work was a little too steady, but buckarooing was rarely steady enough. Vet bills and feed costs and truck repairs, the want of a new saddle or the need for a younger horse could occasionally send us looking for employment completely outside the field. One year I was driving log truck and there was a popular song on the radio about a girl sitting on her daddy's knee and her daddy telling her she could be anything she wanted to be. When I finally got a day off to ride, Jake asked: "Is that what your daddy did to you to make you want to ride bronc's and drive big trucks?"

I told him the only thing I remembered about my daddy's knees was being laid across them for a whipping. We didn't talk too much about our families. I knew he had been married once or twice and had grown children he saw from time to time. He knew I had never been married, never had children, and had no regrets about either. That was all the family history we cared to share.

We were more likely to talk about our animals than our people. But we could trail cattle all day without saying a word. We didn't need to fill the distances we covered with conversation when we had all that scenery stretching before us. Sometimes we would pull up our horses to watch a herd of elk spill through the sagebrush like spring runoff, or stop to look down into the breaks of the Snake and glimpse an eagle hunting far below. We would gaze a while and then ride on, never diminishing what we had seen with small talk. The landscape was too big for words and the work so instinctual it wasn't necessary to discuss what we were doing. We'd ridden together enough to know what to expect of each other. We knew how to position ourselves to one another and to the herd, moving as the cattle and the terrain dictated. When we needed to separate, we knew, without saying, which ridges and draws each would ride and where to meet up again.

We were as familiar as an old married couple, although we never once touched that it wasn't in the course of work — helping the other to their feet after a horse wreck; bumping knees if our horses squeezed together at a narrowing of the trail; brushing up against one another while trying to load a young colt in a strange trailer. Jake came from a generation that thought women deserved special consideration, but the only time he showed that side of himself was in town. If we stopped at the feed store for vet supplies or a café

203

for lunch, he always got the door for me. I let him do what he had to in public. When we rode, we were equals and split the work right down the middle, whether it was riding the rougher country, roping the biggest stock, or just getting off to get the gates.

There was one day, though. I was galloping after an elusive bunch of steers when my horse tripped in a badger hole and came down on top of me. My foot was crushed and soon swelled so bad I eventually had to cut my boot to get it off. Jake helped me back on, got every gate, then hauled me home, helped me to the couch, unsaddled my horse, and made me supper. "I expect you'll get a chance to return the favor one day," he said when I protested.

I did, just a couple years later, when a bull ran him and his horse through a barb-wire fence and left them both unable to travel. I rode two hours to get help, and then nursed Jake and the horse for a month. "I'm glad to have you," he said one day when I came in from changing the dressing on his gelding's leg. I told him I was just returning a favor. The horse finally went sound, but Jake had spent enough time around large animals already to have a bad back. It just got worse after that, and he was never again able to shoe his own horses. I kept his and mine all shod for the next few years, until a blue-eyed roan dumped me on a basalt outcrop.

Our backs were both out the day my mare, that had been a young filly when Jake and I met and was now the most dependable horse I owned, slipped and broke her leg. We were deep into an erratic winter of thawing and freezing, and the pasture was a sheet of ice. Maybe it's because I don't have much other family, but I get attached to my animals, and I was more attached to this one than any before or since. Quick and smart and honest to the bone, she was the kind of horse you come across maybe once or twice in a lifetime, if you're lucky. It was a horseman's paradox: you should never let yourself love the good ones, because it will always be the good ones you lose. But when you have a good one, knowing the odds are against you somehow makes you love them even more.

I didn't call a vet; I called Jake, and he was there in ten minutes with his big .44. "A person shouldn't have to shoot their own horse. That's what saddle pals are for," he said, then did what I couldn't.

The sensible thing would have been to rent a backhoe, but Jake and I were neither sensible nor flush enough to hire a piece of equipment. We put on our neoprene and velcro back supports, popped a bunch of Ibuprofen, found a patch of partially thawed ground, and started chipping away at a grave. It takes a big hole to bury a horse, and by the time the sun fell behind the Blue Mountains and started to pink up the sky we were worn out, in need of stronger painkillers, and nowhere near finished. Jake pulled his pickup around and fetched a bottle of whisky from behind the seat. When it got dark, he turned the headlights on and we worked through the night, alternating between a shovel and a whisky bottle. In the morning we winched the mare's stiffened body into the grave. Jake took off his hat and said: "There's one that won't soon be forgotten."

She wasn't. For years afterward I rode the densest, most corrupt horses I could find, just to save myself the emotion of losing another. I ended up with a herd of unlikable creatures that wouldn't die. They never got sick or went lame or tore themselves up on barb wire. I had no vet bills and no attachments. "What the hell kind of life is that?" Jake asked one day when we were sorting pairs and I was trying to justify riding an animal that gave me no pleasure.

Not long after that I started looking for something better. By the time Jake and I took our final ride together, I had a big dun gelding I was starting to like pretty well. "He's gonna make you a helluva good partner," Jake said as we came up out of Cottonwood Cañon, pushing a bunch of late stragglers across a snow-blown flat toward their winter feed grounds.

"Yeah," I said. "That's what scares me. You know what happens to the good ones."

"Nothing lasts forever," Jake said. He was short of breath and coughing quite a bit, and, if I'd thought about it, I would have known what he was trying to tell me. He was a two pack-a-day Marlboro man. I always gave him a hard time about it, telling him we were like the two cowboys riding the range in the anti-tobacco ad. The one with the cigarette in his mouth turns and says: "Hey, Bob. I've got emphysema."

But what Jake got was a faster killer. I must've known it. Looking back, I remember riding through the sagebrush, how sweet it smelled, and how I could feel the vibrations of Jake's horse on the frozen ground coming right up through my own horse. I remember

206

how cold my feet and hands were and how the snow stung and cut into my face and how hard it was see the cows in front of us. I remember hoping we would still have them all when we got to the ranch and wondering if we would make it there before dark; before I started losing digits to frostbite. And I remember thinking, as miserable as I was, there was no place else I'd rather be and no one else I'd rather be with.

He called from the hospital six weeks later. "Take me home," he said, his voice such a rheumy murmur I didn't know who it was at first. "I want to see my horses."

He couldn't sit up without assistance, much less stand and walk. His cancerous lungs were so filled with fluid he had to fight for every breath. "Drowning," he said, gasping for air. "God damn' miserable way to die."

He had already pulled his IV needle. I wrapped a blanket around him and carried him out of there. He was so wasted away, I doubt he weighed more than a sack of feed. A nurse tried to stop us, but backed away when Jake looked at her and she saw the desperation in his eyes. I got him in my pickup and drove to the little house he was renting at the edge of town. I propped him on the couch in front of a big window that looked out on the snow-covered field where three diligent cow horses stood with their backs to the north wind. First one, then the other two swung their heads and saw him watching them. Jake smiled faintly. I turned and went into the bedroom and pulled his .44 from the holster hanging on the bedpost.

"I'll take care of your ponies," I said, laying the big gun in his lap. It was what saddle pals were for.

207

For Two Dollars

JANE CANDIA COLEMAN

Born and raised in Pennsylvania, Jane Candia Coleman majored in creative writing at the University of Pittsburgh but stopped writing after graduation in 1960 because she knew she "hadn't lived enough, thought enough, to write anything of interest." Her life changed dramatically when she abandoned the East for the West in 1986, and THE VOICES OF DOVES (1988) was written soon after she moved to Tucson. It was followed by a book of poetry, NO ROOF BUT SKY (1990), and by a truly remarkable short story collection, STORIES FROM MESA COUNTRY (1991). Since then two more collections have appeared: MOVING ON: STORIES OF THE WEST (1997) which includes her two Spur Award winning stories, "Lou" and "Are You Coming Back, Phin Montana?", and BORDERLANDS: WESTERN STORIES (2000). She has also won three Western Heritage Awards from the National Cowboy Hall of Fame. DOC HOLLIDAY'S WOMAN (1995) was her first novel, followed by I, PEARL HART (1998). "For Two Dollars" was written expressly for this collection.

You see, it happened this way . . .

Joseph Peña and I were out with the goats and sheep on the north side of the mesa where the grass was still green. We were young. And curious. And like all children we were bored staying in one place while the sheep grazed, the sun passed overhead, and the cottonwoods by the river did their dance in a breeze we could not feel.

Joseph lay on his back, staring at the steep cliff above us, and I felt the tension in him like a bowstring pulled back.

"What do you see?" I asked.

He squinted, his dark lashes covering most of his eyes. "A cave," he said. "There's a cave up there."

I looked, made out a small opening in the rock I'd never noticed, and that was strange. I have always seen the small things, always understood the voices of the earth.

"Let's climb up," I said.

"You might fall."

"I never fall."

Joseph, I understood, was just being a boy, acting tough, showing off his superior strength. He got up, stretched. "I'll go first."

It was a dangerous climb. The soft rock crumbled under our feet and finding handholds was scary, but at last we stood on a narrow ledge with the small opening behind us.

I looked out then — across the yellow valley that shimmered between black, volcanic hills — and the beauty of the land was a sweet taste in my mouth, like honey from mesquite flowers. All around me that day there was magic.

Joseph was peering into the cave. "It's a little house," he whispered.

I knelt beside him and saw what he meant. In the roof of the round room was a small hole, a natural chimney, and light came in like the light of a lamp shining down on a fire pit so old that even the ash had turned to dust.

"Whose?" I whispered back.

"I think maybe the Old Ones."

I shivered. The Old Ones had lived in these valleys before our people came. What had happened to them, no one knew. But in that cave, on that hot, late summer afternoon, I knew they were still with us, that their spirits surrounded us like the dance of dust in the ray of light from above.

And I was even more sure of their presence when I saw the broken pot and gathered the pieces with their strange designs, black brush strokes on white clay. It seemed to me that the shards were talking, humming like a swarm of bees, making of the dark an enchantment that has stayed with me all of my life.

I filled my pockets to show Grandmother, who still made her pots in the old way, and who always took me with her to dig the clay from a place only she and I knew. Then, when the buckets were filled, I would carry them home, walking slowly because they were heavy, and behind me, slower still, came Grandmother, leaning on her stick, her face a map of earth with its seams and cracks, and her voice rusty with age.

"I learned this place from my mother. Now it's yours, but tell no one," she would caution.

I never have. I have only dug the clay for myself, taking the long way around and listening to the songs of earth — a spring of clear water, a thread connecting all things.

Joseph, that long ago afternoon, said: "Maybe you shouldn't touch anything. Maybe the old gods will be angry."

But I was determined. "These are mine," I said, fingering the cool, shattered pieces. "They've been waiting for me."

We walked home slowly, breathing in the dust kicked up by the sheep, both of us silent, thinking of those who had gone before.

Grandmother was under the elm tree that grew to one side of our house. She was washing and cleaning the clay we had brought back the day before, picking out sticks, stones, leaves, anything that would come between her fingers and the shaping of her pots.

I went and stood beside her, waiting for her to recognize me. After a minute, she smiled and patted the ground beside her. "Sit," she said. "Tell me what has happened."

In my hands the shards shone as if they had just been polished, and one by one she took them, studied them, put them in her lap.

"Where did you find these?"

I explained, and she nodded.

Then she asked: "Why did you bring them to me?"

It was a difficult question. There are times when, between the word in my mind and my mouth there is a space in which nothing exists. And that day, as a child, I could not speak about what was in my head. I could not duplicate the reality so that Grandmother would understand.

"I . . . because . . ." Speech was useless. With my hands I made the shape of a bowl in the air. "I want to do what you do, Grandmother," I said, and then was quiet, hunched into myself.

"Your mother needs your help. She'll be angry if you sit all day with me."

My mother was always angry, although she tried not to let it show. We were poor, and she worried about having enough to eat, about our debt at the trading post, about growing old and useless and still hungry.

Twice a year, though, my father took the wagon filled with the pottery Grandmother had made and drove to the train station where the white tourists came and bargained for her pots. Sometimes she got as much as fifty cents for a bowl or a jar, and once or twice a dollar. For a few weeks after, my mother was happy. Money paid for the food we couldn't grow, the things we got from the trading post where, most of the time, my

212

mother's jewelry was pawned until we could pay what we owed.

I picked a shard from the pile in Grandmother's lap. On it was painted a horned toad with a triangular head and wicked eyes that seemed to be making fun of me. It was easier to answer him than to describe what I felt inside.

"Someday," I said, "someday I will make pots that sell for two dollars."

Light gathered in Grandmother's eyes and touched the brown earth that was her face. She seemed like a *santo*, her head circled in gold.

"May it be so." She reached for my hand. "Now help me up. Tomorrow you can begin."

I remember how, on that first day, the clay began to speak. *I am this . . . bring me to myself . . .*

First, as Grandmother showed me, I made the coils — long, damp snakes that wrapped around and around and that had to be kept wet so that the actual piece could be shaped.

"Thin as a cat's ear," Grandmother said. "Thin as the shell of a new-hatched bird."

Always, from that day, I listened to her and to the clay, learning when to stop, when to move on, making the growing life between my hands symmetrical — a word I didn't know then.

"Balance," Grandmother called it. "One side the same as the other, like what you see when you look at your face in the river."

213

I closed my eyes so nothing could come between us, turned the birth shape between my hands, and let the voices come to me.

It was a kind of freedom but with always a price. Spin a form and you become that form. It inhabits you, and the debt you pay is to keep on, always attempting perfection but never achieving it, no matter if you live, as I have, almost a hundred years.

In the beginning, Grandmother was beside me — a presence like the Old Ones, a blessing like the summer rain — her hands guiding mine so that her spirit came into me, and her seeing that held everything she saw or knew in her aged body.

Of course, my mother was angry. She thought my apprenticeship was a waste of time, that I was bothering Grandmother and avoiding what she saw as real work — weeding, watering, tending the sheep, learning to cook our simple meals.

"Do you think white people need so many bowls and *ollas*?" she asked. "They have water that comes into their houses all by itself, and fancy plates, and their food comes out of cans. All you're doing is wasting time. No man wants a lazy woman for a wife."

I ignored her, even though what she said was partly true. I did what I did because I couldn't stop, each step in the doing bringing me closer to the heart of a great mystery. And besides, I had Joseph, who because he had been with me when we found the cave of the Old Ones often came to watch Grandmother and me as we shaped and polished our work. It was Joseph who brought the wood for our fires, who gathered the

214

manure used to smother the flames so that, somehow, those pots being fired turned black. I don't know why to this day, even though it's been explained to me. Grandmother never knew, either. That's just what happened. Some pots remained the color of the clay. Others, smothered by manure, turned black as the black, volcanic rock of the hills.

Just as at times there is an emptiness between thought and words, the same happens between desire and ability. When I started to paint my pots, I was a child with a vision I was too young to bring to life. How I struggled to control my hands, make them do what I wanted, drawing on ruined pots, on smooth rocks — struggled and cried from frustration.

It was Joseph who, one day, took up the yucca brush and drew a long-stemmed flower up the curving side of a jar — a graceful stem topped by yellow petals that came to life as if it grew there.

Grandmother nodded at him. "Where did you learn that?"

He shrugged and looked puzzled. "I don't know. It just came out of my hand."

His was a gift, always. What I did was through determination. My mother laughed her bitter laugh. "What kind of man wants to spend his life painting flowers? Next he'll be wearing a skirt! Tell him to go help his father and make something of himself."

But neither of us could help what we were, any more than a young bird can stop from flying. Joseph closed his ears to the taunts as if they were no more than pebbles tossed into the river, but I was hurt by them, by

215

mother's inability to understand the difference between herself and me. It was always so.

One morning Grandmother went to sleep under the elm tree, and her spirit flew up into the branches where the sparrows were building nests and the smoke from the fire was caught in the new leaves. And I wept because in her place was a space nothing could fill.

Joseph tried to comfort me, but I wouldn't listen. Finally he said: "You're just sorry for yourself. Not for her."

The way he spoke made me angry. "She wasn't your grandmother! How can you know what I feel?"

"Because I was there, too."

Oh, he was so sure of himself, standing outside the church where Grandmother lay in a wooden box, her hands still, her eyes closed to me forever.

"You're as bad as Father Roy," I said. "Him like a piece of wood saying prayers, giving blessings that don't mean anything. The same words all the time, over and over without thinking. What good do they do?"

He agreed with me. I could see it in his face, but all he did was reach into the sack he was holding. "I want to do something for her," he said. In his hands were two tiny jars we'd made as children. I remember how impatient we had been as we waited for the fire to burn down, and how Grandmother had scolded us in that gentle way she had.

"Sit still! Nothing happens before the right time. You can't hurry the sun along, can you?"

"No," we had said together.

"Well, then." She had leaned against the tree and closed her eyes, and after a while she had begun to talk. It had sounded like a prayer. "Take the time to look around you. To see things before they're gone and it's too late. Life is long, but it's short, too. One day you're a child, and the next you're old, and what went before is like a dream. When I look at you two, I see myself. I see another way opening, and it makes me happy."

While I had been seeing the past, Joseph had been watching my face. "Now do you see?" he asked.

I reached out and took one of the little seed jars. It fit in the palm of my hand. "You want to give them to her so maybe someday somebody will find them just like we did," I said, startled at the way I suddenly saw the flowing of life just as Grandmother had described it.

He took my free hand in his. "Come on. We'll have to hurry before Father Roy gets here."

Like two bad children we opened the carved church doors. Inside, it was cool and dark. Light came in from high overhead, a thin light that seemed to have passed through water, and a few candles burned, their flames dancing in the wind that came in with us.

We moved softly down the stone aisle, past the *santos* in their niches, past the handmade benches, the paintings of corn and sheep, lightning and rain on the walls that someone, a hundred years before, had made. The paint was flaking off now, and some of the pictures were only faint outlines, their colors faded, and I thought again of the shards that had lain in the cave for a thousand seasons.

What we do in life stays behind, just as what we say spins off into the sky but is never lost. A thread, invisible as the silk of a spider, connects us all, living and dead.

The lid on the coffin was shut with a few bent nails, but Joseph pried them loose. When I saw Grandmother's face, I stepped back, my legs trembling. She looked young and as if she were smiling. "She's not dead," I whispered, and it sounded very loud in the little church.

"Hurry up!" Joseph hissed. "I can't hold this open much longer. Anyhow," he added, "she's alive where she is."

Quickly I put the gifts in the folds of her best skirt and stepped back, my heart beating so loudly my ears hurt. Just before Joseph fastened the lid, I heard Grandmother's voice from long ago.

Why did you bring these to me?

This time, my words came easily. "Because I love you."

Joseph bent the nails into place, looking solemn, and the slump of his shoulders made me sad.

I said: "Thank you. That was nice. A good thing to do."

"I loved her, too. She never scolded. She never laughed at me like the rest."

"I never laughed at you."

He reached out and took my hand. "Why would you? We're the same."

My mother caught us coming out of the church, her mouth a thin, dry line that broke her face into two pieces. "What were you doing in there?"

"Praying," I answered.

She gave us a hard look. "Pray when Father gets here. I need help. We have to feed him after Mass, and who knows where the money's coming from? But maybe now you'll stop your foolishness, both of you."

Whatever had happened in the church, it had changed me forever. I shook my head, knowing Grandmother was still with me.

"No," I said, and my voice rang the way a good piece of pottery rings when struck. "Next week we're going to Santa Fé. If I make any money, you can have it to pay for whatever you want."

"A few dollars. Spent in a minute. How long did it take you to make those things? Six months? Five years?"

I was, I suddenly realized, taller than she was. I looked straight into her eyes and knew victory when she turned away. "It took me all my life," I said, then I, too, turned away.

So many white people! So many loud voices mixed with the sounds of horses and wagons and the new automobiles that fouled the air and made me long to be home again in the silence.

My father left me and Joseph to set up our display, which we did, not talking to each other or to any of the rest who had come to sell jewelry that glistened like the sky, and rugs of many colors already spread out in the best places. We had come late, so we had only a little space corner at the very end of the *portal*.

I felt small, a person of no identity, an ant crawling across the sand of this city that, had I known it, was still a village, but which seemed to me to reach to the horizon. Shy, miserable, I sat looking at the ground, at my feet in their old moccasins, my hands motionless in my lap.

What would happen to my painted children if they were not sold? What would happen to Joseph and me? We were in love, although we hadn't spoken of it, being young and just as hesitant about ourselves as we were about selling what we had made. The link between us was there, however, forged long before. We knew each other's moods and silences, strengths and weaknesses, as if we shared the same skin.

Oh, that day! Behind my eyes I can still see the men and women in their strange, white people clothes, and how the shadows of the trees in the little park in the center of the plaza made crooked lines and patches of darkness on the sun-bright ground.

For a long time, I don't know how long, no one stopped to look at what we had, and I was discouraged, thinking maybe Mother was right, and the voices, even Grandmother's, had all this time been false.

Joseph was watching me as he always did. "Stop frowning, Angelita. The look on your face would frighten a bear." He laughed to make me feel better.

"They don't even stop." I was whining and hated it.

"They don't know how to see."

"I want to go home."

220

"Wait," he said. "We can't make anything happen."

Grandmother's words thrown back at me. I hated him. I hated how we sat there, like two beggars, our hands held out for white people's pennies. I said: "I'll smash everything."

He moved close to me. I saw his face, its roundness, like a bowl I could hold in my hands. "Stop it!" His voice was as sharp as a shard. "Remember who you are!"

That was hard. I was nothing but a dream.

"Oh, look! How sweet!" A woman stood in front of me. A woman with the face of a ferret, wearing a green skirt and buttoned boots that had never known the dust of a trail through the desert.

She picked up a bowl — my favorite — black on white with the old designs of mountains, lightning, patterns of clouds — that I had worked on for many months.

"How much?"

I hadn't been wrong. She did look like a ferret, all sharp nose and small eyes. My pride fought with desperation. I hesitated. The bowl was not meant for her. She'd treat it like a toy or something to be tossed out when she got tired of it.

I said: "Two dollars."

Her eyes turned into slits. "Fifty cents. You Indians think you can get away with anything."

Beside me, Joseph stiffened. He knew what I knew. That the bowl was my heart, and that I was angry. "Two dollars," he repeated.

The woman's laughter burned through me the way lightning burns into the core of a tree. "It's not for sale," I said.

Her thin lips turned in on themselves, and she tossed her head that had on it a silly, feathered hat. "I'll find something better," she said.

I nodded. Perhaps she would. But the bowl was still mine. When she was gone, when the sound of her little feet in those fancy boots had clicked away, I looked at Joseph.

"I'm a fool," I said. "I threw away money."

His smile softened the angles of his face. "No, Angelita. You must never sell the hours of yourself too cheap. Your grandmother wouldn't forgive you."

Relieved, dizzy, I closed my eyes. When I opened them again, a man wearing a dark suit and a wide-brimmed straw hat was standing there.

Slowly he knelt down, not caring that his knees were in the dust, and slowly he picked up the bowl. When he spoke, I heard the wonder in him. It pleased me. "You made this?"

My throat was dry as sand. I nodded.

"And this?" He lifted a jar with a slender neck.

Joseph answered for me. "She made them all. Some I paint myself."

One by one the man examined each piece, touching them as if they were sacred. *He understands*, I thought, amazed that there was such a person.

He sat back on his heels and looked at me, and from somewhere I found the courage to look back. "Are there more of these?"

222

Once again I nodded.

"It's what we do," Joseph said.

"This one . . ." — I found boldness and pointed to the black on white — "this one is two dollars."

A smile hovered at the corners of his mouth, and the pupils of his eyes became small black dots like I'd make with a drop of paint. When he spoke, it was slowly, as if he thought we wouldn't understand. "You're cheating yourselves. What you've done here . . ." He stopped and shook his head at what I assumed was our stupidity. "Three hundred dollars," he said at last. "For all of them."

Maybe he was crazy. Three hundred dollars would buy everything we needed for months, maybe a year. Joseph reached for my hand. He was thinking of marriage — and children who would not grow up shouted at or hungry. And a mother-in-law whose tongue would be silenced once and for all.

"These designs," the man was saying. "I've never seen them on contemporary pieces. Only in some of the digs."

"Digs?" The word was unfamiliar.

"Old sites. Where your people lived who knows how long ago."

"The Old Ones," I said with a smile.

"The Anasazi. The Hohokam. What they did . . ." Again he shook his head. "What they made out of nothing was magnificent. Is that what inspired you?"

Well, maybe. If inspiration means the reaching out to something that is nothing more than mist over the river

223

on a cold morning, or the guidance of Grandmother's hands.

I said: "What they did . . . the Old Ones . . . was sacred. What we do is only an echo."

He looked as if he heard that echo, as if he was straining to hear the whole past and the future as it was shaped by the past. An unusual man, not like the rest of his people who came and saw what was on the surface like a photograph and went home thinking they understood all those who lived here and what the land was saying.

"Art can only *be* an echo." He expected me to answer, but I didn't know what he was talking about. He waited a minute, then said: "Don't you think so?"

If I understood, he was saying that my pottery was art. I thought art was the painting of pictures, if I had ever thought about it at all. It seemed we — he and I — were talking across a chasm, each of us bewildered by the other but needing to communicate. How to explain to him?

"I only do what I do because . . ." I looked to Joseph for help.

"Because that's who she is," he said.

"But this speaks for all of us," the white man said, still holding my bowl as if it were a treasure — or a woman's body.

"This thing . . . this art," I said carefully, "it means that the voices choose you."

Those clever, half-yellow eyes of his lit up like the mesa in the morning sun. "It's a calling. For a few. You're one of the lucky ones."

224

How good it was to be known by a stranger! The happiness began in me in that moment, and it has never left. Not once. From that time, my mother's anger was like a wind that swept past and disappeared. From that time, I began to see a larger and more compassionate world, a world full of people different from me and yet the same.

I heard the familiar rattle of my father's wagon before he turned the corner and stopped at the curb. He tied the team and came to stand beside me, all the time looking curiously at the white man.

Laughing, I said: "This is my father. Give the money to him."

Astonished, he stood there while my new friend counted out three hundred dollars. "What is this?" he asked.

"Give it to my mother," I said.

"She'll think we robbed somebody."

The white man chuckled. "Your daughter and her friend earned it. There will be more, I promise you."

Pride and disbelief fought in my father's eyes. Trust in white strangers was harder for him than for me, but finally he let himself smile. "Maybe so," he said.

The white man handed me a card with his name on it that meant nothing to me. Marks on paper, what are they? A name is what is given. A calling is what is heard.

He said: "If I may, I'll come to see what else you have. Is it all right?"

I liked him — his eyes, the dust on his knees and worn boots, and how he held my bowl, with a kind of tenderness.

"You come," I told him. "We will be happy to see you."

I thought how my mother's face would be full of astonishment, how her hands would fumble over food for our visitor, and how her words would come out in no understandable order. She would look at me, her daughter, and see a woman she did not know, would never know, not if she lived a thousand seasons.

Sometimes birds hatch in a nest not their own. So it was with me who had been and would always be a stranger to her. Who knows why, for sure? But trouble is as necessary as happiness. It makes us strong; it speaks loudly of what we already know to be the truth.

And now, you see, how it happened to me. When the time was right, my life began.

Thursdays at Snuff's

GRETEL EHRLICH

Often called the Whitman of Wyoming, Gretel Ehrlich's poetic prose has defined the landscape, the culture, and the people of this state. It was personal tragedy that led Ehrlich ultimately to writing in 1979, three years after she had left her native state of California. Since then her output has included a fiction set in Wyoming during the Second World War — HEART MOUNTAIN (1988), a novel, and DRINKING DRY CLOUDS (1991) — as well as non-fiction ranging from biography — JOHN MUIR: NATURE'S VISIONARY (2000) — books of essays — THE SOLACE OF OPEN SPACES (1985) and ISLANDS, THE UNIVERSE, HOME (1991) — of spiritual journeys — QUESTIONS OF HEAVEN (1998) — of memoirs about life-changing experiences such as having been struck by lightning — A MATCH TO THE HEART (1995) — as well as many collaborative efforts on a variety of Western topics. "Thursdays at Snuff's" was one of the short stories collected in DRINKING DRY CLOUDS.

Suddenly I saw the cold and rook-delighting
 heaven
That seemed as though ice burned and was the
 more ice,
And thereupon imagination and heart were
 driven
So wild that every casual thought of that and
 this
Vanished and left but memories, that should be
 out of season
With the hot blood of youth, of love crossed
 long ago . . .

W. B. Yeats
From "The Cold Heaven"

Bright floodlights shone down on the mill at night,
on the long dusty sheds, the front loaders, and railroad
sidings. Sunrise lay pink across great mounds of tailings
and left again so that by mid-morning the mineral
looked white. The mill was located at a bend in a road
that came from nothing and led to nothing for a
hundred miles. The only other structure was a bar
across the road called Snuff's Place. Between the two,
human lives were caught and suspended the way
floating tree branches become snagged on sandbars.
Snuff's took in and gave out people whose nervous,
sour smell made the green paint peel prematurely, and

the mill's pink dust blew back over the gaunt building as if to conceal its ramshackle edifice and clothe it decently.

Out back an archipelago of small cabins made a line up the hill. In the 'Twenties, they had housed the only black madam in the state and her three employees, though after a few years, because business there was brisker, they moved back to Butte, Montana where they had come from. When the Depression hit, Snuff opened the cabins again, fitted the beds with worn but clean blankets, and let jobless men and women coming through on freights sleep in them.

Now only one cabin was occupied. Someone called the Wildman lived there. He had fallen from a moving train just beyond the mill on a forty below zero night and, when he was found, the tops of his ears had to be cut off because of frostbite. After, he stayed. At the height of the Depression he was seen acting as Snuff's chauffeur, parodying the decorous door-openings and gestures although both men wore rags.

In the one uncurtained window at the end of the bar, shaped like a porthole, a geranium plant laden with double blossoms pressed at the grimy pane. Its gnarled stalks bent over themselves, straining to soak up the autumn light. From there Snuff watched for Carol Lyman's car every Thursday. When he saw her coupé glide in under the bloodshot pulse of the bar's neon sign, he snapped on his bowtie and poured the Manhattan he had mixed for her into a stemmed cocktail glass.

229

Thursdays were Carol Lyman's declared "days of freedom," days on which she donned the darkest dark glasses and assumed an air of anonymity so complete she hardly knew herself. Sometimes she walked in the badlands, collecting rocks in dry washes, or, when she had enough gas, she'd drive to another town and drink a milkshake at a drive-in restaurant there. She thought of her ability to step out of routine as a discipline — the way some women of her age do volunteer work or take up ballet.

Carol Lyman came to Wyoming in the summer of 1941. It was already the fall of 1942 and still no one knew her well. She had arrived husbandless, with a pear-shaped retarded son, and she wasn't questioned about her past. If there had been a son, certainly there had been a husband, although his whereabouts and fate were unknown.

She took part-time jobs at the shipping yard café and the Heart Mountain Relocation Camp and lived in a house on the very edge of the small town of Luster. The neighbors next door had a yard full of roosters who awakened her each morning. They strutted and crowed and brawled until Manuel came out and fed them. Carol looked like a bird herself. She had long arms and legs and gnarled toes and the skin on her neck showed gooseflesh in the winter. Yet she had a handsome, haughty presence, a posture that was never less than regal, and carefully kept red fingernails.

She began going to Snuff's the day the Mormon women invited her to their Relief Society Meeting. They had felt sorry for her and because wartime heightens people's sense of community — in direct proportion to their experience of bereavement — the women issued an invitation to the solitary Carol Lyman. She attended once. To show her gratitude she baked a banana cake and made a gallon of non-alcoholic punch, but she sat back as the women made Christmas ornaments and never joined in. During a break she went outside to have a smoke. From behind a currant bush she watched the kindly women reconvene. They kept looking up, expecting to see her return. Instead, she stubbed out her cigarette and drove north with her dark glasses on. That was a Thursday. She decided she would be obligated to no one from that Thursday on.

Carol drove to Snuff's on a whim. She was a guarded person who realized she had nothing to guard: her life had become as narrow as a pine needle. Snuff's bar straddled two state lines and was the loneliest place she had ever seen. That's what made her stop there.

The first time, she stepped out of the car, straightened her hair, took a deep breath, and walked in. A chandelier in the center of the room swung in the draft of the opened door. Its bottom tier was bent and only four crystal prisms remained. A long cord descended through the middle of the fixture, and a bare bulb hung down in the room like a punching bag. She walked to the middle of the floor and turned slowly. It was a big drafty place with a cream-colored tin ceiling blackened by soot. A sour smell moved stiffly through the air and mixed with something antiseptic. Flannel curtains with scenes of ducks, and hunters pointing their shotguns hung limply over unwashed windows, and the ten-by-ten linoleum dance floor was badly stained. There were tables and chairs and spittoons randomly arranged, and, at the back, a card table sparsely padded with green felt. Snuff stood between the cherrywood back-bar and the marred counter where cowboys had carved their brands with pocket knives.

"You want to buy the outfit," Snuff asked jovially, "or do you want a drink?"

Carol Lyman turned to him. He was tall and dapper and nearing fifty. He wore a trimmed mustache, and his hair rose in a wild tuft at the top of his skull. His bright eyes danced, and, when he smiled, his thin lips turned white.

"A Manhattan," Carol said. "Do you know how to make one?"

Snuff looked askance and went to work. He poured and shook and strained and in a moment held out the drink she had requested. She ate the cherry first, returned the stem, then drained the glass of its reddish-orange liquid.

"Very good. Thank you," she said, handed Snuff the correct change, and left the bar.

During the week, between one Thursday and the next, Carol Lyman put in time at her two jobs. Every morning she drove her son Willard to the grocery store where he swept floors and dusted canned goods. She watched as he careened down aisles with a wide broom and scattered fresh sawdust behind the polished butcher's case, while above his head cones of string spun and bounced on their spindles and were threaded down through black eyelets to the counter, then wound around white packages of meat.

It was shipping time, and the café was crowded. Sugar and coffee had been added to the list of rationed foods and were considered two of the worst small sacrifices, although, when the coffee pot emptied early in the day, no one complained. The outer ring of world misery — the Death March in Bataan, the war in North Africa, Nazi burnings and killings, the arrest of Gandhi — gyrated around local commotions: the accident in which Pinkey was hit by a car; the arrival of more Japanese-Americans in guarded trains; cockfights and violent snowstorms; and the coming home of the war dead.

The next free day — Thursday — Carol drove directly to Snuff's. She had not intended to, but that's where she ended up. When Snuff saw her black coupé glide in, he made a pitcher of Manhattans. Just inside the door Carol pulled a compact from her purse, primped her brittle hair, then proceeded to the bar. When she saw the drink waiting for her, she gave Snuff a hesitant, surprised smile.

"How very sweet," she said, and slid onto the barstool one hip at a time.

"Hello. I'm Snuff," the tall man said.

"Carol Lyman," she said, then felt the stiffness leave her body. "It's legal to gamble in Montana, isn't it?"

"More or less."

"I'd like a card game. Is that possible?"

233

Snuff looked at the woman quizzically. Then he snapped on his red bowtie, for luck he said, and led her to the table at the back of the room. A pool of light lay on the green felt like a full moon. Snuff opened a new deck. His bony fingers were so long they seemed to wrap twice around the cards. He shuffled, she cut, he dealt, she asked for a card, and, when she turned her hand face up, he saw that she had won.

She raised the stakes for the next game and the next and won again. By mid-afternoon the pile of chips in front of her had grown tall. She looked at Snuff and started laughing self-consciously.

"I can't take all this," she said, pushing the chips back toward him, and left the bar.

During the week snow blanketed the northern part of the state, and there was a bad ground blizzard. The canary and saffron aspen leaves froze prematurely, blackened on the limb, and were blown unceremoniously to the ground. One rancher brought his steers off the mountain through the middle of town. They trampled rose bushes and vegetable gardens, ran onto one old woman's front porch, right into her living room. Then the weather turned warm.

Thursday morning Carol Lyman drove to the badlands behind her house. Wild horses ranged there in the fall, and she hoped to catch a glimpse of them. She followed a road so faint it sometimes disappeared and the tops of the sagebrush scratched the underside of her car. Finally she stopped, got out, and knelt down. The white scarf she wore, a present from a man she

234

loved twenty years before, whipped her face. In front of her were the cold hoof prints of horses. They overlapped and moved out from under her body as if running from her. The wind howled. When she looked up, she saw the sky had turned violet-black — the color of a bruise. Hail fell. She pulled the scarf over her head and tied it tightly. Hail battered the back of her head, and, when the wind shifted suddenly, it beat on her face. She stood, put on her dark glasses, and drove away. Behind her the horse tracks, carved into soft soil, filled with white stones.

She arrived at Snuff's in the early afternoon. As she unwound the white scarf from her neck and head, she thought it was like taking off a bandage. Her cocktail teetered on the scarred counter. The liquid swung from side to side, and, where it ran down the glass, it left an orange residue that looked like gasoline. Snuff watched Carol drink. The dimples that showed when he smiled gave him a youthful, mischievous look. They took their usual places at the blackjack table, and Carol won every game.

When the bar door swung open, the chandelier swung slightly. A short man on crutches hobbled to the middle of the floor. His gray Stetson was cocked sideways on his head.

"What can I do for you, Pinkey?" Snuff asked.

"Oooooweee! Look at all that money," he exclaimed.

"It's hers," Snuff said flatly.

Pinkey doffed his hat to Carol. One of the crutches fell from under his arm as he did so.

"I need a saw," Pinkey said.

"What in hell kind of drink is that?"

Pinkey squinted hard at the tall man. "Well, you're dumber than I thought you was. What's wrong, don't you savvy English?"

Snuff grinned.

"You've got to let me outta this son-of-a-bitch, that's what I mean," Pinkey said, and kicked his broken leg into the air.

When Snuff refilled Carol's glass, Pinkey peered over the rim.

"What's that hummin'bird food you're drinkin'?" he asked.

"Here, try it," she said.

"Hell, no, that'd clog my pipes."

Carol inspected the mutilated cast. It was blotched with mud, and the bottom edge was badly frayed.

"How long have you had that on?" she asked.

"Too long . . . a couple of weeks, I guess."

Snuff disappeared and came back, carrying a meat saw.

"What are you going to do with *that*?" Carol asked.

"Pinkey, lay back on that big table over there, will you?" Snuff said. "Carol, grab his heel and kinda steady the thing."

Pinkey lay back on the long table, a relic from the neighboring town's one lawyer who died and whose office sat idle for twelve years. Pinkey watched as the saw sank into white plaster. Soon the cast was halved, and Snuff pried it apart. They peered down at the leg.

"God, it looks wormy, don't it?" Pinkey said. "Can't you put that thing back on?"

Snuff held a piece of the cast up and laughed.

"Then get me a shot of whisky," Pinkey said.

Snuff brought the drink, and Pinkey gulped it down. He slid off the table slowly until both feet, the one with the boot on and the pale one covered by a sock, touched the floor. He put weight on the broken leg, then lifted it gingerly. He tried again. Then he looked at Snuff, and at his foot.

"I'm healed! I'm healed!" he cried, and waved his crutches in the air like wings. He stood up. The leg held.

"Just send me a bill, Snuff," he said, and hooked the crutches on the chandelier's bent frame. They watched as he hobbled out the door.

Carol Lyman turned on her heel and gasped. The Wildman stood directly behind her. Clean-shaven, his black hair was long and matted. He had olive skin and a dappling of black moles — beauty spots — on his jaw, a dent that flattened the bridge of his nose, and penetrating eyes.

"What are you afraid of?" he asked.

In confusion, Carol looked imploringly at Snuff.

"Carol, that's the Wildman. He lives out back," Snuff said quietly.

"My dog is sick. Maybe you can help him," the Wildman said.

Carol nodded, and she and Snuff followed the man to the cabin. Inside, it was cramped but tidy. A narrow bed had been shoved up against one wall, a steamer trunk against another, and, leaning sideways, there was a tall bookcase crammed with a miscellany of titles:

237

The Virginian, War and Peace, a set of the *World Book Encyclopedia,* and a stack of 1942 *Saturday Evening Posts.*

Carol looked at the dog. A kelpie, used for working livestock, he was smaller than a wolf but with a wolfish nose and ears.

"I found him abandoned in an irrigation ditch. He was just a little rat, a few days old. I guess they tried to drown him, but someone forgot to turn the water on," the Wildman explained.

"Let's take him to the bar where he'll be warm," Snuff said.

The Wildman bundled the dog in a torn blanket and carried him to the green building. Carol had not noticed before but the afternoon was nearly gone. In the northwest dark clouds humped up and moved toward this desolate bend in the road. Despite heavy snows the week before, the air felt tropical, and Carol thought she could smell the sea.

They made a soft bed for the dog under the oak table where he had always liked to sleep. He gave them a grateful, sad look. Snuff went to the porthole window and looked outside. In the distance lightning domed the dark sky with its ghostly hood of light. There was a terrible explosion of thunder overhead. Then the lights in the bar went out.

"Snuff. What's happening?"

Snuff pressed his face against the grimy porthole. Outside it was dark, too: the neon light off, the mill dark, no moon. The door swung open. A small figure stood in the entry and did not move.

238

"Come on in," Snuff said.

Still the visitor remained motionless.

"Who's there?" Snuff asked again.

When there was no answer, Snuff came out from behind the bar and fell once against the bottles.

"Snuff, god damn it, can't you light a match or something?" Carol yelled. She heard a match being struck behind her, then another. The Wildman held up a silver candelabra.

"Where did you get a thing like that?" Carol whispered as they approached the silent figure at the door. A wizened Japanese man appeared before them. When the light shone on his face, he hid his head in his hands. Then he regained his composure.

"They leave me. Cannot find way back. So confused . . . ," he began.

"Who left you?" Snuff asked. "Are you Japanese or American?"

The old man looked at Snuff timidly but gave no answer. Snuff took the candelabra from the Wildman and went to the phone. The line was dead. He put the receiver back slowly.

"Christ," he mumbled, then rejoined the others.

A plane flew over. It made a high uneven whine that deepened into a drone as it veered away. Snuff and Carol looked up at the ceiling. Then they heard a car and two gunshots.

"What's going on around here?" Snuff said. "Maybe we better find some cover for a while."

"Oh, Snuff . . . ," Carol protested, but when Snuff led the old man away from the door, Carol and the

Wildman followed. Snuff helped the old man down, and they all joined the sick dog under the great oak table.

"Here, give me that light," Carol said, and held the candelabra up to the old man. Under coal black eyebrows he had an elfish face and a delicate upswinging nose. Gray hair was swept back from a long, grooved forehead.

"I know you," she said. "From the camp."

"*Hai*. Heart Mountain. *Hai*," he replied cheerfully, and broke into a timid smile.

"You better blow those out now," Snuff said quietly.

The Wildman held the dog close to him, and in the dark they could hear the animal's labored breathing. Another plane droned overhead. This one was farther away.

"War and Peace," the Wildman whispered, and chuckled at his private joke.

In the confusion Carol's hand touched Snuff's under the folds of a coat he had thrown down for them, and she did not move it away. They braced themselves, although for what they weren't sure — for a bomb to be dropped, for a Japanese army to burst in, for sudden death. Snuff positioned himself so he could see out the porthole at the end of the bar. Beyond the bent geranium the sky was a blank. Even the North Star, the axis around which the other stars revolved, had been obscured.

Carol leaned back against the table's thick pedestal. It was like a tree, she thought, the trunk curved and smooth and branching into a sheltering canopy. For a

240

moment the window went white with lightning. A clap of thunder jangled the chandelier's crystal prisms. Carol imagined she was on a boat. Wind whistled, and the air slipping under the door into the stale room smelled of a failing sun and seaweed.

They waited. Each tried to comfort the dog, passing him from lap to lap, stroking his hair. When the dog was passed to the old man, Carol whispered: "He's just old. There's nothing to be afraid of." Then she looked at the man again. "I'm Carol Lyman," she said.

"Nakamura. Hello," the old man replied.

"Where did you relocate from?" she asked.

"Los Angeles. I was a flower grower. Then had to come here. Plant garden. No good, no grow," he said forlornly.

The Wildman looked at him. "Nothing grows here except cactus, rattlesnakes, and jack rabbits," he said dryly.

Mr. Nakamura gave the dog back and looked the Wildman in the eye. "Maybe he die tonight," he said.

"Yes," the Wildman said, and rocked the dog tenderly in his arms.

The night was divided by long silences and short interludes of whispered talk. Snuff spoke first. He told of an upbringing in the mining town Butte.

"I worked for Marcus Daley. He owned just about everything in Anaconda and Butte. Besides the mines he had a big hotel. It was quite a place. Everything in it was made of copper . . . even the toilet seats. All kinds of people came through . . . boxers, opera singers,

241

movie stars, gangsters. They said Butte was an island of easy money entirely surrounded by whisky. I was an orphan. My dad died in the mines. Oh, death was common. One man died every day in those mines . . . the cemetery held forty thousand. Money was easy. Death was easy. I guess it was living that got to be hard.

"I grew up on Venus Alley. Do you know what that was? A whole street of whorehouses. When Mister Daley put me to work, I didn't have a dime. He taught me something about making money. I even had a little string of racehorses all my own. Then I lost them in a poker game. And in exchange I got this place."

Snuff paused and looked at his surroundings, then laughed.

"I think of myself as a priest in a hardship post. I might have had a gentleman's life, but things get lost along the way," he said wearily.

Snuff's story was followed by silence. The rumbling of the Wildman's stomach broke the spell. Carol smothered a laugh, then crawled on hands and knees behind the bar. She returned with a handful of elk jerky and four pickled eggs. They were shared by all. The Wildman broke his egg in half and gave the yolk to his dog.

"What about you?" Carol asked, looking at the Wildman.

He smiled, and his dark eyes bounced like wild berries stripped from a green vine.

"I fell out of a boxcar across the road. Snuff took me in."

Carol looked at him intently. "Is that *all*?"

The Wildman's eyes widened. Then he shrugged and continued.

"My ears were frostbitten. After I healed up and spring came, I commenced to work as an irrigator. It's a job, like child's play. I like water. You can't hang onto it. You have to keep letting go."

A silence followed. All eyes were on the Wildman. His matted hair sprouted straight up from his head as if he were electrified.

"Before that I was enrolled at a place called Harvard. One day I came home from class, and my house had been robbed. Then I looked out at the streets, and I knew why. It was the 'Thirties. I had lots of things and other people had nothing. I wanted to know what it was like to be poor, so I rode the rails. When I returned, my parents had lost everything. I wanted to spare them the embarrassment of having an extra mouth to feed so I took off again and landed here."

Carol's head dropped. For a moment tears stood in her eyes and dropped at an angle away from her face like a pair of dice. The small dog groaned, stretched his back legs, and collapsed again in the Wildman's lap. Snuff looked through the window. Two stars shone, then one was overtaken by clouds.

"I wonder what's happening out there," Snuff said.

The Wildman looked at him. "Nothing. The lights went out, that's all. Who would bomb this desiccated piece of real estate anyway? Did you ever think of that?"

No one answered.

"What about you, Mister Nakamura?" Carol said.

The man looked at her timidly. "Oh, no, is no very good story."

"All stories are good," she said.

He looked from one to the other, then sat up straight and began.

"I come on ship. I'm opposite him," he said, and pointed to the Wildman. "I start out with nothing. Come here to make money. Ship take long time. Very rough. People sick all over. Only one other man on board. All others . . . women. Picture brides. You know them? Mail order. They have photograph of man they marry. That's all. Never meet before. Just picture. Well, one woman, she so scared she jump overboard. Then her friend and I fall in love. She very beautiful. We write poems to each other every day. Like in Heian times. The day we are coming to port, we don't know what we will do. She stand in bow of ship all day looking at pictures of her man. As soon as we see land, she tear it and throw it to the birds. When we get off boat, there he is. Right in front. Oh, so ashamed. She grab my arm like married woman, and we walk by. It is very bad thing we do, but in those days love matches not very common. Not common at all.

"After, I work for farmer. Then lease own land. Very beautiful. Right on coast, hill overlook ocean. Like Japan. We grow daisies. Many, many acres of them. So thick, I think they look like snow."

The Wildman rearranged the ailing dog and covered him with a torn blanket. Carol thought of all the places these people had lived; how they looked as if a river had run through them and swept all the small comforts

244

away. Because it was dark in the bar, her eyes were closed sometimes, sometimes open. Maybe she would die tonight, she thought, flanked by three strange men. Yet her body felt light. She had not touched any part of a man for many years and now Snuff's arm pressed firmly against her back. A fly trapped under the dog's blanket buzzed, then stopped. The dog's eyes opened, an ear twitched, then sleep overtook him again.

"Carol?" Snuff said.

"I can't."

"Why not?"

"Because I've never told anyone."

Nakamurasan looked at her. "Nothing to lose, huh?"

Carol smiled. The Wildman relit the candelabra, and their faces glowed. Carol cleared her throat.

"I spent a summer near here twenty years ago. I was young and had come to stay at a ranch. In August there was a party at a ranch on the other side of the mountain. We started out on horseback and rode all day. We arrived just as the fiddle players were tuning up. It was a lovely party. Paper lanterns had been strung across the verandah and through the trees. There were tables and tables of food. Everyone came. Even the sheepherders. I remember how they stood at the door and wouldn't come in at first. They had their dogs with them.

"During the evening I wandered down a long hall into another part of the house. I heard someone coughing, so I peeked in. A young man was lying in bed. He was the handsomest man I had ever seen. He had thick, wavy hair the color of chocolate and a

245

straight nose and big glowing eyes. Every feature was perfect. He looked like a young god lying there. He told me he had pneumonia. His cheeks were very flushed, and he kept clutching my hand and asking me to stay there and talk to him. So I did. We talked about everything . . . there seemed to be no inhibitions. I had never talked that way to a man before. Only once did someone come in and check on him. We were alone for the rest of the night."

Carol paused, then continued.

"He was the father of Willard. I say 'was' because he died a week later. I saw it in the paper the day I was leaving to go home."

Carol looked at the others. All at once the arbitrariness of their lives seemed absurd. This bend in the road and the little towns on either side, linked by great acreages of desolation, had neither accepted nor refused them. There was room here, that was all — a geographical accident. What they had done, how far they had drifted was of no concern. The convulsions of weather and seasons would always be greater than they were. That was a comfort, too, Carol thought. The bigness and strangeness of the landscape had acted on her like a drug and try as she did to reason why any of them had ended up here, she could push no clear idea into her mind.

She felt tired and cold suddenly and lay her head against Snuff's knee. A warm wind rattled the doors and windows of the bar. After a while she slipped into a light sleep. She dreamed she was on a boat, although the sea-swells she thought cradled her were Snuff's arms and the back legs of the dying dog and the Wildman's knees and Nakamura's folded hands. The boat passed over a school of fish. Then she could see herself from up in the air as though she were flying. It was not water that held the boat, but light. A clap of thunder woke her.

"What time is it?" she asked, startled.

Snuff looked toward the grimy window and shrugged. Rain undulated across the darkened mill, slapped at the road and against the windowpanes, then ceased. A car drove by. There were three gunshots this time. The Wildman stood up excitedly and ran out the door, shaking the candelabra like a staff. A smell of wet sage tumbled into the room as if it had been accumulating there for years. He ran to the middle of the road and yelled: "Here I am . . . here I am! Can you see me? Shoot me. Go ahead. You can have me. Come on," he said, taunting an empty sky. As he spoke, wind extinguished the candles one by one.

Carol and Snuff went after him. A wide band of red stretched across the eastern horizon, and the black began to drain from the sky. Each took an arm and led the Wildman back to the bar. Nakamura was holding the dog and singing something in Japanese. The dog's body had stiffened; he was dead.

The Wildman knelt in front of the old man and put his head to the dog's chest. After, he sat up limply. Carol put her arm around him, and, when he turned his head into her shoulder, they could hear his muffled sobs. Carol's eyes passed over the Wildman's clotted hair and met Snuff's. They had never really looked at one another. She felt as if her body were being pressed through a screen, the soft parts flowing forward. The screen was a last restraint beyond which there were only openings.

When Snuff looked through the porthole, he saw daylight. Simultaneously they got to their feet and went outside. The red belt of first light had widened: it looked like a pink shield held up to do battle with night. The sky was neither blue nor black, but pale as if the gases had been burned from it. The Wildman walked away from the others. They watched as he clambered up the pink dune of mineral tailings: over the lip of one, down the backside, up another. Nakamura pointed to the mounds.

"They are the color of fallen cherry blossoms," he said. Carol looked at the wizened old man. She thought she had never seen a morning like that, a more exquisite bend in the road. She wrapped her long arms around herself and felt ribs under her sweater. Trembling from the cold that comes just before sunrise, she rocked back and forth on her feet. Snuff looked at her.

"You look like a bride," he said.

The pink came out of the sky all at once. Now the cherry blossoms looked like drifted snow. The air took on a transparency like the hottest part of a flame. She thought she could see the stories she had heard that night skittering above the horizon, the troublesome human parts — the pain and blame — burning into the blandness of day.

A car barreled down the highway toward them. It was Pinkey and two other cowboys. They waved wildly as they passed, then the one in the back seat drew a pistol and shot three times into the air.

Perched on a pink mound, all the candles escaped from the candelabra. The Wildman started laughing. He lay on his side and rolled from the crest to the bottom of the mound and stood up at Carol's feet, his face and hair powdered thickly with dust. He did not brush himself off but walked toward the bar, his shoulders drooping slightly. As Carol, Snuff, and Nakamura followed, the neon sign over the door buzzed suddenly, lit up and began its habitual blinking once again.

Acknowledgements

"The Woman at Eighteen-Mile" by Mary Austin first appeared in *Harper's Weekly* (25/9/09).

"Shootin'-up Sheriff" by Cherry Wilson first appeared in *Western Story Magazine* (15/6/29). Copyright © 1929) by Street & Smith Publications, Inc. Copyright © renewed 1957 by Condé Nast Publications, Inc. Reprinted by arrangement with Golden West Literary Agency. All rights reserved.

"The Drought" by Dorothy Scarborough first appeared in *Century Magazine* (5/20).

"Wilderness Road" by Janice Holt Giles in WELLSPRING (Houghton Mifflin, 1975). Copyright © 1957, 1958, 1963, 1975 by Janice Holt Giles. Reprinted by arrangement with Houghton Mifflin. All rights reserved.

"Brother Shotgun" by Jeanne Williams first appeared in *Ranch Romances* (2nd June Number: June 14, 1957). Copyright © 1957 by Literary Enterprises, Inc. Copyright renewed 1985 by Jeanne Williams. Reprinted by arrangement with the author.

About the Editor

VICKI PIEKARSKI was Associate Editor on the Close-Up on the Cinema series for Scarecrow Press (1976–1981), a contributor to *Twentieth Century Western Writers* (Gale, 1983) and the second edition (St. James Press, 1991), and editor of *Westward the Women: An Anthology of Western Stories by Women Writers* (Doubleday, 1984; reprint: University of New Mexico Press, 1986).

She was Co-Editor-In-Chief on the *Encyclopedia of Frontier and Western Fiction* (McGraw-Hill, 1983), the first reference book which sought to catalogue comprehensively the complete works of some 300 authors of Western fiction and which is currently being revised for publication by the University of Nebraska Press, expanded to include over 400 authors. In addition to contributing approximately one-third of this reference book's entries (consisting of biographical sketches and critical literary analyses), this undertaking has involved exhaustive research, establishing an entry format, editing and copy-editing of all entries, and verifying all biographical and bibliographical as well as factual information.

For The Frontier Experience: A Reader's Guide to the Life and Literature of the American West (McFarland, 1984), on which she was also Co-Editor-in-Chief, she contributed sections covering a wide variety of topics, again based on extensive historical research into the available literature, oversaw and edited all contributions by others, and developed a house style.

Co-founder of Golden West Literary Agency, Vicki Piekarski currently co-publishes thirty-nine hardcover books a year in two prestigious series, the Five Star Westerns and the Circle V Westerns, and is the co-editor of The Morrow Treasury of Great Western Stories, an anthology that contains significant contributions by women authors of Western fiction.

She lives in Portland, Oregon with her husband and daughter.